Praise for QUIVER

"*Quiver* is good. It's really very good—with some cracking dialogue, clever plotting, and an enjoyable bloody climax."

—*The New York Times*

"[The] prose is clear, paunchy, and free of what his father calls 'hootedoodle.' His villains are so scuzzy...the story moves so quickly that there is no time for the novel to drag."

—*The Daily Telegraph*

"*Quiver* is a spectacular debut....With a large cast of characters—each presented as meticulously as an Andrew Wyeth portrait—and numerous points of view, all funneling inevitably to a stunning conclusion, you will be holding your breath until the final page."

—*The New York Sun*

"A strong debut that combines a tight plot (about a deadly double-cross in the woods of Michigan) with memorable characters and dialogue—come to think of it, not unlike what Leonard's father, Elmore Leonard, creates."

—*Seattle Times*

"*Quiver* is a fast-paced, cleverly plotted thriller...the reader is left somewhat breathless as the plot accelerates toward a climax involving plenty of gunfire and bodies, eventually, everywhere."

—*Uncut*

Praise for TRUST ME

"As anyone who read his debut novel *Quiver* knows, Leonard really is the equal of his father, Elmore. Set like *Quiver*, in Detroit, *Trust Me* is a knockout caper comedy, packed with unexpected twists, improbable entanglements, and wry, paint-fresh dialogue you could read all day without getting bored."

—*The Guardian*

"Leonard is starting to show some real individuality...he's crafted a pleasantly twisty thriller and a central character who could give Jackie Brown a run for her money....The plot is smooth and Leonard conveys the menace with assured ease. Promising."

—*Observer*

"*Trust Me* is about gasping for air. Peter Leonard, like Leonard père, depicts physical violence not so much in terms of sharp pain, and there's plenty of that to go around, as it is about controlling the flow of the air to the solar plexus. Breathtaking is a reviewer's cliché. But it is simply the best way to describe the pace of Peter Leonard's latest offering."

—*The Washington Times*

"Razor-sharp dialogue and a plot that races like a souped-up Mercury Cruiser; from turbocharged start to explosive finish. Brilliant!"

—R. J. Ellory, author of *A Quiet Belief in Los Angeles*

Praise for BACK FROM THE DEAD

"*Back From the Dead* is a one-sit read; there is no good place to pick up from where you left off. One page flows seemlessly into the next, so quickly that there should be skid marks on the pages on the final quarter of the book. The beginning will hook you, and there are passages that you will underline and write down elsewhere."

—*BookReporter.com*

"Leonard gets better and better."   —*Uncut*

Praise for VOICES FROM THE DEAD

"If you haven't read Leonard before—and you must—this is a great place to start."

—*The Guardian*

RAYLAN
GOES TO DETROIT

A RARE BIRD BOOK
LOS ANGELES, CALIF.

RAYLAN
GOES TO DETROIT

A NOVEL BY

PETER
LEONARD

Publisher's Cataloging-in-Publication data
Names: Leonard, Peter A., author.
Title: Raylan Goes to Detroit : a novel / by Peter Leonard.
Description: First Hardcover Edition | A Genuine Rare Bird Book |
New York, NY; Los Angeles, CA: Rare Bird Books, 2018.
Identifiers: ISBN 9781947856219
Subjects: LCSH Fugitives from justice—Fiction. | United States Marshals—
Fiction. | Detroit (Mich.)—Fiction. | Criminals—Fiction. | Suspense fiction.
| FICTION / Thrillers / Suspense
Classification: LCC PS3612.E5737 .R39 2018 | DDC 813.6—dc23

For Dante Salazar, Aaron Garcia, and J. B. McVay

ONE

DIAZ SAT IN THE long line of cars waiting to cross the border from Mexicali into Calexico, watching the beggars and the window washers, looking at the high wall that separated Mexico and the United States. When it was his turn, he handed his passport to the Hispanic border agent.

When the man asked why he had been in Mexico, Diaz said he was a parts manager working for Volkswagen and had visited the plant in Puebla and then the Hermosillo Assembly and Stamping Plant. Now he was returning home to Virginia to see his family. He drove a Passat with a registration that listed the car as owned by Volkswagen of America on Ferdinand Porsche Drive in Herndon, Virginia, near the nation's capital.

"Mr. Perez," the border agent said, "welcome home."

Diaz drove across the flat green fields of Imperial County that smelled of manure and something else, but he could not decide what it was. He could see migrants in the far distance, bodies bent over, picking vegetables, and a tractor crossing a dry parcel, dust trailing behind it.

And then he entered El Centro, an ugly little town of auto dealerships, strip malls, and fast food restaurants. With the GPS he found Elm Avenue and the address, a small one-story house surrounded by a chain-link fence, as many of the houses were in this quiet neighborhood inhabited by members of the cartels, by members of the border patrol living with their families, and by members of the US Marshals Service.

He parked in the driveway, got out, and walked to the front door. Pelon, a fat, oily man he had met on a previous occasion, invited him in and closed the door. "Care for something—*agua, cerveza, tequila?*"

Diaz shook his head. The fat man walked across the room and disappeared down a hallway. Diaz glanced at the room, the empty beer bottles, the ashtray on a table next to the couch overflowing with cigarette butts. He heard angry voices and a door slam, and now Pelon was coming toward him carrying a small suitcase.

Diaz said, "Is there a problem?"

"My woman," the fat man said, eyes on the floor, "she can be difficult."

"Sure, like any woman, uh?" Now Pelon's eyes met his and the fat man grinned.

"My concern, your woman can make trouble for me."

Embarrassed, the fat man said, "No, señor, nothing like that. *Le aseguro que.*"

"Something happens, you know who I come after."

"*Todo está bien.*"

The fat man handed the suitcase to him.

"Open it, let me see."

Pelon laid the suitcase on the couch, unzipped the top, and pulled it back. Diaz glanced at the guns, reached in and picked up the .22 Sport King, felt the weight and balance, ejected the magazine; it was full. He screwed the suppressor on to the end of the barrel and set the .22 in the case. He picked up the SIG Sauer, aimed the red dot laser sight on a lamp across the room, lowered the gun, and put it in the case. There were boxes of cartridges for both guns. There was a roll of duct tape and a set of picks. Everything he had ordered.

Diaz zipped the suitcase closed, dug a folded wad of bills out of his trouser pocket, and handed it to the fat man. He carried the suitcase to the car and lifted it into the trunk. He drove east across desert and scrub, a dark line of mountains in the distance, the outside temperature registering 119 degrees. He stopped for gas, tacos, and a Coca Cola in Yuma, a desert town that made El Centro look like a resort.

Diaz arrived in Tucson at four o'clock and checked in to the Arizona Inn. He changed into a bathing suit, walked to the pool, swam, and lay in the searing afternoon sun, enjoying a Grey Goose and tonic, admiring the lush grounds, the sculpted shrubs and flowers.

When the sun was fading over the mountains, Diaz returned to his room, showered, dressed, and drove to El Torero. Luz, the bartender, noticed him when he walked in but didn't say anything, didn't acknowledge or welcome him. He sat at the bar and waited for her to come his way, and when she did, she said, "What can I bring you, señor?"

"You don't remember me?" Although Luz was married, he had spent the night with her the last time he was passing through.

"You remind me of someone, a man who made many promises and has kept none of them." Her expression was stern as she looked into his eyes. "What do you drink?"

"Surprise me," Diaz said, smiling, trying to loosen her, pry her out of this dour mood. Minutes later, Luz placed a lowball glass in front of him. It was red and fizzy and had a cherry floating near the bottom. She watched as he picked up the glass and took a drink. It was something a child would order, and now she broke into a grin.

A little after two in the morning, Diaz awoke Luz and told her she better go home. This time he promised he would take her with him to a resort in Cabo and on a shopping vacation to Buenos Aires. Luz believed him cause she wanted to. He wondered if he would ever see her again.

Dressed in black, Diaz drove north to the foothills of the Tucson Mountains. He parked on North Tortolita Street and walked down into the wash, moving on the sandy bottom, camouflaged by saguaro, choya, octillo, and desert trees he could not identify. He heard dogs barking and smelled the javelinas before he saw them—a feral reek that was worse than a skunk. He climbed up the sandy rock-strewn slope and crouched behind a giant saguaro, saw their red eyes glowing in the dark as the herd, at least twenty javelinas, passed by him.

Four in the morning, it was still ninety-two degrees, sweat running down his face, blotting the shirt that clung to his shoulders and back. He passed a chicken coop and thought it would be bad to be a chicken in the Arizona desert, wild animals staring at you, licking their chops.

A decorative fence wrapped around the back of Frank Tyner's property. Diaz opened the gate and crossed the pool enclosure to the French doors. He could hear the hum of an air conditioner. He used the picks to unlock the door.

Inside it was cool and quiet. He went in the kitchen and dried his face and hands with a dish towel, pulled the .22 Sport King from the belt behind his back, and moved toward the bedrooms.

Peeking through the open door, Diaz could see the shape of someone in bed, under the covers in the dark room. As he moved closer, he could see Frank Tyner on his back asleep. Diaz shook the man. Tyner opened his eyes, a knowing look on his face, as if Frank had been expecting him, knew he would show up sooner or later. Diaz took a step back, aimed the gun and said, "*Plata o plomo.*"

Frank Tyner raised his hands in surrender. "No, it's a misunderstanding. I can explain."

"Señor Rindo say is too late for explanations. *Que Dios te ayude.*" Now Diaz made the sign of the cross and shot him in the forehead, and again in the chest, and it was over. He made a final check of the room, picked up the casings, and went into the bathroom to relieve himself. He glanced at the tub on the other side of the room, shower curtain pulled all the way open. He did his business and walked out.

•••

SHE WAS COMING OUT of the bathroom, half asleep, saw a man with a gun approaching the bedroom, ducked back in, moved to the tub, got in on her back, held her breath, and tried not to move—more afraid than she had ever been in her life. She heard what the man said to Frank and heard the *pffft* sounds of the suppressed rounds being fired.

She heard him come into the bathroom, shoes clicking on the tile floor, and listened to him urinating. Her body frozen, heart thumping in her chest, sure he was going to come over and look in the tub.

She heard the sliding door to the pool *squeak* as it opened and *thud* as it closed, got up and went into the bedroom, checked Frank's pulse. He was dead. She found her purse, grabbed her weapon, and ran out to the street. Down to the right a silver Volkswagen sedan was making a U-turn. She ran toward it but was too far to read the license before the car turned left on El Camino Del Cerro.

She had to call this in, but wasn't sure what to say and needed to think it through. Maybe it would be better to wait, say she'd tried calling Frank for a couple hours and he didn't pick up. She was worried and stopped by his house. Frank's wife was out of town. Somebody would have to tell Claire. The main thing was not to panic.

•••

WHEN DIAZ WALKED OUT the rear gate, the sun was peeking over the Santa Catalinas. He moved quickly to the car, thinking about the contract. He never became involved in the politics of the hit, never questioned who or why. Diaz was paid to do a job and he did it.

Even with his Catholic upbringing, there was no feeling of contrition for what he had done. He remembered being taught the catechism of the Catholic church—that confession of even venial sins was important. Diaz's sins were of a more grievous nature. One day he would go to confession. He imagined the dialogue with the priest.

"Bless me, Father, for I have sinned," he would begin.

And the priest would say, "My son, what do you have to confess?"

"I have killed many men and even some women, but never a child."

"How many are you talking about?"

Diaz did not know what the final count would be, but estimated the way he was going it would be close to fifty.

The priest would say, "What did they do to you?"

Diaz would say, "They did nothing, Father."

"Why did you kill them?"

"I was paid to do it."

"Paid to take the lives of other human beings?"

Diaz saw himself fidgeting, anxious and impatient in the narrow confines of the confessional, waiting to be absolved of his sins through the sacrament of reconciliation, receiving God's mercy. He would not mention other sins he had committed—venial or mortal—in his adult life. The priest would conclude by asking him to do penance and forgiving him his sins so he would be accepted by God in heaven.

TWO

"WE LIKE TO HIT them before they take their first piss in the morning," Bobby Torres said. "Man doesn't have the same fight when you catch him in his underwear."

"I don't know," Raylan said. "I've seen them buck naked, sitting on the toilet with more fight than a pit bull."

They were passing decorative storefronts with signs in Spanish. Bobby turned left on a street named Clark from Vernor, the sun coming up over fields of tall grass, houses scattered here and there—some in decent shape, others leaning left or right, looking like they were going to fall over any minute—and in the distance the skyline of Detroit.

"Been to any foreign countries lately?"

Raylan glanced at him.

"Cause you just drove through two: Lebanon and Mexico." Bobby grinned.

"What was that we just passed?"

"Mexicantown. Know why they call it that?"

"I'll take a wild guess, say that's where the Mexicans live."

"I like your instincts." Bobby paused. "Town before that with all the signs in Arabic's Dearborn. We've got like three hundred thousand Arabs living in the Motor City." Bobby Torres pulled over, the nose of the Ford SUV pointing at a Victorian house with a porch in front, maybe a hundred yards down the street.

The neighborhood was quiet as Raylan brought binoculars to his eyes, zooming in on the house but not seeing anyone. There was a car in the driveway and two more on the street.

Raylan lowered the binoculars, glanced at the wanted poster on the console. Jose Rindo, a tough-looking guy with a shaved head and a square jaw, resembled someone he'd seen fight in the Octagon, the UFC.

Name: Jose Cardenas Rindo
Race: White or Hispanic
Gender: Male
Hair Color: Black
Eye Color: Brown
Height: 5' 10"
Weight: 165
DOB: July 19, 1985
Names/Aliases: Pepe, Snow, Snowman
Scars/Marks/Tattoos:
  Tattoo: Back—Grim Reaper
  Tattoo: Right Forearm—Skull
  Tattoo: Right Bicep—Praying Hands
  Tattoo: Chest—Dragon
  Tattoo: Left Forearm—Ant Dog
  Tattoo: Left Bicep—Get It Bitch
  Tattoo: Left Calf—Pitbull
  Tattoo: Right Calf—Cross with Wings
  Tattoo: Right Hand—Tribal Design
  Scar: Left Shoulder—Knife Wound
  Scar: Right Shoulder—Gunshot Wound

Rindo, a known narcotics trafficker, was wanted in connection with three drug-related murders. They'd seen one the night before. Detroit

Police Homicide had found the body of DeShonte Moore, a rival dealer. Dude's street name was "Money," also answered to "Boo Money."

The crime scene was behind an abandoned factory, yellow tape slung between two Detroit Police cruisers, marked units, lights flashing. Raylan smelled the body before he got out of the car, burned meat and sulfur, and now it was in his nostrils and on his clothes. He and Bobby approached the group standing there: uniformed cops, homicide detectives, and an evidence tech shooting photographs—different angles of the man, what was left of him, charred beyond recognition, a red gas can on its side a few yards from the body.

Bobby Torres pointed at a shell casing in the dirt. "Looks like DeShonte was shot first. One in the head the brothers call the *Fo' sho.*"

Some distance away was a tricked-out Jag with a personalized plate: *Money.*

"This is what happens," Bobby said. "Someone doesn't know what the fuck they're doing, tries to set up shop in Mr. Rindo's hood. Now you see why he's top fifteen."

Bobby picked up the radio handset. "Paco on the eye. No sign of S-1. Grab a slab, let's give it a few."

Raylan said, "How do you know he's in there?"

"One of his exes had Rindo's kid, dude says it wasn't his, dumped her, she's pissed off, gonna show him. You can see it from the woman's point of view, can't you?"

"I can see it from his, too."

"You don't like women?"

"Sure I do. Married the wrong one when I was young. Now, finally, I think I know what I'm doing. It only took twenty years."

"Here's the best: Rindo's seeing his ex's BFF, girl named Heather Lopez. How you think that went over?"

"I've gotta believe that's why we're here. The ex tell you who's in the house with him?"

"She didn't know for sure, but Rindo has drugs and money, so there are always *pegote*, man, the crew hanging out." Bobby paused. "I been meaning to ask: someone your age, what're you doing in Detroit?"

"Churning, but it's a long story. I'll tell you sometime. Anything else you want to know?"

"Yeah, what's with the hat?"

Raylan shrugged.

"Think you're in the old west or something? Guys don't wear hats like that in Detroit less they're going to a rodeo or a costume party. Though I hear you're a cowboy, like to pull your gun, uh?"

"Isn't that what they're paying us to do?"

Bobby picked up the binoculars but hesitated before bringing them to his eyes. "Man, I don't know how you did things in Kentucky, but here you don't want to call attention to yourself cause that also calls attention to me and the other members of the team. You understand?"

Raylan took off the Stetson, reached behind him and placed it on the back seat next to Bobby Torres's Remington 870, and combed his damp hair back with his fingers. Straight ahead past the house he could see an F-150 parked at the end of the street, James Thomas Proctor, a young hotshot from College Station, Texas, everyone called "Jim Tom," behind the wheel.

In the side mirror, Raylan could see Calvin Rice, known as "Street," a low-key black dude in an old Pontiac Bonneville, and somewhere out of sight but close by was a girl deputy marshal, Jill Conlon, who looked about eighteen, and was called "Boom Boom" due to her proficiency with a tactical shotgun.

"Okay," Bobby said, "Ready?"

Raylan nodded. It was 6:42 a.m, the clock on the dash was five minutes slow.

"Want the shotgun?"

Raylan shook his head. "I'll stay with this." He put his hand on the grip of the Glock holstered at his waist.

"I seen you got three hundred on the test."

"I do okay."

"Okay? You know how many score that high?"

Raylan shook his head. "I used to teach care and use of firearms at the academy."

"Why'd you get kicked out?"

"My supervisor was an asshole."

"What'd he do?"

"Made it difficult to do my job."

"So you took his weapon and cuffed him to the steering wheel of his G-ride?"

"Disciplinary board said I have authority issues."

"I bet they did. Wasn't the first time."

"Art, my old chief, went to bat for me. Board said, 'Okay, we got an opening in Detroit.' Not exactly where I wanted to end my career. That answer your earlier question?" Raylan reached in the back seat for the heavy vest.

"How you like it so far?"

"Reminds me of photos I've seen of Raqqa."

"Where's that at?"

"Syria. There's a war going on in case you didn't know. Parts of Detroit look like they've been bombed."

"It grows on you." Bobby paused. "Listen, you have a problem with something, tell me about it, okay?"

Raylan opened the door, stepped out of the car, slipped the UAV over his head, and adjusted the straps. When he got back in, Bobby had the AR-15 across his lap and the radio in his hand. "All right," Bobby said, "let's go get him up."

•••

JOSE RINDO HEARD SOMETHING, opened his eyes, and saw the early morning light around the edges of the window where the blinds didn't cover all the way. Heather was asleep next to him, her caramel shoulder sticking out of the covers. He picked the nine up off the table next to the bed, moved to the window, opened the slats, and saw armed police moving toward the house. Jesus.

One thing Jose knew for sure, he wasn't going back to prison. As he was dressing, Heather turned in the bed, saw the gun in his hand, and said, "What's going on?"

He looked out the side window and saw two police with shotguns moving along the side of the house—now thinking they probably had him surrounded. Heather was sitting on the bed naked, long black hair and little tits, rubbing her eyes.

"Tell me what's happening."

"Is the police. Stay here."

Jose moved along the hall to the second bedroom, opened the door. Albano, in bed but awake, was staring at the nine in his hand. Jose brought his finger to his mouth. "Police," he whispered. "Get the alphabets, man."

In the third bedroom he woke Luis, whose face reminded him of a young Roberto Durán.

And now they stood at the top of the stairs, Albano and Luis dressed and holding AK-47s, looking like Arab terrorists he had seen in the newspapers, the guns with their banana clips unmistakable. Rindo pointed down the stairs and in a quiet voice said, *"Buscalos."*

He went into the room. Heather still sitting on the side of the bed, said, "I am afraid." Now she stood, moved to him and put her arms around him.

Jose said, "There is no need to be. The police are here for me not you," all the while thinking the shooting would begin anytime. On cue he heard a voice say, "US Marshals," and then a loud burst of gunfire.

•••

RAYLAN WATCHED THEM COME down the stairs holding AK-47 assault rifles with their curved magazines. They were young and inexperienced, doing it all wrong, moving across the open floor. Neither appeared to be Jose Rindo.

Raylan said, "Put your guns on the floor, you'll live to tell about this." Instead they aimed at him, and Raylan shot the tall one, who fell, finger on the trigger, firing a wild burst into the hardwood. The second man ran for the kitchen and Raylan shot him in the leg and he went down howling in pain. Raylan walked over, crouched, cuffed him, and picked up the assault rifles.

•••

JOSE KNEW IT WASN'T possible to shoot his way out of this, that he'd have to think of something else. When the firing stopped he brought her down the stairs, saw Albano dead on the floor, and the two police. He was behind Heather, his arm around her neck, the barrel of the nine pressed against her temple. The dark-skinned police, who looked like one of *them*, said, "US Marshals, put your weapon on the deck and release the girl."

"Not the way is going to happen," Rindo said. "Put yours down or I kill her."

"Please do what he says," the girl said, "I don't want to die."

It wasn't the dark-skinned marshal that concerned him. It was the other one. A tense situation and the man was relaxed as though it did not matter what happened. Now the crazy marshal said, "Listen, you can go out of here on your feet or on your back, but you're not taking the girl." He raised his gun, pointing it at Jose. "I know what you're thinking. Can you pull the trigger before I do?"

"Take it easy," the dark-skinned marshal said. "No one is gonna get shot. We're gonna do this peacefully."

"That's up to him," the crazy one said.

"Please," Heather said, "I have nothing to do with this." She was crying.

"Then what're you doing here?" the crazy one said. "How do we know you're not involved, part of the gang?

"I spend the night. I don't do drugs, I don't sell them."

Rindo pulled Heather closer to him backing across the room toward the kitchen. He could smell sweat from his body and perfume from hers. He could see Luis handcuffed on the floor.

"One more step it'll be your last," the crazy one said, speaking hard words in his quiet tone.

Jose believed him, knew it was over or his life would be. He dropped the nine on the wood floor, let go of Heather, and put his hands in the air. The crazy marshal came over and jerked his arms behind his back and cuffed him. Jose made eye contact with him. "I see you again, uh?"

"I doubt it, less it's in a courtroom."

"I think it will happen.

"You better hope not. Next time you won't be this lucky."

"No, I'm going to repay you. Count on it."

•••

ALBANO CRUZ WAS TAKEN to the morgue, Luis Ramirez to the hospital, Jose Rindo to the Wayne County Jail, and Heather Lopez to the police station for questioning.

Standing on the porch, Raylan said, "There you are, a three-for-one special."

Bobby Torres said, "Tell me you weren't really going to shoot him."

"It was up to Rindo. I don't draw my gun less I'm gonna use it." Raylan fixed his attention on a group of neighbors, watching them across the street, young black dudes, shorts hanging low on their skinny hips—hamming and shuck-a-lucking—as a black Crown Vic pulled up in front of the house.

A petite Latina and a big corn-fed linebacker got out and walked up the front steps. Raylan knew they were FBI before they identified themselves.

Special Agent Nora Sanchez said, "What the hell do you think you're doing? You know how long we've had this fugitive under surveillance?"

"How long?" Raylan said.

Special Agent Sanchez said, "Deputy, do you think this is funny?"

"You must've misread something in my expression. No, we take our work serious."

"Jose Rindo is wanted in connection with the murder of Special Agent Frank Tyner. We've been after this man for six months. Ever hear of Deconfliction, the Watch Center? Why didn't you call it in?"

She was a feisty little thing. Raylan was surprised the big guy didn't say anything, letting her run the show.

Nora Sanchez said, "Who's the bonehead in charge?"

"He is," Raylan said, nodding at Bobby.

"I'll be talking to your chief about this."

Raylan said, "What're you getting so worked up about? We've got Jose Rindo, a major drug trafficker with several murder warrants against him, in custody. When we're done with him, he's all yours."

"And who are you?"

"Deputy US Marshal Raylan Givens."

She took out a small spiral notebook and wrote something—probably his name.

On his way back to the office, Raylan said, "That hot little FBI number wouldn't be so bad you pulled the stick out of her ass. What do you think's gonna happen?"

•••

IT WAS HOT IN the cell Jose shared with Rocky Castro, a gangbanger trying to act tough—tats on his arm, the outline of a star with the number five in it and the letters *LC* that stood for Latin Counts. He'd been arrested for carrying a knife and a little weed but said he was bonding out in a couple days, and hearing that gave Rindo an idea. "Hey, look at me, man. Know who I am?"

Dumb gangbanger, still playing, said, "No, who are you?"

"The one's going to make you rich. Money, cars, women, anything you want."

"What do I *have* to do?"

"Give me your bracelet, we switch."

"You crazy? I be out in two days." Rocky Castro glanced at the narrow window that had a view of Ford Field. "What they get you for?"

"Being in the wrong place at the wrong time." Rindo cracked his knuckles. "A million dollars. Tell the guards you were afraid. I threatened you. They won't do nothing to you, and you be rich."

"When do I get the money?"

"When you get out."

"How do I know you do it?"

"I'm telling you, giving my word as a man."

"Your word as a man. What else you gonna give it as, a bitch?"

Jose wanted to fuck him up, kick his little squat ass, but he could see the dude was interested, just holding back cause his little brain couldn't quite get around the idea. "I wire twenty-five thousand to your bank account, show you I'm serious."

"You think I have a fucking bank account?"

"I have cash delivered to your mamacita, or your homie, man, whatever."

"How you know it will work?"

"Don't worry."

Rocky Castro grinned, probably picturing the money, a pile on a bed the way you see it in movies, covering himself and laughing. But then he saw something else and the grin faded. "Man, I don't know. I got to think about it."

"Listen, you don't want to do it, no problem. I find someone else. Is okay, I thought you had it going on. Dudes be standing in line for this." It was a good move. Let the *pendejo* think he had the money, already spending it, and then take it away.

Two days later, Rindo walked out of the Wayne County Jail wearing Rocky Castro's bracelet and clothes: red warm-up, black cap. Caroline pulled up in the Benz, lowered her sunglasses, looked at him with big blue eyes, said, "Really?"

Rindo got in the car.

"I give up, who you supposed to be?"

"Rocky Castro, gangbanger with the Latin Counts."

Caroline smiled now. "They could use some help with their outfits. That's the worst use of three-color I've ever seen." She rubbed his thigh. "What do you want to do? Although I have a pretty good idea."

"First, tell me what you know."

"Albano is dead. Luis, shot in the leg, is in the county lockup. The one who did it is Deputy US Marshal Raylan Givens. Lives in an apartment building in Royal Oak. What you gonna do?"

"What do you think?"

THREE

G OT A CALL FROM an extremely pissed off Special Agent Sanchez of the FBI," Chief Wayne Broyles said. "I understand you're acquainted with her." He picked up the coffee mug from his desk and took a sip, put it down, glanced at Bobby and then Raylan. "She says they've been after this fugitive, Jose Rindo, for six months. Evidently murdered or hired a contractor to take out one of their agents. Now you want to tell me what the hell happened? Why didn't you call it in?"

Raylan said, "It was spur of the moment, a chance to grab Rindo while he was sleeping, minimize the risks."

"You didn't know the FBI was after him?" Chief Broyles said, directing the question at Bobby Torres.

"We knew," Bobby said, "but..."

"You know how this goes. We don't follow the rules, it ruffles feathers up the food chain," Chief Broyles said. "They keep score, we all know that, but we've got to work with them, so let's try to get along." The chief grinned. "Who owns the house, the girl?"

"Sonora Management," Bobby said. "My guess, it's Rindo's."

•••

Two DAYS LATER, BOBBY Torres said, "Jose Rindo walked out of county jail Thursday morning."

Raylan, at his desk in the bullpen, said, "Yeah, right."

"I'm serious, man." Bobby told him about how Rindo and Rocky Castro, this dumbass gangbanger, switched bracelets. Rindo bonded out. "Did the same thing in Tucson, Arizona."

"You're telling me the deputies at county knew this and let it happen again?"

"That's what I'm telling you."

"They don't make sure they've got the right guy?" Raylan couldn't believe it. "Well, you seem to know Rindo's tendencies better than most, so where'd he go, where's he at?"

"How do I know? Dude's mother lives in Mexicantown. According to tower records, she's been talking to someone in Toledo. Why don't we stop by, introduce ourselves?"

Twenty minutes later, they were on Twenty-Fifth Street in an industrial area, Raylan staring at a corrugated fence covered in graffiti, Spanish words he didn't know and symbols he'd never seen before.

Bobby said, "It's the gangs tagging and such, showing their colors. You see the outline of a star with the number five inside the shape, and a big LC? That's the Latin Counts. See the thirteen? That's the Sureños. The Counts and Sureños don't get along."

Bobby drove like it was his first time behind the wheel, glancing at the laptop, going too fast, or too slow, passing inches from parked cars. His cell phone rang. He answered saying, "What you got?" listened, and said, "Uh-huh, okay," and disconnected. "The mother just got another call from Toledo. That's eight in the past couple days."

"You think it's Rindo, boy misses his mom?"

Bobby shrugged.

"Why don't you call the number," Raylan said, "see who answers?"

"What do you do, pretend you're selling something? 'Hey, we're having a special on window cleaning, save twenty percent'— something like that?"

"Or you say, 'Hey, man, I know where you're at, and I'm coming to get you.'"

"That how you did it in Kentucky?"

Raylan glanced out the window at two teenage bangers getting into a Chevy lowrider parked on the street. "You send a BOLO on Rindo to the marshals in Toledo and the PD?"

"I'm a step ahead of you, bro." Bobby made a left turn on a side street and stopped in front of a clapboard house that looked freshly painted and had a garden full of flowers, the Rindo residence standing out, looking good in this neighborhood of abandoned, dilapidated homes, a shiny, brand-new Cadillac in the driveway.

Raylan said, "What's this woman do, she can afford a car like that?"

"Has a son traffics heroin."

Bobby knocked on the door. A woman's voice on the other side, heavy barrio accent, said, "What you want?"

"US Marshals, we need to speak to Maribel Rindo."

Raylan saw the woman looking out the window at them and then heard a deadbolt retract and the door opened. Mrs. Rindo was short and plump with dark hair pulled back in a ponytail and a scowl on her face, but still pretty in her late forties.

Bobby said, "Can we come in and talk?"

"You can talk from there."

"Do you know where Jose is?" Bobby said.

"*No tengo ni idea.*"

"*Está en la casa?*"

"*No, no lo he visto durante algún tiempo.*"

"She says he isn't in the house and she hasn't seen him for some time," Bobby said to Raylan. "But you talked to him on the phone," he said to Mrs. Rindo.

"Pepe call on my birthday."

"When was that?"

"Two days ago."

Raylan said, "Mrs. Rindo, who do you know that lives in Toledo, Ohio's been calling you? It's Jose, isn't it?"

Mrs. Rindo said, "*No lo entiendo.*"

Bobby Torres glanced at Raylan. "Says she doesn't understand." He fixed his gaze on Mrs. Rindo. *"Quien le ha estado llamando de Toledo, Ohio?"*

Mrs. Rindo shook her head. *"No conozco a nadie en Toledo."*

"Says she don't know anyone in Toledo. Anything else you want me to ask?"

"Does she know the penalty for aiding and abetting a fugitive?"

Bobby said, *"Sabes la pena por ayudar e instigar a un fugitivo."*

"No lo ayudaba."

"Okay, we can go," Bobby said.

Walking to the car, Raylan said, "Isn't that nice. Boy's on the run, a fugitive from justice, but doesn't forget his mom's birthday." He paused. "What was the last thing Mrs. Rindo said?"

"She hasn't helped him."

"She knows where he is, doesn't tell us, it's about the same thing, isn't it?"

"You want to arrest her? Cause I was hoping we'd go after Leon Harris."

•••

BOBBY TORRES WAS CHEWING a bite of sandwich as he brought the binoculars to his eyes and, still chewing, said, "Somebody's in there, I can see him."

"What's he doing?"

"Looking out the window at us. Knows all the cars on the street. Sees one he doesn't recognize, gets paranoid. Leon Harris has two warrants for attempted murder. Last week the PD said Leon shot at his brother five times after a verbal altercation outside Cliff Bell's, a nightclub over by Comerica Park."

Raylan said, "Good thing for the brother, Leon doesn't know how to shoot."

They were parked on Westphalia in East Detroit, one of the worst precincts in the city, doing surveillance on Leon Harris's girlfriend's residence. Raylan studied Leon's face on the wanted poster, a black dude with an Afro and big diamond studs in his ears, reminding him of earrings his ex Winona used to wear. They looked better on her.

Bobby took another bite of his sandwich that had a strange smell. "What is that? Raylan said.

"Chorizo and peppers, want the other half?"

"I'm good."

"Last night, Lakisha Bell, Leon's lady, came home in a taxi, went in the house, said she was gonna get money, be right back, and never returned. The cab driver waited and after a time went and knocked on the door. The driver and Leon got into argument. Leon shoots the dude, grazes him. Driver runs to his car, Leon chases, shoots him two more times. Dude's in the hospital."

"Usually, somebody shot three times is in the morgue, but with Leon's track record all bets are off, huh?"

"Read his sheet? Leon likes to drink, likes to get high."

"Well there you go, that's his problem, why his aim's so bad."

"What do you think, send him to rehab so he'll be more accurate?"

"There's an idea."

Raylan noticed a photograph positioned on the dash over the fuel gauge. "Who's that?"

Bobby reached for it and handed it to him. "My wife and boys." The woman was petite, blonde, and attractive. The three boys looked like Bobby. It was interesting to think of Bobby, the tough deputy marshal, having a normal side to his life.

"What about you? No romantic interests at the moment?" Bobby paused. "Got kids from your first marriage?"

"My only marriage. Two boys: Ricky and Randy, grown now, living in LA, and a daughter Willa who lives with her mom."

Bobby's phone rang. He turned it on said, "Talk to me," and listened for a couple minutes. "All right, let me know." He glanced at Raylan. "Guy fitting Jose Rindo's description just shot a state trooper outside Columbus, Ohio. It was a routine traffic stop. Trooper asked for his driver's license, Rindo pulled a gun. He's driving a Jeep Grand Cherokee with a Michigan plate registered to a Caroline Elliott. Detroit Police questioned her, she said the Jeep was stolen from a parking garage downtown."

"You believe her? She have any connection to Rindo?"

"Wouldn't be surprised. Dude's got ladies all over the city."

"Anyone else in the Jeep?"

"Trooper says he only saw Rindo."

"What's the trooper's condition?"

"Critical but maintaining, shot once in the stomach. Ohio law enforcement has a BOLO on Jose Rindo and the Jeep. Someone's gonna recognize him." Bobby reached behind him, picked up the heavy vest, slipped it over his head, and adjusted the straps.

Raylan said, "Meantime, let's go get Leon Harris. What do you say?"

"Soon as the team gets here."

"Man can't shoot, you know that. What're you worried about?"

"That's how we do things. Don't take unnecessary chances. I want to go home tonight, see my family."

"What's your wife think about you being a deputy marshal?"

"Likes it, except that I'm never around." Bobby looked in the rearview mirror. "Okay, here they are."

In the side mirror, Raylan could see their cars had pulled up, and parked a few houses behind them, Conlon and Street crossing the road with shotguns, and Jim Tom right behind them, carrying an AR-15.

At the front door, Bobby knocked and said, "US Marshals." Raylan, five feet to his right, was looking in the big picture window at the living room. There was furniture but no sign of Leon Harris. Bobby gave it a couple seconds and swung the Blackhawk Thunderbolt breeching ram into the door and almost took it off the hinges.

They entered the house, Bobby leading the way, shotgun racked and ready, Raylan behind him two hands on the Glock. They secured the living room and kitchen. There was a warm bucket of KFC on the counter suggesting someone had just picked it up and was in the house. Raylan grabbed a drumstick out of the bucket, took a couple bites—it was good—and threw it in a plastic trash bin.

Bobby called everyone inside. Jim Tom and Street searched the basement. Conlon positioned herself at the top of the stairs while Raylan and Bobby searched the master bedroom. Raylan checked the bathroom, wet towel on the floor. Checked the closet, checking out Leon Harris's hats: sport caps and fedoras, pork pies and Borsalino Panamas. Man liked his lids. He checked under the bed, found an AK-47 with a full magazine.

Raylan searched the other two bedrooms, same result. They met in the hall a few minutes later. Street appeared at the bottom of the stairs, looked up and shook his head. Leon Harris wasn't in the basement, wasn't in one of the bedrooms, so unless he somehow got past them, there was only one place left to look.

Bobby glanced up at the hallway ceiling, pointing to the attic door. It was too high to reach. Raylan walked into the master bedroom, picked up a chair, carried it into the hall, and got up on it. "Listen, man, be careful," Bobby whispered. "Don't take any chances. You see him, come down. We'll light it up."

Raylan reached to take hold of the latch, pulled the door down, and unfolded the ladder. No one wanted any part of a situation like this, going blind into a dark unfamiliar space looking for an armed fugitive with nothing to lose. He climbed the ladder, flashlight in one hand, Glock in the other.

Almost to the opening, he stopped, glanced down at Conlon holding the 870 Remington. Street was at the top of the stairs and Bobby was directly below him. Raylan went up, sweeping the flashlight beam across the attic walls, over a trunk, a bookcase, and a chair; sunlight from two vents on opposites sides of the room made patterns on the wood-plank floor. "Leon, you up here, drop your weapon, let me see your hands. It's over, man, you can relax, no more looking over your shoulder."

But Leon Harris didn't show himself, and now Raylan stepped into the attic, crouching, aiming the flashlight beam and the red dot of the Glock's laser sight. He checked every inch of the room, training the flashlight on layers of insulation between the joists, thinking of the time he'd found an armed robber in a situation like this, hiding under a pink blanket of Owens Corning R-13, sweating, covered with threads of fiberglass.

Raylan climbed down the ladder, folded it up, and closed the attic door. He looked at Bobby and pointed at the stairs. They all went into the living room where Jim Tom was standing sentry. "Well I guess he's not here," Raylan said, winking at Bobby, and whispering, "Leon's in the house. Man, I can feel him."

"I hear you. Okay, let's do it, let's go."

•••

LEON HARRIS SAW THEM in the front yard, the US Marshals with all their guns. Watched them cross the street and get in their cars. Motherfuckers think they good, can't find a brother in a house. He saw em drive away, Leon still in his secret hiding place where he kept his stash, guns, and money. Had a little bed, had a little window with a screen over it that look like an air vent.

Leon heard the motherfuckers bust in, heard em downstairs, upstairs, heard one motherfucker in the closet bout six inches away on the other side of the wall—Leon wanted to say, "In here, motherfucker." Heard em overhead in the attic, and then heard them drive away. Young niggers across the street having fun with it. Like being in a video game: *Mayhem In the Hood.*

Though he was jonesing for the pipe, Leon held off, give em like fifteen minutes. He sat on the side of the bed grinning, enjoying the gangsta life. And then, when he thought enough time had passed, he stoked the pipe, inhaled deep, felt the buzz settle over him, put the nickel plate in his waistband, and now it was time to come out of the closet.

Raylan heard what sounded like a sliding door closing, and then the floor creaking in the bedroom directly above him, and then a man's voice was talking; he was on the phone. Raylan couldn't make out what he was saying, but it didn't matter. Leon would be coming down soon enough. What Raylan didn't expect was a car pulling up. He stood at the picture window watching the skinny black girl in a pink ensemble approach the house, walk up on the porch, stop and take a long look at the front door and the shattered molding.

Raylan was crouching behind a chair when she came in, crossed the living room, and went upstairs. On the landing he heard her say, "What happen your door?" Next thing he heard was the headboard banging against the wall, the girl moaning and screaming. Leon didn't waste any time. Probably his last chance doing it with a woman.

It went on for a while, and then silence. He heard a toilet flush. Next thing the girl was at the top of the stairs. She walked down, holding onto the banister, looked up, and said, "Nigga, what'd you do to me? I can't hardly walk."

"Call, you want some more."

The girl left the house and Leon Harris came down carrying a backpack by one of the straps, and a nickel-plated semiautomatic, a show-off gun in his waistband, Leon singing:

I can give a fuck bout no hater.
Long as my bitches love me.

And he didn't have a bad voice. When Leon was halfway across the room, Raylan approached him from behind. "Feeling pretty good about yourself, huh?"

Leon glanced over his shoulder, right hand dropping to his waist, going for the gun. Raylan's Glock was holstered but he didn't have any worries about drawing it. "Leon turn around. I want to give you a fair chance." Leon turned facing him. "Now I've got to ask you. Can you pull your pimp gun before I pull mine? That's what's on your mind, isn't it, making you hesitate? Best you can do is a tie, and you'll be dead." Raylan let that sink in before he said, "I want you to pinch the grip with your thumb and index finger, raise the weapon out of your waistband, place it on the deck, and slide it over."

Leon Harris did it just as Raylan had instructed.

"Well, you give yourself an A for following directions. Now drop the backpack and put your hands behind your head."

When Leon was cuffed and sitting on the stairs, Raylan called Bobby and said, "You still looking for Leon Harris? Cause he's here waiting for you. Come and get him."

FOUR

"CAROLINE ELLIOTT IS GETTING calls from the same Toledo number's been calling Jose Rindo's mama," Bobby Torres said. "What do you think of that?"

"You check her for warrants?"

"I ran her all the way around. Did one hundred and twenty days for possession of a controlled substance in 2012. Been clean since." Bobby paused. "First, though, I got us set up with Rocky Castro, gangbanger switched bracelets with Jose."

They met him in a conference room at the Wayne County Jail, Bobby and Raylan sitting on one side of the table as Rocky Castro hobbled in wearing yellow fatigues and ankle chains, his hands cuffed to a transport belt, a rig the Detroit marshals called a three-piece suit. The guard sat Rocky across the table from them.

Bobby said, "First of all, congratulations. In my experience no con has fucked up bigger than you did. Two days to bond out, you give your bracelet to a man wanted for three homicides. What is it about this place you like so much? Is it the food? The company? Tell me, will you?"

"Said he was gonna have me killed I didn't give it to him."

"Tough guy like you, that's hard to believe. What really happened?" Raylan studied the homemade tats: a green-and-yellow snake coming up the left side of his neck, and the number 5 on his forehead.

"Happen like I tole you."

Raylan said, "You know what they're gonna add to your sentence? Instead of getting out, you're gonna do a year, maybe two, less you can tell us something."

"We tell the court you been totally co-op," Bobby said, "they gonna take it easier on you, cut you some slack." He paused. "Either that or ask Mary, the Blessed Virgin, for help. Might also want to have her inked on your back, the hard-timers won't make you their bitch."

Raylan said, "Where's Rindo?"

"You think he tole me where he's going?"

•••

MIDAFTERNOON, THEY WERE ON the Lodge freeway in heavy traffic. Bobby said, "Think Rocky was being straight with us?"

"You mean did Rindo threaten him? No. I think Rindo offered him money or drugs for the bracelet. And Rocky was dumb enough to take the deal."

They rode in silence for a few minutes until Bobby said, "Hey, that was some good work this morning. I'm impressed. How'd you know Leon was in the house?"

"Bucket of chicken on the counter, food in the refrigerator, dishes in the sink, carryout containers in the trash. There was a car in the garage and a wet towel up in the bathroom."

"Okay, looked like someone was living there, but how'd you know he was hiding?"

"I've found fugitives in crawl spaces, attics, under floorboards, behind hot water heaters, in car trunks, you name it. I just had a feeling."

"You look at Leon cuffed on the porch, see his eyes?"

"I must've missed that."

"There was no light behind the windows," Bobby said. "Dude's stone cold, got the black eyes of a predator."

Raylan said, "Where he's going, that'll come in handy."

Bobby took a lane and cut somebody off. Raylan heard the horn sound behind them and the car in question, a Ford Taurus, came around Bobby's side honking, the driver with his arm through the sun roof giving Bobby the finger.

"You gonna let him get away with that?"

Bobby looked at Raylan and grinned.

"All the people to fuck with, he picks a US marshal with a shotgun in the back seat."

"Luck is with him, man," Bobby said. "He should buy a lottery ticket, play the horses, go to the casino."

The sign said Park Place. They drove into the complex of redbrick row houses, Bobby following the nav system on his laptop till he found the right address, pulled over, and parked. Raylan said. "What's Caroline Elliott do for a living?"

"She's one of Rindo's bitches, a kept woman."

Raylan followed Bobby up the steps to the front door. Bobby knocked and it opened as if she was expecting them.

"Deputy US Marshals. Are you Ms. Elliott?"

"What's this about?"

"Your Jeep that was stolen."

She brought them into a designer room with a giant flat screen and furniture neither of them could afford. Raylan and Bobby sat next to each other on a leather couch opposite Caroline Elliott, a tall, blue-eyed blonde with a small, cute nose, and a knockout body. She was done up, Raylan looking at her red-painted nails and bracelets clanging on skinny wrists.

"Did you find it?"

"Ohio State Police have the vehicle impounded in Columbus," Bobby said.

She frowned, trying to think of what to say.

Raylan said, "Know who was driving?"

"Whoever stole it."

"Jose Rindo," Raylan said, watching her face, expecting a reaction, but not getting one—not getting anything. She was poised and relaxed.

"This is a nice home you have," Bobby said, eyes sweeping across the room. "You don't mind my asking, what's your occupation?"

"I'm between jobs at the moment." She paused. "I worked in retail for years and then I was a personal shopper."

Bobby said, "What's that all about?"

"I helped my clients find the right clothes. Most men have difficulty deciding what looks good on them, styles and colors that flatter them."

Raylan said, "How long have you been seeing Jose Rindo?"

"I don't know who you're talking about."

He could see a little concern creeping into her expression now.

Bobby said, "Who's been calling you from Toledo?"

"I don't know. It was probably a solicitor."

"You're saying you don't know Jose Rindo, also known as Pepe," Bobby said, "is that correct?"

"I've never heard of this person." Caroline picked up a pack of Marlboro Lights off the glass coffee table, tapped a cigarette out of the pack, lit it with a silver Zippo.

"Let me show you something." Bobby got up, took a DVD out of his sport coat pocket, and handed it to her. "Put this on, will you?"

"What is it?"

"Movies. I think you'll like them. You've got a starring role in one."

Caroline Elliott hesitated for a beat, walked over to the player that was on a shelf under the flat screen, slid the disk in, and turned on the TV. It was grainy footage from a surveillance camera inside a parking garage. A man was walking behind a row of cars. A minivan with its lights on came up behind him. He turned, squinting into the glare of the headlights, and now in close up Raylan could see the man was Rindo. The car passed him and he was standing next to a dark SUV, unlocked the door with a key fob, got in, and backed out of the space. As the vehicle moved toward the camera, Raylan could see it was a Jeep.

Bobby said, "How you suppose he got the key to your car?"

"How do you know it's mine?"

Another camera picked up the Jeep as it drove out of the garage into sunlight, Jose Rindo behind the wheel, and then a shot of the rear deck of the Jeep showing the license plate number: BBQ 6069.

"According to the Department of Motor Vehicles, the car is registered to you," Bobby said. "Now what do you have to say?"

She glanced from Bobby to Raylan but didn't open her mouth.

"Check this out," Bobby said. "You and this person you've never heard of."

The footage was sharp and clean, showing Caroline trying on sandals, boxes piled up on the floor next to the saleslady, and Rindo, cap on backward, a bored expression, sitting next to her.

Caroline Elliott looked worried now. Bobby got up, pushed a button on the remote, and the TV screen went black.

Raylan said, "So what do you think, you want to go to jail, or you gonna help us?"

"I think I should call a lawyer."

Bobby said, "Where's Rindo?"

"You found the Jeep, you must know. Why you asking me?"

Raylan could see Bobby wasn't expecting that. He took the handcuffs off his duty belt. "All right then. Put your hands behind your back." She did, and he cuffed her. "Like bologna and mayo? I hope so, cause that's what you gonna have for lunch and dinner every day." Bobby put his hand around her biceps and led her toward the front door.

Raylan, flanking her on the other side, said, "I see you like to get dressed up, fix your hair, look nice. In county you wear an outfit smells like the con wore it before you."

At the front door, a worried look on her face, Caroline said, "The Knights Inn, East Columbus. I talked to him just before you came here. And you didn't find the Jeep, that's bullshit."

Bobby Torres said, "Let me have your cell phone."

"It's in my purse, in the kitchen."

Bobby went to get it.

Raylan, next to Caroline, smelling her perfume, looking at her fine features and perfect complexion, said, "Tell me something. What do you see in this thug?"

"You don't know how it works, I can see that." She smiled, showing perfect teeth, loosening up a little.

"You sit around this place he bought you, waiting for him to show up."

"If it wasn't him, it would be someone else."

"Doesn't make any difference, huh? They're all the same?"

"In the dark, whether it's Jose doing me or some other dude, I can't tell."

Bobby walked up to them. "Okay, I checked your phone. It's the same number."

"I've cooperated, done what you asked, now let me go."

"We will," Bobby said. "But first we have to hold you for a while."

FIVE

"Y OU GONNA TELL ME what we're doing here?" Raylan said, looking across the church parking lot filled with cars. "We going to services, you going to pray for me?"

"That's not a bad idea," Bobby said.

"What is this?"

"St. Anne de Detroit, part of it built in 1701. The oldest church in the city."

"What're we doing here? This part of the tour?"

"Waiting. You'll see in a few minutes."

A white, full-size van drove into the lot and parked, man behind the wheel, engine idling. A few minutes later, a Trailways Motor Coach pulled in. The van moved close to the bus as the passengers, four couples, were getting off. The driver met the couples and transferred their luggage, nine suitcases, into the back of the van.

Raylan said, "What's next, we gonna watch em play bingo, have the blue plate special?"

"One couple, we're not sure who, works for Rindo, been talking to him. Lot of chatter, lot of noise, lot of people involved. They just drove in from Tucson. They take cash on the way out, bring Grade-A Mexican heroin on the way back. Tucson Marshals kept tabs, told us when they were on their way. What Rindo is doing, man, is smart. These old people are under the radar."

"Think they know what's going on?" Raylan said. "They're doing it, but do they understand what they're doing? You see any sign any of them throwing money around?"

"Not yet."

They followed the van to the first stop, a well-kept, two-story house with a front porch on Campbell Street. The couple got out with their hand luggage. The driver opened the rear doors of the van, carried three suitcases up the porch steps and into the house. The van took off and Raylan could see Jim Tom following it to the next stop.

Bobby drove slow past the house. There was a Chevy sedan in the driveway. "Can you read the tag?"

"QRM 2280."

Bobby punched it into the laptop that was angled on a metal stand to the right of the steering wheel and waited for it to download. "Okay, the car is owned by Eladio Martinez, age fifty-seven."

"Got a warrant against him?"

Bobby checked NCIC as he went around the block and parked across the street from the Martinez house. "Nothing shows up, man appears to be clean."

The radio crackled. "Jim Tom on Ferdinand Street, couple number two, same drill as before, driver carried two suitcases into the house."

"Hang tight," Bobby said. "Grab a slab, let's see what happens."

Conlon followed couple number three to Morrell, and Street had couple number four on Christiancy.

Bobby pulled up a Google map of Mexicantown on the laptop and swiveled the screen toward Raylan. "We're here, the other houses are within a couple blocks of each other."

Now a commercial van with *ACME Carpet Cleaning* on the side pulled into the Martinez driveway. "Go on vacation, come home, have your carpeting cleaned, that the way you do it?" Raylan watched two men get out of the van, open the side door, bring out a big carpet-cleaning machine, carry it to the porch and up the steps into the house. Ten minutes later, the two men came back out with the machine, put it in the van, and drove away.

"They work fast, huh?"

"Or maybe they don't work at all," Bobby said.

Raylan wondered if the cleaners were going to stop at the houses of the other couples. Instead, the carpet cleaners drove to a building on Franklin Street near the Detroit River. The team met a couple blocks away in an empty lot with grass growing through cracks in an old concrete foundation, Raylan looking at flat, vacant land all the way to the GM Building in the distance.

As Bobby laid out the plan, Raylan watched a homeless dude, a raggedy figure, pushing a shopping cart filled with his meager possessions along the street. "Okay, we set up a perimeter around the building, I knock on the door, tell them US Marshals have em surrounded so tight—"

"They couldn't squeeze out a popcorn fart," Jim Tom said, cutting him off.

Raylan said, "Why don't I take a look, see what we're up against?"

"They got cameras all around the place," Bobby said. "How you gonna get close without being seen?"

•••

ARMANDO WAS WATCHING THE monitors, seeing an occasional car pass by on the street in front of the warehouse, and on another was *el tío sin hogar* pushing the cart, wearing a plastic garbage bag like a poncho. He stopped like he was talking to someone, but no one was there. He took a drink from a liquor bottle and shook his head. It was funny to watch this *hombre loco* coming close the building now.

•••

"GET ME OUTTA HERE," Jill Conlon said in the basket of the shopping cart under a pile of the homeless dude's clothes and plastic bags full of empty cans and bottles. Raylan had given him eighty dollars—all he had in his wallet—to borrow the rig.

When they were next to the wall under the cameras, Raylan tossed off the clothes and bags, tilted the cart forward, and Jill came out feetfirst with a Glock in her hand. "I was suffocating," she said in a whisper, glancing up at the open second-story windows.

Raylan led the way along the south wall of the warehouse to the end of the building and heard voices. He peeked around the corner and saw two dudes wearing shoulder holsters standing on the loading dock. The one closest to him had a mustache and goatee. The second one was a big man, heavyset. He didn't see anyone else.

•••

ARMANDO SAW THE HOMBRE *loco* again behind the building, talking to Molina and Calderon, who were smoking a blunt. They stepped down from the loading platform, both grinning, talking to the homeless dude. He saw Molina offer the blunt to the man, saying, "Want some of this? It fuck you up."

Calderon said, "Look at him, man. He already is."

Armando, ready for a break, walked out to the loading dock and lit a cigarette.

•••

RAYLAN WAITED TILL HE got closer to the one with the goatee, till he could see into the building, shafts of light angling in from the upstairs windows, but not much else. The man with the goatee, the one closest to him, offered Raylan the joint, reached to give it to him, and as Raylan tried to take it, the dude pulled his hand back. The men laughed. "You have to be quicker," the one with the goatee said. "Let's try again."

To complicate things, another man came out of the building. He said, "Hey, what's going on?"

"Watch this," the one with the goatee said. The man reached to give Raylan the joint again, and this time Raylan grabbed his wrist, hit him in the face with a sweeping right hand, and pulled his Glock, first holding it on the heavyset dude with the shoulder holster and then the man smoking on the loading dock. Conlon appeared now, coming around the side of the building, running into the scene with her weapon.

Raylan crouched inside the loading gate, looking down at the production line of workers weighing and packaging cocaine or heroin at a long table on the warehouse floor. The workers, young women in their underwear, wore surgical masks and rubber gloves. Two guards with shotguns kept an eye on things at ground level. Two more with automatic weapons stood at the railing of a second-floor catwalk.

One of the guards on the warehouse floor glanced toward the loading dock, looked at his watch, and started moving in Raylan's direction. Raylan crouched behind a Hi-Lo as the man approached and walked past him. After taking off his Luccheses, Raylan followed him outside in his socks, and when the guard aimed his shotgun at McGraw, Raylan put the barrel of his Glock in the man's ear and said, "Take your finger off the trigger and do it slow." The guard did. "Now lay the scatter gun on the deck."

Raylan cuffed the man, walked him down the stairs to the driveway, and sat him on the cracked concrete. "Here's what's gonna happen, four of you're gonna stay right where you're at, don't move a muscle or Boom Boom will tase you, and that don't get it done she'll shoot you."

The task force arrived in five mismatched vehicles, reminding Raylan of a scene from *Mad Max*, and formed a perimeter around the building. Standing on the loading dock and amplifying his voice with a megaphone, Bobby Torres said, "US Marshals. We have you surrounded. Put your guns down and come out with your hands up."

That's how they busted Jose Rindo's heroin operation. The Task Force confiscated ninety-six pounds of pure uncut heroin, $1.7 million in cash, four AK-47s, six Mossberg 500 Tactical shotguns, and arrested twelve people with intent to distribute or sell a Schedule 1 drug.

"Rindo and his crew are slinging big time," Bobby said. "Moving some weight."

After the arrests, Raylan drove to his apartment in Royal Oak that was still filled with boxes from the move. He'd towed a U-Haul trailer behind his Durango 4X4 from Kentucky, the trailer packed with all of his worldly possessions, but that wasn't saying a whole lot. Took him eleven hours to drive the seven-hundred-plus miles to an apartment he'd never seen, in a town he'd never been to that was described as lively, full of restaurants, bars, and nightlife.

He heard loud voices next door; sounded like the neighbors he still hadn't met were having an argument. He left the apartment, walked down Main Street in the early evening, looking in storefronts, stopping to study menus that were posted. Raylan wandered farther and went into Mr. B's. He found a seat at the crowded bar, had a couple beers, feeling relaxed for the first time since he woke up.

He heard his phone ring and dug it out of his jeans. It was Bobby. "What's up?"

"Ohio State Police just arrested Rindo. We gotta go pick him up."

"What time you want to leave?"

SIX

SIX IN THE MORNING, still dark out, Bobby met Raylan in front of the Federal Building on Lafayette. Bobby got out of the transport vehicle, a Dodge Charger with a 370-horsepower Hemi V8 under the hood and a steel cage in back, and walked to Raylan's G-ride. Raylan was getting his vest and long gun out of the trunk.

"There's a change in the plan. FBI fucking things up again," Bobby said. "Chief wants you to go with the girl, the special agent. Remember her? The one kickstarts her vibrator."

"This's a joke. You're putting me on, right?"

"I wish."

"Why am I going? You're the case agent. We've got to make sure this gets done right."

"I've got faith in you, so does the chief. I guess she insisted on going and asked for you," Bobby said. "Pick up Rindo, she's gonna interview him, wants to show you how the professionals do it."

"That's her talking, or you?"

"Chief said cooperate, get it over with. Maybe she's not so bad. Maybe you can loosen her up."

"It's only a three-and-a-half-hour drive." Raylan paused. "Know anything about her? She any good?"

"You'll find out," Bobby said, staring at the Stetson. "Jesus, bringing the hat back."

"I missed wearing it, didn't feel right."

"I guess you can get away with it in Ohio. You're gonna pick Jose Rindo up at the Franklin County Jail in Columbus."

"Anyone from the warehouse bust talking yet?"

"It takes time to get through the pile. At first everyone thinks they're tough. Nobody's gonna say nothing. Give em a couple months in a federal holding facility, they're gonna be begging you to talk." Bobby took a business card out of his shirt pocket. "One more thing, you're supposed to pick up Special Agent Sanchez at the Bureau field office, Four Seven Seven Michigan Avenue."

"Why doesn't she come here?"

"You can ask her."

"What time she gonna be ready?"

Bobby glanced at his watch. "Six fifteen, you better get going."

Raylan handed Bobby the keys to his G-ride. Bobby'd park it on Griswold next to the courthouse, leave the keys under the mat.

When Raylan was in front of the building, he dialed her number. "Agent Sanchez, it's Deputy US Marshal, Raylan Givens—"

"You don't have to identify yourself every time we meet," she said, cutting him off. "I know who you are, and you're late."

Friendly as ever, Raylan thought. It was gonna be a long drive. "I'm parked in front. Where're you at?" But she'd already hung up. He set the GPS for Columbus, Ohio, a city he'd never been to. Nora Sanchez came out of the building and down the steps wearing black slacks and a blue blazer, carrying a shoulder bag. As she got closer, he waved to her. She opened the front passenger door, looked at Raylan, glanced at the cage, got in, and fit her bag on the floor.

"Know how to get there?" It sounded like a challenge.

"We'll see," Raylan said, turning in his seat. "Tell me something, what're you doing? Why're you pushing your way into this?"

"Pardon me." Nora looked like she wanted to take a swing at him. "Who do you think you are?"

"The one arrested the fugitive and now's going to pick him up."

"We have as much right to Jose Rindo, and a whole lot more motivation than you or anyone else. And I would think you'd be embarrassed this murderer escaped again."

"We hunt them down and bring em in. We're not involved in their custody. Anything else you want to say?" That's how it started: at odds with each other from the opening bell.

"Should I go back inside, come out, we'll try again?"

"I don't think anything would change." Raylan could hear a little Spanish accent when she got angry. Yeah, he wanted her to go back in and stay there, but he pictured Chief Broyles's face and kept that to himself, put the Charger in gear, and rumbled to the freeway. They didn't say another word to each other till they were crossing the state line. Raylan looking up at the sign that read:

OHIO WELCOMES YOU

"Ever been to Ohio?"

"No," she said, a little friendlier, but still not looking at him.

"One of the most boring states I've ever been through."

Nora Sanchez glanced at him, more relaxed now, and said, "You better stay out of Nebraska."

"It's bad, huh?"

"Halfway through you'll want to head back the way you came, go through Kansas." She smiled for the first time and Raylan saw a good-looking woman.

They were clipping along in the fast lane, just south of Toledo. Raylan checked the side mirror, saw the state trooper coming up fast, light bar flashing.

He pulled over on the gravel shoulder and lowered the window. "See, the problem? You want to get through Ohio so bad you speed, and they stop you."

Raylan watched the trooper get out of his car and come up on the driver's side, bend his frame at the window till he was eye level, and glance inside. "License and registration."

To Raylan, this young muscular hard-ass looked about twenty-two and was cut from the mold. Not too bright, cause the job was monotonous and boring. But the man carried a semiautomatic on his hip and had authority and that had to be a lot of the attraction.

"I'm a deputy United States marshal," Raylan said. "And next to me is Special Agent Sanchez with the FBI. We're armed."

"Let's see some ID."

Nora took hers out and flipped it open. Raylan showed the trooper his star on a chain around his neck.

"What's your business in Ohio?"

"Picking up a prisoner, fugitive warrant, in Columbus," Raylan said. "Shot one of your own a couple days ago, Trooper Watson. You know how he's doing?"

"Died this morning."

"Sorry to hear that," Raylan said.

"Left a wife and two little ones. Call me, you need assistance." The trooper handed Raylan a card. "I'll give the son of a bitch what he deserves and more."

When they were cruising again, Raylan said, "Based on his reaction I'm surprised Rindo made it into custody at all."

"Yeah, but the trooper was still alive when they found him. What would've happened if they arrested him today?"

She was a step ahead of him on that.

"Listen, I just want to be clear on something." Nora said, fixing a hard stare on him now. "Jose Rindo is my prisoner."

"What does that mean?"

The scowl returned. "Before he's tried on the other charges, I want him for the murder of Special Agent Frank Tyner."

"What difference does it make? He's going away and he's never getting out."

"To me it does."

Why was it so personal with her? "That's up to the court. You don't know how this works?"

"I want to question the suspect. I don't know if you have another agenda." She was wound up tight.

"Like what, take him in the woods, shoot him, say he was trying to escape? My agenda is to pick him up and take him back. You want to question Rindo, fire away. You've got three hours and change, less that trooper stops us again and shoots him. That enough time?"

Nora turned the other way now, looking out at the flat Ohio countryside, and didn't say another word till Raylan said, "Want to get something to eat? Be our only chance. There's a service plaza a mile up the freeway. You've got your choice of McDonald's, Taco Bell, or Subway."

"I brought tuna on whole wheat and a bottle of water, but you go ahead."

That seemed like the kind of healthy lunch a sensible, clean-living FBI agent would have. Raylan got off at the next exit, turned into the drive-thru lane at McDonald's, and ordered a double cheese, fries, and a coke. He wolfed it down in the parking lot while Nora took her time, taking small, stomach-settling bites like she was part bird.

"Where're you from?" Raylan said.

"Miami, originally. I went to the academy and was transferred to Tucson. Been there eleven years."

"Got any brothers or sisters?"

"Three brothers."

"Know how to throw a curveball?"

Nora frowned. "What's that supposed mean?"

"Girls I've known that had a lot of brothers knew how to throw like a guy."

"You want to pull over, play catch?"

"I hear an accent when you say certain words."

"I grew up speaking Spanish and English, which comes in handy being so close to Mexico." She drank some water.

"Tell me about this friend of yours, the FBI agent that was murdered. Were you seeing him?"

"He was married." Nora paused, eyes sad like she might cry. "Frank was a good friend."

He could see she didn't want to go there and dropped it.

•••

HALF AN HOUR LATER, Raylan pulled into the sally port at the Franklin County Corrections complex, showed his ID to a sheriff's deputy about his age, and said, "US Marshal here to pick one up. Where's the Criminal Clerks Office at?"

"Third floor. Let me see the paperwork."

Raylan took the forms off a clipboard: "Writ of Habeas Corpus, Extradition Order, and the Criminal Warrant." The deputy gave each page a casual glance and said, "Okay. Come with me." The man took him in the building, showed him where to go, and ten minutes later Raylan came back with the forms signed, and ten minutes after that another Franklin County sheriff's deputy brought Jose Rindo into the sally port, his hands cuffed to a transport belt, ankles cuffed to a fifteen-inch length of chain, fugitive hopping along in jail fatigues.

Raylan said, "Your last hurrah, huh? I hope it was good, cause that's it."

"You think so, huh?" He was locked up tight and still full of swagger.

The sheriff's deputy said, "You've got to sign for him."

"Give me a minute." Raylan led him, hand on his biceps, to the Charger.

"What I tell you, huh?" Rindo said. "We meet again. Remember what you said to me?"

"Next time, you're not gonna be so lucky. You think anything's changed?"

"No, but I think is only a matter of time."

"You trying to tell me something?" Raylan opened the rear door, pushed Rindo in the cage, and fastened the seatbelt around him.

Nora was looking at the prisoner from the other side of the car, and now Raylan walked back to the Franklin County sheriff's deputy and signed the form.

"Think you can hold him this time?" the deputy said without expression. "Switched bracelets on you, I hear." Now a little grin slipped out. "That's not the oldest trick in the book, it's right up there. Need some help, give us a call."

Raylan said, "You've got all the answers, huh? That's why they've got you working cell block." That silenced him, wiped the grin off his face.

Raylan popped the trunk and opened the equipment locker as Nora came around the back of the car and stood next to him. "What's this, you expecting trouble?"

"You better, and be ready when it happens."

"Why didn't you say something?"

"Transport a prisoner, an ambush is always a possibility. I don't think anything's gonna happen, but if it does, we better be prepared. I thought you knew what you were getting into." But it was obvious she didn't. He reached in the trunk and grabbed his UAV. "Put this on." He lifted it over Nora's head and helped her adjust the straps. It was too big, but it would protect her. She tapped the front of the vest with her knuckles.

"You usually run with heavy plates?"

Another strange question. "When I don't know who's coming or what they're bringing."

"Where's yours?"

"I've got a soft one on underneath. I can't drive in a tac vest." Raylan held her in his gaze. "Tell me you're armed."

She patted her shoulder bag. "Got my primary in here." Raylan felt better. Sounded like Nora knew what she was doing after all, till she said, "But I've never fired my weapon in the line of duty."

Now he wasn't so sure.

•••

RINDO HAD BEEN STUDYING the girl. She was a hot little package, but why'd this sexy bitch look so familiar? She didn't wear a star on a chain around her neck like the crazy one. Who was she, man? He watched her standing close to the car, looking in like she knew him, wanted to say something, Rindo thinking, *yeah, dude, she's the angel, the one gonna save you.*

The engine started with a heavy rumble. The crazy one drove through the parking lot. Jose said, "Hey, miss, I was wondering, can you help me with something? You look familiar. Where do I know you from?"

Now the girl turned, held him in her gaze, and said, "Tucson. You killed a friend of mine, or you had him killed, which to me is the same thing. I'm a special agent with the FBI, and I'm going to do everything I can to send you to the gas chamber."

"I don't know what you're saying. I don't know anything about this."

"The shooter used your name, and said, 'It's too late for explanations.' And then murdered him."

Rindo was sorry he asked.

They rode, nobody talking for a while until the crazy one, looking at him in the rearview mirror, said, "Saw what you did to DeShonte Moore. Man was extra crispy when we found him. Be a bad way to go."

"What do you care? Nother drug dealer bites the dust." Rindo sucked a piece of scrambled egg out of his teeth and swallowed it. "Listen, I got a proposition for you, fix you up for life? Let me go, I give you five million."

The crazy one said, "Five million what?"

"Dollars, man. What you think?" He waited a little before he said, "Hey, Miss FBI Special Agent, I can set you up, buy whatever you want, never worry about money again."

The crazy one looked at the FBI girl, and then he was looking at Jose in the mirror again. "What do we have to do?"

"Nothing cept let me escape. What could be easier?"

"And you're gonna give us five million dollars?" the girl said. "Is that right?"

"Yes, that is exactly right."

The girl whispered something to the crazy one Jose couldn't hear.

"It's a chance to retire," Rindo said. "Do whatever you want. Never worry bout nothing."

The girl said, "When do we get it?" sounding like she was interested.

"Look, that's not a problem. We can work it out."

The girl said to the crazy one, "What's trying to bribe a federal officer going to add to his sentence?"

"Not enough to worry about."

Now the girl said, "I think we should turn him loose, and when he starts to run, shoot him."

"He was trying to escape. That's not bad."

Jose was quiet till they crossed into Michigan and saw a rest area sign. "Hey, listen. I got a problem with my stomach, I have to get to a toilet."

"We don't stop," the marshal said. "I told you that."

"This been going on for a few days. I don't know, I ate something bad, or what. I'm gonna shit myself and all over the back of the car, man."

Nora whispered, "What do you think?"

"Maybe he has to go. I'm thinking of the worst that can happen and it doesn't sound very good. I'm okay, long as we do it fast. Next one's forty-four miles, you see the sign?"

The BMW M5 that had passed them twenty minutes earlier—Raylan remembered the car—was angle-parked in front of the building. It had a Michigan plate. He didn't think anyone was in it, but with the blacked-out windows it was hard to tell. There were three other vehicles parked there: a minivan, a pickup truck, and an RV. On the truck side of the complex were two semis.

Raylan scanned the rooflines of the building, imagining a man with a rifle up there watching them. He didn't see anyone, got out of the car, closed the door, and looked in the BMW. No one was in it. Now he moved to the back of the Charger and opened the trunk. Nora got out and came around the car to meet him. "Tell me what you want me to do."

"I'll go in, clear out the men's, give you a sign. You want the shotgun or the long gun?"

"The shotgun."

Raylan pulled the Remington 870 out of the gun locker and handed it to her. He picked up the AR-15, popped a magazine in, and chambered a round. He slipped on a blue windbreaker with US MARSHAL on the back and slung the AR over his shoulder. "Let's let them all come out before we make a move."

It was a windy day. The American flag was flapping in the breeze. He put a hand on top of his hat to keep it from blowing off.

Raylan entered the building, holding the door for an elderly couple that made their way to the parking area in slow motion, and got in the RV. Next a woman and her daughter walked out, moved quickly to the pickup, and took off.

Now two black dudes, one the size of an NFL nose guard, exited the men's room and approached, checking him out. Raylan stood to the left of the doors and watched them all the way to the Beamer. They got in and drove away.

Raylan went in the restroom, yellow cinderblock walls and no windows, found a Smith & Wesson .38 in the second stall taped behind the toilet tank. Had to be from the dudes in the BMW. He went back outside. Nora, holding the shotgun, stood next to the Charger, waiting for a signal.

He moved toward her, glanced at the other side of the rest area where the trucks were parked, saw the BMW circling around, speeding past the semis, and pointed to it. The BMW was a hundred yards away and coming fast. Raylan aimed the AR, trying to steady it in the wind, fired two three-shot bursts at the Beamer and felt the Stetson lift off his head and watched the wind carry it away.

He got in behind the wheel, floored it, jumped the parking block and went straight over grass, bouncing on the irregular surface to the other side of the rest area, seeing the BMW in the rearview mirror, closing fast.

They got stuck behind a semi gearing up on the entrance ramp heading for the expressway. In the side mirror, Raylan saw the BMW coming up behind them and then felt it ram the back end of the Charger and try to pull around them on the right. Raylan jerked the steering wheel going the opposite way, speeding along the left side of the semi, the BMW going along the right side. "You see them, don't hesitate."

Nora had the barrel of the shotgun sticking out the open window, resting on the doorsill. As the BMW cleared the truck, Nora fired and blew out the driver's side window. The BMW drifted to the right. She fired again and blew out the left front tire and sent the high-performance sedan zigzagging out of control. It went off the road and came back, tried to ram them again, and Nora blew out the windshield.

The Beamer disappeared down the embankment, and then came up plowing through a barbed wire fence into a cornfield.

Raylan called the Marshals Service in Toledo figuring it was the closest office. He gave them the license number of the BMW, its current location near Milepost 188 in Monroe County, and a description of the two dudes that were in it.

Raylan reached behind his back, gripped the .38, and handed it to Nora. "This was in one of the stalls waiting for him."

"That was close."

"Can't take anything for granted with this dude."

"What about the money? Let's make a deal," Rindo said, sounding like a Spanish game show host.

Raylan said, "This boy doesn't quit, does he?"

"Trying to play his last card," Nora said.

"Hey, you hear me, man, what I'm saying?"

"I don't hear him," Raylan said. "You hear him?"

Nora said, "I don't hear anything."

"I can change your life, man. Yo, how much they pay you a year? You making seventy, seventy-five? It's a joke. All the risk, put your life on the line for what?"

"One more word," Raylan said, "you're gonna ride in the trunk."

"The fuck difference it make?" Rindo unhooked the seatbelt, lay across the back seat, brought his knees to his chest, and kicked, banging the cage with his shackled feet, shaking the car. He did it again and Raylan said, "Tase him."

"All right, man, I'm chill."

Rindo was quiet till they got to the Wayne County Jail. Raylan took him in and booked him, told the sheriff's deputies his criminal history, his successful escapes, and suggested they put the dude in isolation.

•••

HE DROPPED NORA OFF at the FBI field office on Michigan Avenue. "Thanks for the vest and shotgun." Nora paused. "Listen, you were right. I shouldn't have interfered. I shouldn't have insisted on coming with you. It's not what I do."

"I thought you handled yourself like a pro," Raylan said. "You know how to use a shotgun. I'd take you with me anytime."

Nora smiled. "Well I appreciate that." After spending the day with him she felt more relaxed in Raylan's company.

She was opening the door when he said, "Let me ask you something." Nora stopped and turned to him. "You told Rindo the shooter used his name and said, 'It's too late for explanations,' or words to that effect. That can only mean one thing: you were there."

She frowned, eyes holding on him, but didn't say anything.

"I heard you say it. It's hard to ignore. You were either at the scene or you weren't. Which is it?"

"None of your business." She got out of the car and walked up the steps.

SEVEN

Raylan walked in his apartment after a long, tough day, thinking about his Stetson. He'd had that one eight years, finally broken in and fit like it was part of him. Maybe it was just as well. Wearing it didn't make any sense in Detroit.

He went in the kitchen, opened a beer, took a long drink, guzzling a third of the bottle, and felt better. He'd never had more trouble with a prisoner in transport and was glad to be rid of him. The Toledo Marshals found the BMW, but not the two dudes who were in it, and now law enforcement in Monroe and neighboring counties were conducting a manhunt.

Next door, his neighbors were at it again—third day in a row—angry voices coming right through the drywall, the girl's high-pitched Southern screech and the guy's deep-bass snarl. Raylan heard a plate shatter, a door slam, and something bang into his living room wall. He was starving and hoping for a quiet night, drink some whiskey and watch TV. Raylan liked the whole Wednesday night lineup, starting with Jeopardy.

After five minutes of quiet, he thought the neighbors had suspended their hostilities and come to some kind of truce when it started up again, louder than before. He finished his beer and popped another one, went in the living room, and heard them on the other side of the wall. Another door slammed closed.

They had taken their fight into the hall, yelling at each other, Raylan wondering what could get two people so angry. He heard a knock on his door, and the girl yelled, "Help, he's trying to kill me."

Raylan set his beer down, got up, and opened the apartment door, looking at the girl's long, straight dark hair and small frame in a tank top, right there till she moved left to avoid the big man's ham-shank fist.

In the hall now, Raylan said, "You don't want to do that."

"Who the fuck're you?" He looked a little like Gregg Allman, but bigger, long hair, beard, tats covering muscular arms, and sounded like he had a serious buzz on. A heavy Harlan County accent, but still seemed to have his wits about him.

"A concerned citizen," Raylan said.

"You mean pussy, don't you? Why don't you mind your own fucking business, little man? Fore you get into something you can't handle."

"I'd like to, but you're making so much noise I can't hear myself think."

The girl, facing him now, waited to see how he'd react. She was good-looking, early twenties. What was she doing with this fool?

"Listen," the big man said, "you can either go back in there or I'll throw you in."

"That's a helluva impression you're making on your new neighbor," Raylan said. "Why don't we start over, say hello, see can we get along?"

The big man brought his fists up, menace on his face, ready to take a swing. He rushed Raylan, threw a couple heavy haymakers that missed, and now he was breathing hard, slowing a little, but he wasn't gonna stop. Raylan waited for an opening, stepped in close, and broke his nose. The big man's hands went up to protect his face.

"Hit him again," the girl said. "Hit the son of a bitch." She came over and stood next to Raylan. "You gotta help me. I go back in there, Junior's gonna give me what for, I'm telling you."

Junior said, "Get your shit, and get the hell out."

Two tenants opened their doors and stepped into the hall to see what was going on.

"Will you come with me, make sure he don't do nothing?" She said it with fear in her eyes and a bruise on her upper cheek.

All Raylan wanted was a quiet night and now he was involved in this domestic altercation. "Hang on a second." He went into his apartment, slid the Glock in the waist of his jeans, and covered it with his shirttail. He wasn't taking any chances. This fella Junior was a real wild card, mean and unpredictable. He closed the apartment door and walked in the hall. "All right, let's get your stuff."

"I sure preciate your help. I was thinking *this time* he's gonna put me in the hospital or worse. Junior has a temper on him as you seen."

"What're you doing with him?"

"He was kind and gentle, and a tad shy at first. I don't think he had much experience with girls and that made him more appealing." The girl exhaled with a sigh. "Once we got familiar, Junior turned into his real self. I hung in there thinking I could change him. How do you think I did?"

Raylan felt sorry for her. "Got some place you can go? Friends or relatives in the area?"

"Nobody. You're it."

They entered her apartment, the girl nervous, looking around. She went to her room while Raylan sat and nursed the beer. Junior was on the balcony off the kitchen, the big man holding a plastic bag of ice over his nose, taking swigs of whiskey from the bottle. Junior glared at him, opened the sliding door, and came into the kitchen holding the neck of the whiskey bottle down his leg, dropped the ice bag on the table, and moved toward Raylan. "Want her, you can have her. Just be ready is all. Cause she gonna drive you out of your fucking mind." Now in another voice, trying to sound like the girl, he said, *"Them dishes ain't gonna get clean by themselves. Hell, you're not wearing that shirt again, are you? That's three days in a row. Junior Poole, all you do's sit around, drink."* He took a long deep swig of Wild Turkey. "Yeah, I drink. I better, I'm gonna handle that attitude she give me."

Raylan said. "You don't have to worry about her anymore. Just take care of yourself, okay?"

"Slick, talk to me in a couple days, see how tolerant you are."

The girl said, "Why don't you shut your mouth," coming out of her room carrying a big plastic Samsonite suitcase and a pile of clothes on hangers draped over her forearm.

"Why don't you come over here and make me?"

Raylan took the suitcase, led her out of the apartment and back to his, put her suitcase down on the living room floor, and said, "I don't even know your name."

"Well, I can fix that. I'm Jo Lynne."

"I'm Raylan."

"Why's that sound familiar? Ever been to Harlan County, Kentucky?"

"Born and raised. Worked in the mines."

"What's your daddy's name?"

"Arlo. I get you something to drink? Beer, Coca Cola?"

"I don't suppose you got any shine on the premises."

"Shine, huh? Where you from?"

"Belle Glade originally, east end of Lake Okeechobee. That's in Florida, you don't know it."

"Muck City." Raylan opened the cupboard, took out a Mason jar of shine that had a peach floating near the bottom and poured Jo Lynne a couple inches in a short skinny juice glass.

"*Her soul is her fortune*," Jo Lynne said, quoting the Belle Glade city motto. "We moved to Kentucky I was yet a whippersnapper."

"I worked in South Florida for a while," Raylan said. "I liked it down there." He opened the refrigerator, grabbed a beer, and popped the top. "You didn't happen to know the Crowe family, ran a fish camp near there?"

"Know em? I'm one of em. Full name's Jo Lynne Crowe."

"I knew Darryl Jr., Dilly, Dewey, Dickie, Wendy, Coover, and Pervis. Four of them either shot dead or sent to prison. Now you show up here nice as a sunny day."

"They my cousins, aunt, and uncle. I was living in Harlan County when that jig shot and killed Dewey and Coover and almost put Uncle Perv out of business. Though Pervis Crowe has since departed this world. Passed a while ago. We lost a good one, I'll tell you that. My guess, Perv's up there on that piney ridge in the sky, hunting and drinking shine."

If Raylan was looking for proof it was a small world, there she was sitting at his kitchen table drinking Kentucky's finest.

"Deputy US Marshal Raylan Givens. Oh yeah, I heard'a you. Can't believe I'm consorting with the enemy in his goddamn lair. Uncle Perv's probably rollin in his grave."

"I got no quarrel, but if you do, I don't see anyone keeping you here against your will."

There was a knock on the door. Jo Lynne said, "I can tell you who that is."

Raylan got up, walked through the living room, drew his Glock, thinking Junior Poole could be on the other side with a shotgun to go with his surly disposition. He opened the door. It was Junior all right, he had calmed down and looked like a different person—all the anger gone from his face. "Tell Jo Lynne I's sorry. Tell her JR's here and he wants to apologize for his actions."

"I don't want to talk to him," Jo Lynne yelled from the kitchen. "It's happened too many times."

"I'll be better, you'll see," Junior said in a louder voice that could be heard thirty feet away. "You got my word on that."

Raylan, uncomfortable being in the middle of this soap opera, said, "Give her some time, go back to your place, and take it easy." He closed the door and walked to the kitchen.

"This's what he does," Jo Lynne said, "blows his stack, then turns into a puppy, comes crawling back. I think Junior's got something wrong with his brain." Jo Lynne picked up the Mason jar, poured another couple inches of shine in the glass, brought it to her mouth, swigged the clear liquid, and coughed. "Lord, this stuff'll cure what ails you. Been some time since I had it." She took a couple breaths. "Listen, I'm gonna call my brother, see he'll come pick up his sis. You know Derek? Everyone calls him Skeeter."

"I don't believe I do."

"Meanwhile, since I got no place to go, you mind I sleep on your couch for a night or two?"

"A minute ago I was the enemy, now you want to stay here. I just want to make sure I got it right."

"Less you're kicking me out."

Raylan wanted to but couldn't quite bring himself to do it. Jo Lynne called her brother on her cell phone. Told him she'd broke it off with Junior and was stuck and desperate in Detroit. She listened for a time and shut off the phone.

"What'd he say?"

"That he'd warned me bout Junior and I didn't listen. I told him we all make mistakes and now I needed his help." Jo Lynne frowned, holding Raylan in her gaze. "Why do men always have to be right?"

"I thought it was the other way around."

Jo Lynne smiled. "Skeeter's coming to get me, leaving first thing in the morning. I decided not to mention nothing bout you. Hey, you mind I have another blast?"

EIGHT

A GAINST HIS BETTER JUDGMENT, Raylan left Jo Lynne Crowe at his kitchen table in a tank top and short shorts, drinking a cup of coffee, looking pretty good he had to admit.

"Thank you, Raylan Givens, for your hospitality. You're not so bad after all." That was high praise coming from a member of the Crowe family. "This may sound crazy, but I could see going out with you," she said with a smile, her long tan legs stretched out on the chair next to her.

"That'd go over well with your kin."

"We'd be just like Romeo and Juliet."

Raylan let that pass and said, "Call Junior, will you? Tell him you're leaving, or better yet, you left. I don't want him coming over here looking for you. What time's your brother picking you up?"

"What time'd he say or what time's he really gonna be here? I never heard the words 'Skeeter' and 'on time' in the same sentence."

"Listen, help yourself to whatever, I'll check back with you this afternoon."

"Bless your heart, Raylan Givens."

•••

"THEY STILL HAVE HIM?" Raylan said. "He didn't escape again, did he?"

"Trying to be funny?" Bobby Torres said.

They were on Jefferson, passing the Ambassador Bridge. Raylan's gaze moved past him to the Detroit River and the shoreline of Canada in the distance. "After what happened it's not out of the question."

"They're embarrassed, man. Got Rindo in isolation, locked down twenty-four-seven. Got an eye on him. He's not going nowhere." Bobby turned right on Grand Boulevard. "How was it with Special Agent Sanchez?"

"Interesting."

"The hell's that mean?"

"She apologized for interfering, admitted she was in over her head but got the job done when it counted. We came to an understanding."

"So she's not going to be fucking with us again?"

"Here's something else. I think she was with the murdered FBI agent the night he was killed."

Bobby looked stunned. "She told you that?"

"No. It was something she said to Rindo in the car. The shooter said, 'It's too late for explanations,' before he shot Frank Tyner. If she heard it, she must've been there."

"Did you ask her?"

"Yeah. She said it's none of my business."

"Well, there you go. She doesn't want you anywhere near this."

Bobby turned left on Vernor Highway and now they were passing the decorative, bright-colored storefronts of Mexicantown.

"You think Tyner was involved with Rindo and his gang?"

"I don't know."

"Were Sanchez and Tyler having an affair?"

"I can't imagine. She doesn't seem like the type."

"Come on, you don't think she gets laid?"

"You'd have to thaw her out first."

Bobby passed a delivery truck that was double-parked. "You gonna do something about this? Talk to the chief."

"And tell him what? A murdered FBI agent might have had ties to a fugitive drug dealer? Tyner might have been undercover for all we know. As Agent Sanchez said, it's none of our business."

Bobby pulled up in front of the Martinez residence, same Chevy in the driveway.

Raylan knocked on the door, heard voices in the house. Eladio Martinez opened it, eyeing them with suspicion.

"US Marshals," Bobby said. "Mr. Martinez, we need to speak to you and your wife."

"What this about?"

"Invite us in," Bobby said, "we'll tell you."

"How was your trip to Arizona?" Raylan said, sitting next to Bobby on the couch, facing the nervous Martinez couple opposite them in armchairs. "Summer's an odd time to go to the desert. What's it get up to, the heat, like one twenty-five?"

"You want to know about our vacation, that why you come here?" Eladio Martinez was trying to stay calm but it wasn't working. He frowned. "Got nothing better to do?" Mrs. Martinez kept her eyes glued to her husband.

Raylan said, "I've always wondered about taking a motor coach. Is that a relaxing way to travel?"

"Is not bad," Eladio Martinez said, more in control. "You play cards, read, sleep, stop once in a while, have something to eat."

"I was surprised you had so much luggage," Bobby said. "More than the others you were traveling with. You buy something in Tucson, bring it back?"

"You married?" Eladio Martinez said to Bobby in a friendlier tone. "Ever travel with a woman? When it comes to clothes and shoes, there is no such thing as too much. Tell them." Mr. Martinez turned to his wife.

"What can I say?" the woman said, smiling.

Raylan said, "Know what didn't make sense? You get home from the trip, you been gone a week, and a few minutes after you walk in the door, men come to clean your carpet."

Eladio Martinez smiled. "You know why? They have the wrong day. I say to them: 'Hey, what are you doing here? You come next week.'"

Raylan said, "That explains why they were only there for a few minutes, huh?"

"So you were watching us?" Eladio Martinez said. "You saw them?"

"But it doesn't explain where they went after that," Raylan said.

Eladio Martinez said, "What does it have to do with us?"

Bobby said, "Where're your suitcases?"

"In the closet, isn't that right?" Eladio Martinez said to his wife. She nodded. "Why you want to know?"

"I want to see them. Bring the suitcases in here and let us have a look," Bobby said. "What're you worried about?"

Eladio Martinez got up, walked out of the room, and came back in carrying two big blue plastic suitcases and a gray one.

Raylan pictured the scene, sitting in the car on the street, seeing the driver carrying the luggage into the house. From his recollection these were the same three suitcases.

Bobby opened the blue ones first, ran his hand around the sides and bottoms, and closed the tops. Now he opened the gray one, did the same thing, glanced at his palm, and rubbed his thumb over his fingertips. "They tell you what you'd be carrying? You know what was in the suitcase?" His eyes held on Eladio Martinez and then his wife before she looked away.

"They are for clothes like I tell you."

The Martinezes were both nervous now. Mrs. wringing her hands and Mr. rubbing his face like he had a rash.

"The gray one was filled with money on the way to Tucson," Raylan said. "And on the way back it was filled with something else."

Bobby showed him the powder residue on his fingers. "This is what was in the suitcase: uncut Mexican heroin. You're both gonna go to prison." Bobby's gaze moved again from the husband to the wife. "Or you can start talking. How long you been Jose Rindo's mule? And how many of the others are involved? Help us, man, we help you."

"That's why you come here, uh, to help us?" Eladio Martinez let out a breath. "We don't know nothing about this. Whatever is inside, I think you put it there. You have proof we do something, let's see it. Show it to us."

"I did. And now I'm gonna show you this." Bobby unfolded a piece of paper. "It's a warrant for your arrest. You and your wife, Mr. Martinez. Put your hands behind your back." Bobby took the

handcuffs off his duty belt and approached the man. "Your last chance."
Mr. Martinez didn't respond. Bobby put the cuffs on his wrists.

Raylan asked Irena to stand and cuffed her hands behind her
back. Now her husband had fear in his eyes. Irena glanced at him and
shook her head. She glanced at Raylan and said, "We don't know what
was in the suitcase."

"Are you crazy?" Eladio Martinez said to his wife.

Ignoring her husband, Irena said, "A man contact us, say we take
something for his cousin, a suitcase, and bring something back, he pay
all expenses for us and our friends: the bus, the hotel, drinks, meals,
everything, and give us five thousand dollars."

Raylan said, "When was this?"

"Two weeks before we go."

Raylan said, "What did you think was in the suitcase?"

Eladio Martinez looked like he was in pain, but his wife kept
talking.

"The man say is clothes."

"Did you open it to see?" Raylan said.

"The suitcase, it was locked."

"Was it heavy?"

"Not so much."

Raylan said, "You didn't think it was strange, somebody giving
you that kind of money to take clothes? Paying for you and your
friends? Come on."

"You need the money," Irena Martinez said, "you don't ask."

"What do you think?" Bobby said to Eladio Martinez.

He stared at the floor.

"Tell us what happened," Raylan said to Irena.

"A man meet us at the hotel, take the suitcase."

Raylan said, "What'd he say?"

"*Gracias*, I think," Irena Martinez said. "I don't remember his
words." She rubbed her hands together.

Raylan said, "What'd he look like?"

"I don't know."

"The man met you at the hotel and you don't know what he
looked like?"

"I didn't see him." Irena glanced at her husband.

"Eladio," Bobby said, "who picked up the suitcase?"

"I don't know. I never see him before."

"Describe him."

"*Pecoso.*"

Bobby glanced at Raylan. "He's saying the man had a lot freckles on his face. It could also be his nickname."

"The day before we come home," Irena said, "the man bring the suitcase to take back to Detroit."

"How many times have you done this?" Raylan said, glancing at Irena first and then Eladio.

Irina said, "This was the first and only time."

Bobby said, "Who were you traveling with?"

"Our friends from the church," Irena said.

"Did they think it was strange, you inviting them on a paid vacation?"

"I tell them I win the lottery," Irena said.

Bobby said, "You know them well?"

Irena nodded. "Yes, for many years."

Bobby said, "How long have you known Maribel Rindo?"

The woman looked surprised and hesitated before answering. "A long time. We grow up in Mexicali." Now she made a face, knowing she shouldn't have said that.

Raylan said, "So, of course you know her son, Jose. Pepe, she calls him."

Irena Martinez shook her head. "I don't know him."

"That's a little hard to believe, don't you think?" Raylan said. "You and the mom grew up together, but you don't know her son?" Raylan shook his head, turned to Bobby. "That sound as odd to you as it does me?

Irena Martinez glanced at her husband for support and he looked away, telling her she was on her own.

"Anything else you want to say?" Bobby said.

NINE

Diaz found the address and parked on the street, studying the apartment building. There was a girl sitting on a second-story balcony. She was young and pretty, wearing a bikini. The girl had a magazine on her lap, reading and looking down at him in the car. Her cell phone rang. She stood talking now, leaning a hip into the railing, her bikini top straining to contain her breasts. He enjoyed looking at the girl, his mind wandering, seeing himself coming up behind her, removing the top, the girl afraid or pretending to be, and then falling into his arms.

He seemed to make eye contact with the girl. That's the way he saw it, the girl flirting from the balcony, and now realized she could ID him and the car and it was time to move.

He drove north along the street in this residential neighborhood that was lush and green, so different than the parched, gray-brown color of Sonora in the summer months. He went around the block and parked on the south side of the apartment building. A woman was walking a tiny dog on the sidewalk. Behind him a group of young boys played baseball, reminding him of his own youth, playing *fútbol* in the streets of Zona Centro in Tijuana.

Stretching over the console, Diaz reached to open the glove box, gripping the .22 Sport King. He slid the gun in the waist of his trousers, feeling the suppressor slide in and rest there against his manhood. It was 4:30 p.m. He would go to the man's apartment, enter, and wait for him to return, surprising the marshal walking in the door.

Standing in the vestibule, Diaz scanned the directory, saw the name and apartment number. He went up the stairs to the second floor. The hall was empty and quiet. Now standing at the door, he drew the Sport King, holding the gun behind his back. Diaz tapped on the door with his knuckles. It was possible he was at the wrong apartment. The door opened, the girl in the bikini standing there. She said, "Didn't I just see you parked on the street?"

"Is Mr. Givens here?"

"You mean Raylan? He's at work, should be home soon. Wanna come in and wait?"

Out of the corner of his eye, Diaz saw a man appear in the hall from the next apartment. The man was big, his footsteps heavy. As he approached, Diaz moved out of the doorway.

"The fuck is this?" the man said to the girl. "You seeing him too?"

"No, I ain't seeing him. This a friend of Raylan's."

"Oh, he's Raylan now?" the man said with anger in his voice.

"That's his name. What do you want me to call him?" Then the girl said, "Junior, what the hell you doing here? We done."

The man looked at him. "Why don't you move along, give us some privacy."

"I told you, he's a friend a Raylan's." Now she looked at him. "Mister, why don't you go in, make yourself comfortable. I'm sorry you had to see this."

"Jo Lynne, see the way he's looking at you? Like a dog ain't et for a long while."

"Will you stop?" the girl said. And to Diaz she said, "Go ahead, go on in there."

"Look at you in that skimpy thing, your ninnies hanging out the top, your hams and tenderloins out the bottom. Girl, you are practically naked."

Diaz, not sure what to do, went into the apartment and closed the door. There were moving boxes on one side of the room, and on the other was a couch and a table with an old TV on it. The marshal lived like a bum. Diaz went into the kitchen, looking through a glass door wall at the balcony where the girl had been earlier.

They were still arguing in the hall as a pickup truck parked in front of the building and a wiry man fitting the marshal's description got out adjusting his cap. Now there was a knock on the door. The girl said, "Sir, will you let me in please?"

Diaz opened the door and the girl moved by him into the room. "I apologize. That was Junior, my ex. We are *so* done. What did I ever see in him? I'm asking myself. What a Godsend Raylan's been, I can't tell you. Junior and me got into it last night. Between you, me, and Jesus, it wasn't for Raylan I don't know what I'd a done."

His eyes held on her. "Tell me, what time will Mr. Givens arrive?"

"Raylan said like five, and that's in a couple minutes." The girl paused. "You know something, in all the excitement I don't believe I caught your name."

"I am George," he said, using the American pronunciation.

"Pleased to make your acquaintance." The girl offered her hand. "I'm Jo Lynne, Jo Lynne Crowe. So you and Raylan are old buds? Believe it or not he's like public enemy number one with my family, but you probably already know that. Listen, I'm gonna run in there and change, you just sit and relax. My brother shows up tell him I'll be out presently."

Instinct told him to walk away right now. The situation was complicated and getting worse. He moved to the door, opened it, and the wiry man from the pickup truck was standing there.

"You the one took in Jo Lynne? Hi, I'm Skeeter. How bout Junior? Is he a piece of work, or what? Hell, I warned Sis bout that crazy hillbilly. She could have any man in all of Harlan County, she picks Junior Poole. Jo Lynne couldn't of done no worse."

"What're you saying bout me?" She came into the room wearing jeans and a T-shirt, deep red lipstick, and green eye shadow. "I see you two met."

There were two explosions, shotgun blasts, heavy loads that blew holes through the door. The girl and her brother dove on the floor.

Diaz drew the Sport King, waited, moved to the door, and opened it. The big man had the double barrel broke open, feeding shells into it. Diaz aimed the .22 at him. "Put it on the floor."

• • •

WHEN RAYLAN DROVE UP there were two Royal Oak police cruisers angle-parked in front of the apartment building, lights flashing. There was a man in a suit on his balcony talking to someone in the kitchen. Whatever had happened, he figured Junior Poole was involved.

He walked up to the second floor and was stopped by a heavyset police officer with a crew cut. "Hold on there, Chief, where you think you're going?"

"My apartment."

"Which one is it?"

"There." Raylan pointed to the first door on the right. "I'm Deputy US Marshal Raylan Givens." He showed the cop his ID.

An evidence tech was taking photographs of Junior Poole lying face up on the bloodstained carpeting; half his body was in his apartment and half was in the hall. There was a shotgun on the floor next to him. Raylan could hear Jo Lynne's high-pitched voice coming from his apartment. "You know what happened?"

"They're still piecing it together," the cop said. "I'd talk to the detective."

Raylan moved past the man, walked down the hall, nodded at the evidence tech, and noticed two shell casings that looked like .22's tagged with pink post it notes on the floor near the body.

He went in his apartment and saw two big holes in the wide-open door. There was a skinny, goofy-looking kid with wild red hair sitting on the couch.

"Raylan," Jo Lynne said, moving toward him, eyes red, like she'd been crying, but happy to see him. "Where the devil you been?"

The guy in the tan poplin suit he'd seen on the balcony walked in from the kitchen. He had the look and build of a high school football coach or an ex-jock. "Detective Jardine, Mr. Givens. I understand you're with the Marshals Service."

"Someone want to tell me what happened?"

"Your friend shot and killed Junior," Jo Lynne said. "JR was a bad man but he didn't deserve that."

Detective Jardine put his hand up. "Hang on now," he said to Jo Lynne.

"Your neighbor, Mr. Poole, was bent out of shape about something, came over with a loaded shotgun. You can see what he did," Jardine said, glancing at the door.

Raylan fixed his attention on Jo Lynne. "You said my friend shot Junior. What friend?"

"Told me his name was George."

Searching his brain, Raylan said, "I don't know anyone named George."

"Well he sure knows you. Knocked on the door, introduced himself."

"I'll handle this," Detective Jardine said, giving Jo Lynne a hard stare.

"Describe him," Raylan said.

"You know, kinda Mexican-looking, dark hair and skin, sorta oily, but sorta handsome," Jo Lynne said, her eyes big, holding on Raylan.

"That ring a bell?" Detective Jardine said.

The description didn't register. It had to be someone connected to Jose Rindo, but no faces appeared. He shook his head.

"Take us through the sequence," Detective Jardine said to Jo Lynne.

"After Junior fired through the door, George walked over with a gun in his hand, opened it, and they had words."

Raylan said, "Where'd he get the gun?"

"Must've had it on his person," Jo Lynne said.

Raylan said, "The shell casings are from a twenty-two."

"Was a twenty-two target pistol," the red-haired kid said, "with a silencer on the end of the barrel. Thing looked about ten inches long."

"That's my brother, Derek," Jo Lynne said. "Goes by Skeeter."

Raylan said, "Where'd the shooter go after he shot Junior?"

"Disappeared," Jo Lynne said. "I waited a couple minutes, went in the hall. George was gone and Junior was dead."

Detective Jardine said, "Ever see this guy George before?"

"I did earlier," Jo Lynne said. "I seen him setting in a car parked on the street."

Raylan said, "What was he doing?"

"Tell you the truth, I think he was checkin me out. I was on the balcony in my bikini."

Raylan was sorry he'd missed that. What he'd seen of Jo Lynne's parts was pretty spectacular.

"What kind a car?" Detective Jardine said.

"Was a VW, I know that," Jo Lynne said, "silver four-door sedan."

Detective Jardine said, "What model?"

"I couldn't say for sure, but it wasn't little."

"Michigan tag?"

"No, sir. It was blue and white but different."

"What's your visual acuity?"

"Sir?"

"How good can you see?"

"Twenty/twenty, last time I had my eyes checked."

"I'll need you to come to the station tomorrow," Detective Jardine said, "give our artist a description of the shooter. We'll do a BOLO on the car and a sketch of the killer."

"I hate to say this, but my brother's taking me home tonight. We got no place to stay anyway. Raylan was good enough to put me up last night," Jo Lynne glanced at him, embarrassed, "but now Skeeter's here and we don't want to impose."

"Here's the situation," Detective Jardine said. "I can't let you leave. You're a material witnesses to a homicide. As citizens, you have a duty to perform."

"I hate to break this to you, Detective," Skeeter Crowe said. "But I have responsibilities to perform. I got a job I have to get back to."

"Where do you live and what do you do?"

"Currently, I'm in Watford, North Dakota. I drive a lowboy, transporting modular homes. Keep track of logbooks, fuel books, and permits. Got to make sure you bring materials for setting the homes and such."

"Okay, we get the idea," Detective Jardine said. "It's a tough job but somebody's got to do it."

"But first, I got to take her down to Kentucky, Harlan County." Skeeter nodded at Jo Lynne. "Not exactly a hop, skip, and a jump either."

"Can you put them up tonight?" Detective Jardine said to Raylan. "I can do the paperwork in the morning, get them situated in a motel and their per diem."

"You can stay here tonight," Raylan said. "We'll figure something out."

"Detective, I don't think you heard one word my brother said. We've got to go."

"We'll talk about that tomorrow," Jardine said. "What are you planning to do with the mortal remains of Junior Poole? Does he have family in the area?"

"No, sir," Jo Lynne said. "They all down in Kentucky."

"I'll alert the next of kin, you can give me a name and contact information, ask them to choose a funeral home."

"There ain't but one," Jo Lynne said.

"We'll ship the body there." Jardine paused. "All right, you're on your honor now. Do not leave town. Do not cross the state line. Can I trust you, or do I have to take you into custody?"

"We'll stay," Jo Lynne said, looking at Skeeter. "Cross my heart and hope to die."

"I've got an interest in this too," Raylan said. "I think it's connected to a fugitive we brought back from Ohio, drug trafficker name of Jose Rindo."

Jardine turned, glanced at him, and said, "Maybe we can help each other."

Raylan said, "I'll have ICS send us what they've got on known hit men working for local drug traffickers or the cartels."

"All right," Jardine said. "Talk in the morning."

Skeeter said, "Mr. Givens, you got a glass a whiskey or something's got a kick? I've had me one long nightmare of a day."

Raylan went in the kitchen, grabbed the jar of shine and two juice glasses, and put it all on the table. "Okay, come and get it."

"Oh my God," Skeeter said. "Sweet Jesus. Have I died and gone to heaven? It even has a peach."

While Skeeter and Jo Lynne drank shine, Raylan closed and locked the front door and covered the holes with duct tape. Then he made a bed on the couch and covered a chair with a sheet and blanket. Let them decide who got what. He went in his room, unhooked his holster, put his Glock on the bedside table, and washed up.

All the while he'd been thinking about the dark-haired, dark-skinned shooter, drove a VW, and claimed to be a friend of his. Raylan didn't have any friends that fit that description and decided he was lucky cause the man was probably there to kill him, but Junior got in the way. Raylan had made a lot of enemies over the years. He'd bet the farm the shooter was a contract killer, a hit man hired by Rindo's people. So he had a personal interest in seeing if Jo Lynne could ID the man.

Raylan closed the bedroom door and got Bobby on the phone, told him what happened. Bobby said, "You really think this is connected to Rindo?"

"Who else could it be? I'm new in town, already made two enemies, but I don't see Harris has the juice."

"Maybe it's someone from your past."

"How's this someone know where I'm at? I barely know. Has to be Rindo. Can you think of anyone else that has the motivation and the means to make it happen?" Raylan paused. "I was lucky this clown next door and his girlfriend got in a fight, or I could've walked in my apartment and he's sitting on the couch waiting for me. My concern, the shooter might also be looking for you. I'd get your family out of there."

Bobby didn't say anything.

"You still there?"

"I'll think about it. What about you?"

"What about me what?"

"You worried he's going to come back?"

"With all that's happened I can't imagine him taking that chance. He does, I'll be ready."

"Give me his physicals?"

"As described by my neighbor, he's six feet, dark hair, goatee. Drives a silver VW sedan. He may not be looking for you, could be a false alarm, but what if it isn't?"

When Raylan went back to the kitchen, the shine was gone and the Crowes were either drunk or on their way. "You want more, help yourselves. I'm out of shine but there's a bottle of Russell's single barrel in the cupboard and some Four Roses. I'm turning in."

"Sir," Skeeter swayed trying to hold himself upright, "you mind I eat the peach?"

"Knock yourself out."

"Raylan, thanks for everything," Jo Lynne said, slurring her words.

•••

HE WAS ALMOST ASLEEP when he heard the bedroom door open and reached for the Glock. "You're not gonna need that," Jo Lynne said, sliding next to him under the covers, her warm body against his. "I wake you?"

"What're you doin'?"

"Snuggling. I want to pay you back for being so nice." Jo Lynne had a dreamy look on her face in the dim light. "Why don't we wake little Ray up, see he wants to have some fun."

"Listen, I can't do this." It didn't feel right this young girl half his age coming on to him. Not to mention she was a member of the Crowe family. He scooted over, creating some distance between them.

"All right, I'll just lie here for a minute."

And then she was snoring.

TEN

RAYLAN OPENED HIS EYES. It was light in the room. He glanced at Jo Lynne wedged against him on his left side, touched her bare shoulder and shook it gently. She opened her eyes, smiled, and said, "What time is it?" in a small tired voice.

"Quarter to eight."

"All I want to do is sleep." She yawned, closed her eyes, and opened them. "But I guess that ain't gonna happen." She pulled the covers back, got up, and stood next to the bed. "Mind if I take a shower?"

"Help yourself."

Jo Lynne went in the bathroom and closed the door. He heard the toilet flush and the shower turn on.

Raylan dialed Bobby Torres's number and listened to it ring half a dozen times before Bobby said, "Yeah?"

"Well, you're still talking, that's a good sign. Get any unwanted visitors last night?"

"I took Nancy and the kids to her mother's, spent the night. What about you?"

"Nothing. Just wanted to make sure you were okay. See you later."

He put on a pair of Levis and a T-shirt, slid the Glock in the waistband behind his back. That's when Jo Lynne opened the bathroom door, let out a cloud of steam, and walked into the room in a T-shirt and panties and hair so wet it looked dark brown instead of blonde. "Raylan, least I can do is make you breakfast?

"I'm not gonna turn it down. There's bacon, eggs, and pumpernickel bread in there, coffee and some raspberries in the refrigerator."

They went into the living room. Skeeter, sitting on the couch said, "Y'all sleep well?" with an edge of disapproval in his voice.

"Skeeter, be thankful Raylan gave you a place to rest and a roof over your head," Jo Lynne said.

A few minutes later, Raylan smelled bacon frying as he went through the kitchen out on the balcony, holding binoculars. He scanned the street as far as he could in both directions, didn't see a VW sedan, but if the shooter was any good, he'd be driving something else by now.

Raylan went back in, sat at the table, and watched Jo Lynne dry the bacon on a folded sheet of paper towel. She looked at him and smiled. "You mind your eggs scrambled?"

"Scrambled, fried, I like em each way."

She dropped slices of bread into the toaster, poured the egg mixture into the frying pan, and scrambled the eggs in bacon grease. The bread popped up and she buttered the slices, set out three plates, loaded them up with eggs and bacon, but only two had toast.

Raylan said, "What's the matter, you don't like bread?"

"I've got to watch my girlish figure."

Skeeter didn't say a word, sat across from him staring at his plate, shoveling food in his mouth. Maybe he wasn't a morning person.

Raylan said, "How's it living in North Dakota? I was there one time, went to a wedding in Minot. All I remember, it snowed like a son of a bitch in mid-October."

Skeeter looked up from his plate. "Most boring place I ever been to. You work, get drunk, sleep, get up, do it all over again."

Jo Lynne said, "Any girls?"

"A few, but dudes is fighting over em. I can't imagine what would happen, Jo Lynne walked in one of them bars—God help her."

"You don't have to worry, I'm not planning a trip to Watford anytime soon."

"I wish I wasn't." Skeeter shrugged.

Raylan said, "You don't like it, why don't you quit?"

"They're paying me too goddamn much," Skeeter said, showing a mouthful of eggs. "You'd have to have your head examined give up twenty-two fifty an hour."

They finished eating. Raylan did the dishes and called Detective Jardine. "You want, I'll bring the Crowes to you. As I said, I've got a stake in this too."

•••

RAYLAN STOOD WITH Jo Lynne and Skeeter next to Jardine's desk in the crowded bullpen, waiting for him to get off the phone. Raylan could see the other detectives checking out Jo Lynne, eyes holding on her like men anywhere would. He studied framed photos on the neat desktop. There was one of Jardine posing with a good-looking woman and two little girls. And another one of Jardine in a football uniform. When the detective hung up, Raylan said, "Who'd you play for?"

"Western Michigan, the Mustangs."

"What position?"

"Fullback," Jardine said, pushing his bulk away from the desk, getting to his feet. "Come this way, will you?" He led them out of the bullpen, down the hall to a conference room that had a laptop already set up on the table. Based on Jo Lynne's description and Raylan's hunch, they had a place to start.

Jardine said, "You're saying this man, George, is Hispanic, is that right?"

"You know what? As I think back, he weren't as Mex as I thought." Jo Lynne looked a little unsure of herself. "I mean, he had dark hair and he was suntanned, but he could've been totally white."

Jardine said, "I thought he had an accent. Didn't you tell us that?"

"I can't be sure now," Jo Lynne said. "Let me look at the pictures, see if anyone's familiar."

"Here's what ICS sent," Raylan said. "Hit men associated with drug traffickers and cartels. Fella we picked up yesterday, Jose Rindo, had a big operation and the money to hire someone knows what they're doing. He was born in Detroit but he's also a Mexican citizen. The shooter might be American and he might be Mex."

Raylan opened the ICS email and stood next to Jardine behind the Crowes sitting in chairs, Jo Lynne scrolling through head shots and physicals, rough-looking white cons staring without expression, bald Hispanic cons with tats on their heads and faces, one guy with the whites of his eyes tatted black, another one with the word KILL inked on his tongue. One crazy bastard had eyes tatted on his eyelids, so when he closed them he was still looking at you.

Then she got to the kids, thirteen-year-old Hispanic boys taught to kill. Jo Lynne glanced over her shoulder at Raylan. "These ones ain't even in high school, they're killing folks. What's the world coming to?"

"It's going to hell in a handbasket," Skeeter, the elder statesman, said.

After a while, Jo Lynne glanced at Raylan and said, "I'm dizzy looking at all these lowlifes. They come in all sizes and shapes, don't they? Don't see no one resembles who shot Junior."

"I dint see him either," Skeeter said.

"Well then," Raylan said, "maybe he's never been arrested."

Jardine brought the crime artist in, guy in his forties with a scraggly beard and black horn-rimmed glasses, wearing a blue work shirt. Raylan would've described him as a nerd hippie. He sat across from Jo Lynne and Skeeter, sketchpad on his lap below the level of the table.

"Listen," Raylan said. "We're gonna step out of the room, let you talk to this gentleman without any distractions or interference."

•••

"RELAX," THE ARTIST SAID, looking at Jo Lynne and then Skeeter. "There's no pressure, no worries. I'm here to work with you, to help you remember details. But it's your show. I want you to do me a favor, get comfortable, sit back, take your time, and try to remember the crime scene. Think about what the man looked like, get a picture of him in your head. Before we start, you need anything: soft drink, cup of coffee, have to go to the restroom?"

"I'm okay," Jo Lynne said. "Skeet, what about you?"

"I'm fine."

The artist took a drawing pencil out of his shirt pocket and rolled it between thumb and fingers of his right hand. "Think about physical qualities, defining marks: scars, moles, tattoos. Did he have facial hair?" The artist let out a breath. "Did he have defining features you can recall? A long face, big nose, bug eyes, buckteeth? Is there an actor, an athlete, or musician you can think of who resembles this man? Close your eyes and tell me what you see. What was the shape of his face? Describe his eyes, his nose, his mouth and jawline."

With her eyes closed, Jo Lynne listened to the artist she thought looked like a pervert but had a soothing voice. Jo Lynne was so relaxed she thought she might fall asleep and heard Skeeter snoring like a chain saw. She opened her eyes and looked at the artist. "Sorry about my brother, I'll wake him." She touched his shoulder and shook him.

Skeeter came to, opening and closing his eyes. "The hell's going on?"

"You fell asleep."

"Jesus, my bad." He rubbed his eyes.

"You need a minute, or can we proceed?"

"Fire away," Skeeter said.

"Picture the man's head. Was it long? Was it round?"

Jo Lynne said, "His face was thin and more long than short. Jaws came down to a pointy chin."

"What style and color was his hair? Was it long or short? Thick or thin?"

"Black and short," Jo Lynne said. "I think he was losing it on top, so he combed it forward." She glanced at Skeeter. "That sound right to you?"

"I'd say so."

"Describe his eyes," the artist said.

"Dark," Jo Lynne said. "Brown. And he had good eyebrows. They was long and full. Oh, and he had a goatee."

"What about his nose? Big, small, medium? Does it hook or turn up, or was it flat against his face?"

"It was straight, I think, and not big or small." Jo Lynne glanced at Skeeter and he nodded.

"Sounds about right to me."

"Tell me about his lips and mouth."

"Nothing special, about like Skeeter's."

"Thanks a lot."

The artist didn't show any expression, picked up his pad, and went to work. He sketched while Jo Lynne checked her emails.

Twenty-two minutes later, he turned his pad to show them his sketch that was a pretty damn good likeness of the man said his name was George. The artist said, "What do you think, this in the ballpark?"

"You don't mind my saying," Jo Lynne said, "the nose is too big and the eyebrows are too long, the mouth isn't quite right either, other than that it looks like him. What do you think, Skeeter?"

"What you said." Skeet was good with his hands, but when it came to using his head, things ground to a halt.

The artist did some erasing and more sketching and turned his pad to show them the changes he made. "How's that?"

"Is that him or what?" Jo Lynne said. "Skeet, don't you think so?"

Her brother's blank face didn't exactly support her conclusion. She glanced at the artist and said, "My God, you're another damn DaVinci, aren't you?"

He smiled big, crooked teeth crowding his little mouth, reminding Jo Lynne of an opossum.

•••

RAYLAN HANDED HER A piece of paper that read:

ARMED AND DANGEROUS

And under that was the sketch of the suspect, and a photo of a silver VW Passat like the one he drove. Raylan said, "This is going out to local police departments, US Marshals Service, FBI, ATF, and

DEA. It's called a BOLO: *Be on the lookout.* I think he's still in the area. He's got unfinished business. Somebody's seen this boy and his car."

"You think he's really coming to kill you?" Jo Lynne said.

"He showed up once," Raylan said. "I think it's pretty certain he'll try again."

"Skeeter and I can stay with you. He's good with a rifle, and I ain't bad either."

"Let's see what Jardine says. You got us closer with your description. I think you'll probably be free to go."

"I don't know that I want to," Jo Lynne said. "What about us?"

"What're you talking about?" Raylan said. "There is no us."

"I can't help what my heart's telling me."

"Previous time your heart told you to come to Detroit with Junior Poole. I was you, I'd take a break for a while. Your heart talks, don't listen."

"Thanks a lot."

ELEVEN

WHEN HE WAS WORKING, Diaz never stayed in the same hotel or motel more than two nights. He was getting ready to leave when he looked out the window and saw a police car in the parking lot behind the VW. The police would be knocking on the door in a few minutes. Diaz considered his options. He could climb out the bathroom window and jump into the dumpster directly below his room. Or he could leave the suitcase, walk out the door, take the stairs down, and disappear.

Standing at the window, he saw another police car drive into the lot. He tucked the Sport King in the waistband behind his back, left the suitcase, went out the door, and glanced down as a policeman was getting out of his car. He walked along the second-story balcony, taking his time, trying to appear relaxed, in no hurry. Diaz went down the stairs and pushed through a high wall of shrubs onto an auto repair shop parking lot. There was a restaurant next door. He walked behind the building to the entrance, went in, sat at the counter, and ordered eggs over easy, sausage, hash browns, and black coffee.

Still eating, he heard a siren and saw a police car speed by on Woodward Avenue. When he was finished, Diaz paid his bill and asked the hostess to call a taxi. It was after noon, the restaurant was filling up.

He waited, looking out the window, and when the taxi appeared, he went outside and got in. When they passed by the motel, there were four police cars in the parking lot. The door to his room was open and there were police in blue uniforms standing on the balcony.

The driver said, "Where you going?"

•••

"THE VW'S REGISTERED TO Efrain Perez, works for Volkswagen of America," Raylan said. "Only, they've never heard of him. Has a Virginia driver's license and a US passport, the real deal."

Bobby, on the other side of the conference table, sipped his coffee.

"We ran him," Raylan said. "Turns out he's Joaquin Diaz, a contract shooter, works for the cartels."

Bobby said, "So you were right, Rindo sending his regards."

"Royal Oak Police just missed him, and it's probably a good thing. Diaz has killed forty-one people. Hostess at the restaurant two doors south of the motel recognized a photo of him, said she called him a taxi. Driver said he drove him downtown, dropped him off at Woodward and Grand Boulevard. Man fitting Diaz's description bought a ticket on the train to Chicago, leaves tomorrow morning at seven ten." Raylan paused. "We've got to do it quiet. I want this jitterbug relaxed. We take him before he gets on the train. He has no idea what's happening."

"Or we go in," Bobby said, "let him see us in our UAVs, get his stress knob turned up."

"Maybe he bought the ticket to throw us off. We show up in the morning, he slips out of town another way."

•••

Diaz sat at the bar drinking Dos Equis, watching the bartender, a Mexican woman in her late forties but still had her figure. He smiled when she brought him a fresh beer, and when the crowd at the bar thinned out, customers escorted to their tables in the dining room, he was able to attract her attention.

"When you are not serving drinks, what do you do?"

She seemed embarrassed by the attention and wasn't sure how to respond.

"Why do you care what I do?" she said, not angry, but not friendly, either.

"I am here in Detroit on business. I do not know anyone. I apologize if I have offended you." He drank some beer.

Her expression softened and now she smiled. "Not at all. What do I do? I read. I watch TV. I cook."

"Why don't you invite me for dinner? What time do you finish?"

"What do I get out of this?"

"The pleasure of my company." Diaz smiled now and the woman met his smile. "Unless, of course, you are married. I should have asked."

"Thankfully, no." She shook her head. "It ended a long time ago." Her eyes held on him. "Why am I telling you this?"

"You are curious. You are wondering if I am honorable."

"Are you?"

"Of course. Tell me your name."

"Benita."

"So you are blessed."

Two men walked in and sat on the other side of the bar. She glanced at them, said, "Excuse me," and moved to greet them. She talked and laughed with the men while she made and served margaritas in stemmed, salt-rimmed glasses.

Diaz drank his beer and watched her come back to him. "Where're you from? I hear an accent, but I cannot identify it."

"Tijuana originally. Now I live in Herndon, Virginia, and work for Volkswagen. Forgive me, I am Efrain Perez."

"I get off at five. What do you like for dinner?"

•••

DIAZ PURCHASED AN ACCEPTABLE bottle of Pinot Noir and a bouquet of flowers at a market down the street from Los Galanes, the restaurant where she worked. Benita lived in an apartment building on Clark Avenue. He arrived by taxi a few minutes after six, Benita smiling when he handed her the gifts. She was wearing too much makeup and heavy red lipstick and reminded him of a TJ whore. "What is that I smell?" he said, following her into the kitchen.

"Something good."

There was a whole fish in a shallow baking dish on the counter and liquid bubbling in a pan on the stovetop.

"Will you do this?" She handed him the wine and a corkscrew. She opened a cabinet, took out a vase, poured in a little water from the faucet, cut the stems with a scissors, and fit the flowers in. There was a TV on the counter tuned to the news.

"Is a pleasure to be here," Diaz said. "Thank you for inviting me."

"I think you invited yourself, but it is nice to have company. I usually eat alone." Standing next to the stove, stirring the sauce with a long wooden spoon, Benita looked over her shoulder at him. "I hope you like Snapper Vera Cruz."

"My favorite."

"Is this true?"

"Yes, of course. I don't lie about Snapper Vera Cruz." He poured her a glass of wine and one for himself. Then he said, "To Benita, my number one Detroit friend."

They clinked their glasses. Everything was going well until he saw a grainy photograph of his face filling the TV screen, a voice saying: "Efrain Perez is wanted for questioning in the homicide of a Royal Oak man. He is considered armed and dangerous. If you see him, contact the police immediately."

Benita dropped her wine that shattered in an explosion of glass and Pinot Noir. She stepped back to the counter in shock and picked up a curved boning knife. Diaz could see panic in her eyes as he reached behind his back, drew the Sport King, aiming it at her chest. "Put the knife down," he said in a calm voice. "Please. There is no other way. I do not want to hurt you."

The woman hesitated, staring at him, realizing the hopelessness of the situation. "What are you going to do?"

"Wait for the fish to cook, sit at the table, and enjoy the dinner."

"I have to clean this," she said, looking at the floor.

He stepped aside as a stream of wine came toward his shoe. Now the woman—more concerned about the appearance of the floor than the situation she was in—unspooled a long strip of paper towel and dropped it, blotting the wine. She crossed the room, opened a cabinet door, and came back with a broom and dustpan. Benita cleaned the mess, dropped the soaked paper and broken glass in the trash bin.

In the meantime, Diaz had returned the gun to his waistband, poured the woman another glass of wine, and handed it to her. "I think this will help you relax." Her hand shook, accepting the wine. "It is all right. Make the fish and don't worry."

The woman could cook, but she did not eat. Diaz sat across the table from her, feasting on the delicious snapper, thinking it was one of the best he had ever tasted.

The woman stared at the table, her mood sullen.

"You should have your own restaurant. This is very good, amazing really. Eat, enjoy it as I am?"

Benita did not respond and continued to stare at the table as if in a trance. Maybe another approach would work. "How long were you married?"

"Twenty-six years."

"What happened?"

"The only thing we had in common, we were both from Guadalajara." Now the woman's eyes moved up and held on him. "I have a question for you? How do you become what you are, someone who kills people?" She drank some wine. "How do you do it? Walk up, put the gun to their head, pull the trigger? Or do make them sweat like you are doing to me?"

Diaz was about to put a piece of fish in his mouth but lowered his fork to the plate. No one had ever asked him this. "How do I make you uncomfortable? We are talking and drinking wine. How is this unpleasant?"

"It makes you feel good, I think. Gives you pleasure."

She was in his business now, her tone angry and accusing. The woman telling him he was sick in the head, cruel, heartless, even sadistic. In Diaz's mind, this was worse than killing someone. "Not true. What I do is a job, a profession. I take no satisfaction in hurting people."

"It is a job. Like you are a plumber or electrician. You say it as though there is nothing wrong. Your job is to kill people and you think that is okay. Do you know how crazy that sounds?"

Maybe she was right. Of course she was. Diaz had been doing it so long he had lost perspective.

She stood now. "I no hungry. Seeing you across the table, hearing your voice, I lose my appetite."

"Sit down. Wait until I finish."

She picked up the plate, turned toward the sink, and threw it like a Frisbee. The heavy stoneware hit him in the chest, hot fish and sauce splashing in his face. He was blinded, wiping his eyes with the napkin as she ran out of the room. Benita was at the apartment door when he aimed and fired, her body jerking as the rounds hit her and she slid to the floor.

In the bedroom, Diaz pulled the striped serape blanket off the bed, spread it on hardwood next to the woman, and rolled her body into it. In the bathroom he wiped red sauce from his face with a wet towel. He removed his stained shirt, washing it in the sink and hanging it over the shower curtain to dry.

He dragged the woman's body into the kitchen, took his glass and the wine bottle into the front room, and turned on the TV. Now he could relax, watch a movie, and sleep without concern.

TWELVE

Six in the morning, Raylan entered the Amtrak Station, a duffle bag with an AR-15 in it over his shoulder, glancing across the room that was filled with travelers, some standing, others sitting in the rows of seats. He leaned against the wall, trying not to look obvious, scanning the room, but didn't see anyone who resembled Joaquin Diaz.

Bobby on the other side of the waiting room, carrying a suitcase. The rest of the team was outside or hanging around the building. Raylan saw the men's room sign and headed that way. With any luck, Diaz was in there doing his business and Raylan would cuff him and take him out to the car. But Diaz wasn't there. Raylan went back into the waiting room, looked at the departure times, and saw that the train to Chicago was boarding.

Bobby walked over and said, "You see him?"

Raylan shook his head. "I think he's already on the train."

"I think he changed his mind," Bobby said. "He's not coming."

"We're here. He's not on the train, we get off at the next station."

Bobby followed Raylan out to the crowded loading platform. "What end you want?"

"I'll take the caboose," Bobby said. "We'll meet in the middle."

Raylan walked along the edge of the platform, scanning the people waiting to board, glancing in windows and between the train cars. He stood in front of the locomotive, gaze moving down the open track. And when Raylan turned, looking back at the loading platform, he saw a few late passengers running to board, and a couple of porters wheeling their carts back to the terminal, and called Bobby. "Got anything?"

"Man, I don't think he's here."

"I'm telling you he's on the train."

"How'd he do it without us seeing him?"

"I don't know. You want to talk about it, or get on and find him?"

"Okay, but you see him, you got to be cool, got to wait to take him. No cowboy bullshit."

We'll see how it goes, Raylan thought, sliding the phone in his shirt pocket, and climbing up the steps into the train. He stood at the end of the first railcar, scanning the passengers who were facing him. Worst-case scenario: Diaz would shoot an innocent civilian. Second-worse: Diaz would take a hostage and draw things out, making it a long, difficult day. Raylan moved along the center aisle through the car, carrying his bag.

There were two dark-haired guys, one looked vaguely familiar, could've been Diaz, but on closer inspection he was too young. Raylan went through the double doors at the end of the car and stared through the glass panels into the next one, studying faces.

•••

IT WAS STILL DARK when a taxi drove Diaz to the Amtrak station, arriving at 5:45 a.m., wearing a cap to hide his face. There was a man in the ticket office and a few people sitting in the waiting room. The train to Chicago would depart from Track 3. He walked outside and stood on the deserted boarding platform, looking down the length of the train to the locomotive. Two workmen with tools were climbing a ladder into the cab. The inside lights were on, and he could see a cleaning crew moving through the train.

He waited till they went into the next car and hoisted himself up onto the gangway, went into the restroom and locked the door. This was a precaution in case the police were looking for him. They might walk through the train but would get off before it departed.

From the window, Diaz could see the passengers come out to board the train, people packed in tight, spreading along its length. And then he saw the door handle move. And then someone knocked. Diaz froze trying not to make a sound.

Twenty minutes later he felt the train jerk forward and braced himself, holding onto the sink. The train was gaining speed now, passing neighborhoods of broken-down houses that looked worse than the barrios of Tijuana. When it was time to find his seat, Diaz opened the restroom door and stood in the gangway, opened the door to the car, and moved down the aisle.

•••

RAYLAN SAW THE MAN come through the door on the opposite side of the car. He was wearing a Detroit Tigers cap, brim pulled down like he was trying to hide his face. The man, with a goatee and Diaz's height, stopped, glanced to his left looking around, and sat in the window seat, second or third row. Raylan could feel a rush of adrenaline as he stepped back into the gangway outside the car, called Bobby, and told him the situation.

"Don't do anything till I get there."

"Diaz sees the two of us, he's going to know something's up, do something crazy," Raylan said. "You can count on that. We've got to surprise him."

"What do you have in mind?"

Raylan told him.

"I don't know. Give me a few minutes to get there."

Raylan walked down the aisle with the duffle bag over his shoulder all the way to where the man was sitting and lifted it onto the luggage rack. The man ignored him. Raylan nodded and sat next to him in the empty seat, "How's it going?" he said, watching the man's hands that were in his lap. Where was his gun? Diaz wore a jacket, so it was easy to conceal. Probably had it behind his back. Might've also had one in an ankle holster. "Live in Chicago?"

"No," the man said.

"Where you from?"

"What does it matter?" Diaz turned his head, already tired of small talk, looking out the window.

Raylan tensed as the man reached into his jacket pocket and then relaxed as he brought out a cell phone, checked his messages. Diaz put the phone away, closed his eyes, and leaned his head back, face angled toward the window. Raylan got up, walked to the end of the car through the door and into the gangway, where Bobby was standing.

"You sure it's him?"

"Positive," Raylan said.

"What's he doing?"

"Trying to sleep."

•••

DIAZ SAT UP AND glanced over his shoulder as the man walked away. The .22 was digging into his back. He reached behind and brought the gun out, resting it on the seat next to his left thigh, removed the jacket, and folded it over the gun. When the door behind him opened, Diaz turned and saw the man coming back, and there was someone behind him, a shorter Hispanic man. Were they together? Diaz reached under the jacket, gripping the Sport King. He could see them approach, their reflections in the window glass. He waited till they were at his seat, saw the Hispanic holding a black semiautomatic down his leg, and now the man was identifying them as US Marshals.

Diaz should have raised his hands in surrender. He brought up the Sport King and squeezed the trigger as heavy rounds punched him in the body, sending him sideways off the seat onto the floor, too weak to move, wondering—could he ask for a priest, confess his sins before he died? The sounds of the gunshots started to fade as he lost consciousness.

THIRTEEN

THERE WERE STATE AND local police cruisers and EMS vans parked next to the train, lights flashing. The railcar was a crime scene and had to be uncoupled from the train. Disembarking passengers looked tired and on-edge as they got off and were routed to another car.

Bobby Torres had been shot and was suffering from a gunshot wound that shattered his collarbone just above the vest and was in serious condition but maintaining. Bobby was choppered to Henry Ford Hospital in Detroit. The fugitive, Joaquin Diaz, had been shot four times. He was alive but in critical condition and was taken to St. Joseph Mercy Hospital in Ann Arbor.

Raylan surrendered his weapon to the field supervisor, Keith Cullen, and gave a statement. He'd have to be cleared by the Office of Internal Investigations, a formality any time a deputy marshal was involved in a shooting.

•••

A LITTLE AFTER NOON, Raylan walked through the apartment door that still hadn't been replaced. He'd have to call the manager again. First thing he saw were two suitcases upright in the middle of the living room. Second thing was Jo Lynne Crowe at the breakfast table with a pen in her hand. "I was just leaving you a note," she said as he came in the kitchen and sat across from her. "I'll be heading out fore too long never to return," she said with sad eyes holding on him, "less a course somebody makes me an offer." She grinned now. "I want to thank you for your hospitality, for sharing your home."

Raylan, trying to think of a way to change the subject, said, "Where's Skeeter?"

"On his way to the high-paying job in Watford, North Dakota."

"What about you?"

"Going back to Kentucky. In all the confusion I forgot, or it didn't occur to me, Junior's truck's downstairs in the parking lot. I'm gonna have Junior boxed up, put in the bed, and drive him home. It's only a little over five hundred miles. I'll listen to a book on tape. Or hell, Raylan, you can come along, keep me company. What Crowes is still living down there'd have a conniption fit featuring us together."

"That's what I've been trying to tell you."

"I know it's crazy." Jo Lynne stood, picked up the letter, scrunched it into a ball. "Since I just told you, I guess there's no point in giving you this." And threw it in the trash. She walked over to Raylan, reached up, put her arms around his neck, and kissed him on the mouth with feeling. "Think our paths will ever cross again?"

"You never know."

"I'll take that as a positive."

•••

SIX THAT EVENING, RAYLAN stopped by the hospital to see Bobby. His eyes were closed and his head was propped up on pillows. The poor guy was hooked to machines that were beeping and blipping behind the bed. Raylan introduced himself to Nancy Torres, a petite blonde who looked like she'd been crying. "How is he?"

"Bullet shattered his clavicle," she said, tears sliding down pale cheeks she dabbed with a Kleenex. "But the doctor says after surgery he'll be good as new." Nancy Torres took a breath. "Bobby said you saved his life. I don't know how to thank you."

She put her arms around Raylan, gave him a hug, and held on for several seconds before letting go.

"He'd have done the same for me."

"Hey, Raylan, you met my better half, huh?" Bobby said, weak-voiced, eyes open now. And to his wife he said, "Babe, this is who you want with you when things go sideways." Bobby coughed, and his wife moved around the bed, picked up a cup with a straw angled through the top, and put it in Bobby's mouth. He sucked some water and shook his head. Nancy Torres put the cup back on the table. "Babe, give us a minute, will you?"

"I'm going to go down and get something to eat. I'll see you in a while. Nice meeting you, Raylan." Nancy Torres walked out of the room.

Standing next to the bed, Raylan said, "You okay?"

"You know the CIRTs are gonna ask me if I can still cut it, tell me I don't have to go back out. I can take a break from the task force for a while or forever. Nancy wants me reassigned. Said she can't go through this again."

"You don't have to decide right now."

"You see me doing admin, a deputary?" Bobby frowned. "I'd lose my mind."

"Getting shot has a way of changing you."

"How do you know?"

"I've seen what it can do. Deputy marshal in Harlan, tough dude, went to arrest a fugitive bank robber, was shot twice. Vest saved his life but being shot had a profound effect on him and he never went back in the field again."

"You think it's gonna change how I do things?"

"I don't know. You'll find out when you go back, if you do. You don't, no one's gonna think any less of you."

"That's bullshit and you know it."

"It's Marshals Service protocol. So just accept it," Raylan said. "And take it easy, will you? You're supposed to be relaxing, getting better."

"What happened to Diaz?"

"He was DOA."

"Deserved it, no doubt about that. But how do you feel taking another man's life?" Bobby said, giving it to him now. "I can see them checking you out. Maybe this traumatic event will prevent you from doing your job." Bobby smiled. "How do you like it?"

"Want me to answer your question? Diaz chose a high-risk profession, and there was no other way to handle it." Raylan had justified shooting Joaquin Diaz as he had the other men he'd killed. It was called *in the line of duty*.

"What else you got?"

Raylan didn't want to do anything to stress his partner, but Bobby was gonna hear it sooner or later, so why not get it out of the way?

"Jose Rindo escaped again."

"Don't tell me he switched bracelets." Bobby tried to sit up, groaned, and made a face.

"No, it wasn't the bracelet this time."

"How'd he do it?"

FOURTEEN

Barry Brink, his lawyer, told Jose he was going to be transferred to another facility. He'd been in isolation for a week, locked down in a six-by-eight-foot room twenty-three hours a day, going out his mind. Dudes was watching, had a camera pointed at him 24/7. Watching him piss first thing in the morning. Watching him take a dump, Rindo waving at the half-moon-shaped lens in the ceiling, saying, *wanna see what I made?* Watching him under the bright, never-ending lights. How's a motherfucker sleep with that shit on?

Sitting across the table from Barry, Rindo said, "Yo, you gotta get me bail, man. Gotta get me the fuck out of here."

Dude in his kick-ass blue suit looked at him like he was a seven-year-old, said, "Get you out? I'm trying to save your life."

"Yo, what you got on there, that custom?"

"Are you referring to the suit, or what?"

"Yeah, motherfucker, the suit, what you think I'm talking about?"

"The trouble you're in, you want to talk about my suit? Yeah, it's custom. I pick a fabric, tailor makes it up for me." Barry Brink

turned his sleeve toward him. "Real button holes, how about that?"
Barry Brink nodded.

"I want me one of them."

"That can be arranged. Trade in your fatigues, you'll be styling."

Jose pictured himself in a suit like that, but without the tie.
Wearing a hand-tooled holster underneath to hold his SIG forty.
Now his mind went back to Barry's opening remark. "Why they
gonna transfer me?"

"You're a security risk. You've escaped twice."

"Gonna escape again, I get the chance." He stretched his arms
over his head. "Where they gonna move me to?"

"Ionia. Also known as I-Max. It's a hundred and thirty miles from
here. They'll probably put you in segregation awaiting trial."

"Trial for what?"

"Trafficking a Schedule I narcotic, for starters. Which, if convicted,
would put you away for life."

"The fuck you talking about?"

"Your heroin operation."

"Oh."

"And then there are the warrants for the contract murder of an
FBI special agent in Tucson, Arizona, the three felony murders in
Detroit, the murder of an Ohio state trooper, and the two escapes
from custody."

"They gotta prove it, don't they? Why I hired you."

"I'll be fighting for you, but the evidence on two of the five is
overwhelming. People in your heroin operation are offering to turn in
exchange for leniency."

"Who you talking bout?"

"Their names haven't been disclosed."

"When they are, I want you to give em to me." Rindo paused.
"Anything I say to you is just between us, is that right?"

"It's called attorney-client privilege."

"Yeah, that's it. Listen, I need you to do something for me, make
a phone call, okay?"

•••

TWENTY-TWO HOURS LATER, JOSE Rindo was in the Wayne County Jail sally port in yellow jail fatigues had *Wayne County Prisoner* in black letters going down one of the pant legs. He was also wearing a three-piece suit: hands cuffed to a transport belt, leg restraints, and a fifteen-inch ankle chain. He was escorted by a Wayne County sheriff's deputy, hopping toward a blue Chevy van said *Sheriff* on the side in gold letters, and had mesh screens over the windows.

There were two deputies up front separated from the three prisoners by a steel cage. The other two dudes were black and seemed like they cool till one looked at him, grinned, and said, "Got a beaner with us."

Jose, half black, got his looks and light skin from his Mexican momma, and his surly disposition and quick temper from his father, a big mean Detroit jig, name of Leroy Blakey, everyone in the hood called Do—cause he did.

Rindo's memory of his father was hazy, like looking at an old photo that was out of focus. What he did remember, Do would whip him with a belt when Jose acted up, and would push his mother around she didn't have supper ready when he walked in the door. One day Do took off, they never saw him again, and it was a blessing.

Now Rindo glanced at the black con who'd dissed him, and grinned. He had more important things on his mind.

The black con said, "Got something to say, motherfucker?"

Rindo ignored him, looked out the rear window, saw the Audi SUV a couple cars back, following them through the city.

The black con said, "I dint think so."

Rindo waited till they were on the freeway before he started pulling on the mesh screen over the side window. Pulled hard as he could with his cuffed hands attached to the transport belt—not much room to move.

He'd take a break, look up front at the deputies. The one in the passenger seat saw what he was doing, got up, and stood at the entrance to the cage. "Hey, get away from there. Sit down."

Restrained or not, Rindo knew the deputy wasn't coming back there with three prisoners. He said, "Why don't you come and make me?"

"I'm gonna Tase you, you don't sit."

Rindo gripped the screen with both hands and yanked till his fingers burned and thought his shoulders were gonna come out their sockets. He felt the screen loosen, saw a screw pop out, and another one.

"I'm not gonna tell you again," the deputy said. He was at the cage door, a Taser in his right hand. The black cons had an interest too, waiting to see what was gonna happen.

His fingers were all cut up, but he went back to work, grabbed the mesh, and with everything he had, he pulled it away from the window. Now the deputy was on the phone. "We've got a situation. Prisoner's trying to escape. We need backup." The deputy listened. "Yes, he's restrained for transport. We're on I-Ninety-Six approaching Novi."

The Audi SUV was still a couple cars behind them. He head-butted the window. "Get the hell away from there," the deputy said. Rindo drove his forehead into the glass a couple more times, felt something wet on his face and saw blood smeared on the window, banged into it again, and now it was loose. He knelt on the seat and pushed the glass out of the window frame and watched it fly off.

The driver was pulling the van over to the side of the freeway when Rindo went headfirst through the opening, the van still moving when he dropped, hit and rolled on the gravel shoulder, dazed, the wind knocked out of him, trying to breathe.

The van slowed and stopped. The front passenger door opened and the deputy ran toward him. Rindo tried to get up and the deputy was on him, man kneeling on his chest. "Stay the fuck down." The deputy didn't see the Audi pull up behind the van.

Thunderbird, carrying a shotgun, and Mr. Boy, with a .45, got out and walked toward them. "Yo, Officer, look like you need some help," Thunderbird said, aiming the shotgun at him. "We take him off your hands, let you be on your way."

To the deputy, Rindo said, "Where's the key at?"

Now the driver came around the front of the van with a semiautomatic in his hand. Aimed it at Thunderbird till the dude saw the shotgun. The driver froze, didn't know what to do, young guy trying to stay strong, stay tough, but outgunned and beyond his experience. "Yo, put it down, I come over there, blow you in half," Thunderbird said.

The black con that had dissed him was staring from the empty window, watching the show. Rindo made a gun with his hand, index finger and thumb, shot the motherfucker.

"Not gonna say it again," Thunderbird said to the driver.

"I can't do that," the young red-haired dude said, like he was apologizing.

Mr. Boy came over and put the barrel of the .45 on the other deputy's temple. "Better do like the man say," he said to the driver.

Thunderbird said, "You gonna lose respect, but you be alive. Want to play it another way, tell me."

"Need the key," Rindo said. "Get all this off me."

"Give it to him," Mr. Boy said to the driver, taking the pistol out of his hand.

The driver, unarmed now, handed the keys to Jose. He unlocked the cuffs and ankle restraints and tossed the key to the black cons, let them take off, create a diversion.

Thunderbird cuffed the two deputies together wrist-to-wrist and the driver to the steering wheel, took the keys to the van and their cell phones, and yanked out the radio handset. Rindo watched the black cons, in their yellow outfits, running toward the snow fence fifty yards away.

Mr. Boy took the first exit and crossed over the freeway. Rindo looking at his massive shoulders that overlapped the seat on both sides. He was in the back of the SUV, changing, taking off the jail fatigues, putting on his own clothes, when he heard the sirens and saw police cruisers on the other side of the freeway. He could always rely on his boys from the old hood no matter what. "Yo, give me a blast."

Thunderbird reached over the seat, handing him the vial. Rindo unscrewed the cap, brought the spoon to his nose, slammed it twice, and felt the rush, closed his eyes, and let out a breath.

"Feel better, motherfucker?" T-Bird said.

•••

FIRST STOP WAS THE storage place in Auburn Hills. They loaded half a dozen banker boxes—each filled with money—in the back of the

Audi. Rindo had to get out of Detroit permanently and was working out a plan in his head.

They pulled up to the house in Oakland Township he had purchased in his sister's name. It was in subdivision full of mansions out in the middle of nowhere. Jose was surprised to see Caroline's BMW in the driveway, wondering what she was doing here. He hadn't talked to her since he was arrested in Columbus.

There were moving boxes in the kitchen filled with his shit. One had the Astra A 2000 One-Touch espresso/cappuccino coffee maker, cost seven grand. Caroline came into the room, a stunned look on her face, but recovered fast, said, "Baby, I been worried sick about you." She ran across the kitchen, put her arms around him, and held on tight. "I prayed you'd get out and here you are."

He didn't return the hug. "You're the one told the marshals where I was at, didn't you?"

"They had surveillance footage of you driving my Jeep out of a parking garage in Detroit, and they knew you shot the trooper. Shoot a cop, they come after you. I didn't have to tell them where you were, they knew. Marshals kept me in a holding cell for two days so I wouldn't try to call you. And you're accusing me?"

Caroline should've been in Hollywood. She was a natural. "Okay. What you doing here then?"

"I left some clothes. Came to pick them up. I was looking around and thought: nobody's going to be using this stuff, so I might as well."

"Uh-huh. Let's see what you got there." Rindo didn't like the situation. How could he trust her after she talked to the marshals? He could see her making a deal. *"Ms. Elliott, we know you've been talking to Jose Rindo, tell us where he is, we'll release you, let you go home."* He could hear someone in law enforcement saying that to her. And her going along with it.

He didn't want to pop Caroline—Rindo liked her—but under the circumstances, how could he let her leave? He could give her to Thunderbird and Mr. Boy, have them keep an eye on her. Or he could take her with him. But that wasn't gonna work either. No, there was only one way out of this.

FIFTEEN

Thirty-two years in law enforcement, I've never heard of this," Chief Wayne Broyles said. "Handcuffed man pulls off the mesh screen that's screwed into the sheet metal. Then he head-butts the window out. This guy Rindo's a fifty-one fifty." The chief sipped his coffee that had a marshal's star on the mug. His sleeves were rolled back twice. He had the big hands and thick wrists of a hockey player.

"Man looking at four life terms without the possibility of parole will do anything to escape," Raylan said. "What's he got to lose?"

"These are the two that picked him up and drove him away. This is movie stuff. If I hadn't seen the photographs, I'd have trouble believing it happened."

"Where were the sheriff's deputies?"

"One was trying to subdue the escaped fugitive when these two pulled up in an SUV. The driver got out of the van and was summarily relieved of his weapon. The other prisoners escaped but have since been apprehended." Chief Broyles slid a wanted poster across the desk. Raylan studied it while the chief summarized Melvin Gales's criminal history.

Name: Melvin Antwan Gales, Jr.

Race: Black

Gender: Male

Hair Color: Black

Eye Color: Brown

Height: 5' 11"

Weight: 315

DOB: 8-16-87

MDOC #: 753 549

Status: Probationer

Assigned Location: Wayne / Detroit Eastern district / Probation

Security Level: N / A

Aliases: Mr. Boy / Fat Albert

Scars / Marks / Tattoos:

> **Scar:** Lower Back—Gunshot wound
>
> **Tattoo:** Left Bicep—Jr.
>
> **Tattoo:** Right Bicep—Mr. Boy
>
> **Tattoo:** Right fist—Smiley face
>
> **Tattoo:** Left Arm—Fat Albert
>
> **Body Piercing:** Right ear
>
> **Body Piercing:** Left ear

"Has two warrants against him: assault with intent and assault with a dangerous weapon. And one inactive sentence for possession of a controlled substance. He was arrested with fifty grams of heroin." The chief sipped his coffee. "Weighs three hundred and fifteen pounds. How's a person get that big?"

The chief handed him the second sheet.

Name: Demarco Hall

Race: Black

Gender: Male

Hair Color: Black

Eye Color: Brown

Height: 6' 1"

Weight: 155

DOB: 10-12-86

MDOC #: 846 903

Status: Probationer

Assigned Location: Wayne/Detroit Eastern district/Probation

Security Level: N/A

Aliases: Thunderbird, T-Bird, Marco, Slim

Scars/Marks/Tattoos:

> **Scar:** Left Bicep—Long scar from a knife
>
> **Tattoo:** Center Chest—"What goes around comes around"
>
> **Tattoo:** Right Bicep—Valencia
>
> **Tattoo:** Left Shoulder—Skulls facing each other
>
> **Tattoo:** Back Left Arm—Slim
>
> **Tattoo:** Left Forearm—Stick figure and "OUCH"
>
> **Marks:** Mole Right Face

"Demarco Hall also has a prior for possession—seventy grams of heroin. And two warrants. One for homicide and the second for possession of a firearm by a felon." The chief sat back in his chair. "Couple of beauties."

"Seeing them at the rest area, I knew something was up."

"Why'd you stop? You were almost home." Chief Broyles lifted his arms and stretched.

"Rindo convinced us he had to get to a bathroom. It was an emergency."

"But it wasn't. Deputy, with your experience, I'd think you'd have seen that one coming. You must believe in yourself."

"Or maybe it's legitimate. You gotta go, you gotta go. And if it is, we don't stop, we're all gonna be paying for it. I went in, found the gun, and knew what was coming next."

The chief sipped his coffee before looking at Raylan again. "A motorist saw the BMW drive off the road and obviously hadn't seen what happened prior to that. Stopped to help, they carjacked the man, put him in the trunk of his own automobile."

Raylan leaned back in the chair and crossed his legs, looking at a scuffmark on one of his Dan Posts. He wet his finger and rubbed the leather.

"These two are old friends of Rindo, grew up with him, neighborhood near Grand Boulevard and Linwood, and now work for him."

Raylan said, "Think they're still in town?"

"I doubt it. I'd say they're out west, or on their way. Rindo's known to spend time in Tucson, and Baja Mexico. Brings heroin, cocaine, and meth over the border at Mexicali into El Centro and then ships it to Tucson or San Diego. From there he sends it east to Louisville and Detroit." The chief paused. "This one's red hot. Rindo's been designated a major case by the Marshals Investigative Services Division. And as you know the FBI wants him too for murdering one of their agents. They're asking for our help. Now, we get him, you know they'll take credit for it. They've gotta keep score, show us how good they are. They're bean counters. They get Rindo, they'll take a bean, put it in their pot."

"How do they get away with it?"

"You kidding? They're the FBI. I'd send Torres if he were fit for duty. Bobby knows Rindo, how he thinks, how he works. But then, so do you. I want you to liaison with the marshals and the female FBI agent in Tucson. Start there. It seems to be the logical place to begin. Help them any way you can. Let's get this lunatic off the street."

Nora Sanchez's face popped into his head. Raylan didn't like the idea of working with her again. She was difficult, a pain in the ass, and she knew more than she was saying about Frank Tyner's death. But he wasn't going to say anything to the chief.

"One more thing. This is what happens when you're out of favor with Jose Rindo." He slid a morgue photograph across his desk to Raylan. It was Caroline Elliott in repose, wrists, ankles, and mouth duct-taped. She had been shot once in the head. "Body was spotted at the Bald Mountain State Recreation area by a jogger."

Raylan said, "Why would Rindo want to get rid of this good-looking girl?"

"Doesn't trust her, would be my guess. Which is understandable since she gave him up. Rindo lives in a paranoid world. Anyone might sell him out at any time."

"Caroline Elliott lived in Southfield. What's she doing way out there?"

"Rindo owns a ten-thousand-square-foot house not far from there in Oakland Township. It's in his sister's name. Asset Forfeiture's going to auction the property or sell it. Go out, look around, will you? Maybe you'll find a clue about the murder, or something that tells us where he's going."

•••

RAYLAN PULLED UP TO the gatehouse that was made out of fieldstone, entered the code on the keypad, and the gate swung open. He could see the house in the distance, red brick, slate roof, and six chimneys, ten thousand square feet of structure that stretched east to west several hundred feet on 5.2 acres of manicured lawn, gardens, and woods. It reminded him of houses he'd seen on *Lifestyles of the Rich and Famous.*

Inside it was all marble floors and high ceilings, with a staircase that swept down from the second floor. Raylan could kind of understand why Rindo, growing up with nothing, was now overcompensating, going for it. Saying, *"Hey, motherfuckers, look at me."*

It took an hour and a half to search the house that had six bedrooms, ten bathrooms, a library with thousands of books, a billiard room, a wine cellar, a sauna, and a gym. Raylan went outside and stood by the pool, gaze sweeping across the yard and tennis court to a small fieldstone out building, built away from the house where the grass and woods met.

He walked across the lawn to the building, opened the garage door, looking at all-terrain vehicles and snowmobiles. He walked through the space to a tool room with a workbench and a pegboard lined with tools, Raylan looked around, studying the scene. There were scratches on the sealed concrete floor where something had been dragged to the door. He went outside and saw tire tracks on the grass that extended all the way to a six-car garage attached to the house.

Raylan walked back into the tool room, trying to imagine what happened. Pictured Caroline Elliott standing on a canvas tarp when they shot her in the head with a high-caliber pistol. He could see that the wall on one side of the room had been repaired and painted, but whoever did it was in a hurry.

Raylan stepped into the adjoining room, studied the wall from the opposite side, and saw traces of blood spatter.

Now he inspected the all-terrain vehicles. One of the four had dried grass in the tire treads. Was it used to carry Caroline Elliot's body after she was killed?

The only vehicle in the six-car garage was an Audi Q5, which according to the license number had been used in Rindo's daring escape from the prison transport. He checked the papers in the glove box. The Audi was registered to VIP Limousine Company, an address on Griswold in Detroit.

•••

RAYLAN ENTERED THE SMALL lobby that had two chairs opposite a glass window with a view of an office bullpen. Closest to him was a hot-looking brunette at a computer station. Raylan tapped on the glass. The girl glanced at him and he showed her his star. "Deputy US Marshal Raylan Givens. I want to speak to the owner."

The girl picked up the phone on her desk and said, "Joey, there's a US Marshal wants to talk to you." She listened, staring at her computer screen, and then smiled at Raylan. "He wants to know what this is regarding."

"A vehicle registered to VIP Limousine was involved in a crime."

A couple minutes later, the lobby door opened, a stocky forty-year-old Chaldean with a big nose said, "I'm Joey Yalda, the owner. Come on in."

Raylan thought Joey looked like a Metro car driver who took people to the airport.

Raylan followed him down a hall with framed photos of Joey posing with Detroit celebrities: Joey and Miguel Cabrera, Joey and Matthew Stafford, Joey and Justin Verlander, Joey and Steve Yzerman.

Raylan said, "You know these guys?"

"All dear friends."

The walls of his slick office were lined with more pictures. Joey Yalda sat behind a big glass desk, Raylan in an armchair facing him, trying not to breathe in his cologne.

Joey Yalda fixed his dark, serious eyes on Raylan. "Okay, what's this about?"

"Why would a 2015 Audi Q5 registered to VIP Limousine Company be in Jose Rindo's garage at a house in Oakland Township?"

"Wait, who? What's his name?" Joey's cell phone rang. He glanced at the screen, turned it off, and met Raylan's gaze. "I have no idea. We own a lot of cars. I can't tell you where they're all at."

"You know how this looks?" Joey kept his gaze on Raylan. "You're participating in a criminal enterprise." Raylan handed him the Audi registration.

Joey gave it a casual glance. "For all I know, it was stolen."

"You accept cash payment for cars, provide registration and insurance that can't be traced back to the purchaser. Does that explain it?"

"No, but I'm going to explain it to my attorney before I say another word."

"What's Rindo driving?"

"I don't know who you're talking about."

Raylan stood and took handcuffs out of his pocket. "Tell you what, come over here, put your hands behind your back. I'll take you in, we can finish this at the Wayne County Jail."

"I want to talk to my attorney."

"You'll have plenty of time for that after we book you."

"Wait a minute," Joey said, a look of recognition on his face. "Did you say Jose Rindo? I think I do remember him."

•••

"I don't know where Rindo is," Raylan said, walking into Chief Broyles's office. "But he's driving a 2015 Cadillac Escalade, license number DMB 0531."

The chief frowned. "How do you know that?"

Raylan told him.

"You send out a BOLO?"

"I'm a step ahead of you, Chief."

"Looks like you're several steps at least. When police locate the vehicle, Rindo is going to know who told us. Limo company owner's going to be in deep shit." Chief Broyles grinned. "Where is he?"

"Packing for an extended vacation in South America, if he's smart."

"When are you leaving?"

SIXTEEN

AN IMPERIAL COUNTY SHERIFF pulled Wiggy over after crossing the Coachella at drop eight. He stopped next to the canal, a bright blue stream that cut across the flat, dusty, dun-colored landscape for as far as he could see.

Looking in the side mirror, Wiggy watched the man get out of the cruiser, square his campaign hat on his head, and move toward the van. "License and registration," the sheriff said, standing eye level with Wiggy. The brim of the hat cast part of his face in shadow, and the sunglasses hid his eyes.

The license was attached to the visor by a rubber band. Wiggy pulled it free and handed it to the man. "I left the registration in my other shorts," he said, wondering if the sheriff would believe that.

"Next you're gonna tell me it's with your proof of insurance and smog decal, is that right Mr. Dentinger?"

"Yes, sir." Wiggy had no idea where the registration was at, and he didn't have insurance or a decal. He'd bought the van, a 1991 Ford Econoline with 213,560 miles on her, at Case Towing in Niland for $750.

"I see a post office box. Where in hell do you live at?" The sheriff had beads of sweat rolling down his face, and dark half circles of sweat in the armpits of his tan uniform shirt.

"The Slabs, sir."

The sheriff made a face. "Why do you live in that trash heap?"

"That's where I was brought up."

"Why's a nineteen-year-old kid driving a full-size van? You don't by chance transport illegals, do you?"

"No, sir."

"What's in the back?"

"Nothing."

"You don't mind I have a look inside, do you?"

Wiggy didn't think he had a choice. He got out, walked to the rear, and opened the doors, filling the cargo area with sunlight. There was nothing in it. Just the bare metal floor with nothing on it. He got a little whiff of BO from the last batch of wets.

"I catch you with a load, you're going right to county lockup. Want to spend time with *chalupas*, they got your room ready." The sheriff wiped sweat off his face with his shirtsleeve. "Son, we understand each other?"

"Yes, sir, we sure do."

•••

THREE HOURS LATER, WIGGY was on the driveway, backing the van toward the garage. Lori, a Virginia Slims 100 wedged in the corner of her mouth, came out of the house, met him, and opened one of the garage doors with a remote. He backed all the way in, looking at fifteen wets standing in the empty space where another car would fit.

Lori closed the door and turned on the light. This group looked like all the others—men and women with tan faces and sad eyes. Wiggy felt sorry for the illegals, these poor folks spending their life savings, or borrowing enough to come to the U S of A in search of a better life, and there was no guarantee they were gonna find it. He also thought of them as *his* wets, and he was gonna do right by them.

He walked over to the group. "Hey, everybody, I'm Wiggy. You can call me that or Wiggs. I'll be your driver. I'm gonna get you to LA." He glanced at Lori who was pointing at her watch. He opened the cargo doors and said, "You can all get in the van now."

They picked up their backpacks, duffle bags, jugs of water, and loaded in the back. Wiggy'd bought a case of Gatorade at a 7-Eleven in El Centro and slid it on the floor behind them. "This here's for you. Get thirsty, help yourself." Nobody moved, so he pulled a couple plastic bottles out of the case and handed them to the wets that were closest to him, then handed out a few more and a few more till everybody had one. Now they were smiling and saying *gracias*.

"It's gonna be about three and a half hours till we get to LA, okay? We're gonna be going through mountains with some pretty hairy turns, so I need you all to chill, okay?" They looked at him with blank faces, and Wiggy didn't know if they understood him or not. He said, "*Benvenido America*," smiled big, and they smiled back. He closed the doors and moved along the side of the van. Scared shitless as they were, he didn't tell them they were gonna be driving through the Aerial Gunnery Range, a godforsaken stretch where the Navy practiced dropping bombs and such.

"I'll call you," he said to Lori.

"Watch out for Johnny Law," she said every time he took a load, and he said, "I will." She was like his mother or something—always concerned about him, saying things like: "When're you gonna leave the Slabs, get out of that hell hole, come live with me?" He couldn't imagine sharing space with this wrinkled, chain-smoking desert woman and her four dogs. Her saying, "Jerome, honey, I want you to see a dentist. Tooth decay can lead to more serious problems. I'm gonna make an appointment for you." Or saying, "You've got to have better hygiene, take a shower, clean yourself up, and pop those zits."

Wiggy couldn't remember the last time he'd had a shower, but once in a while he'd jump in the canal to get the stink off. And anyway, Amy, a girl he was seeing, didn't seem to mind how he smelled. As a guy from the Slabs who made money, he was, as Lori said, a catch.

It was dusk when they got to Niland and full dark when they got to the canal, taking drop eight again, a clean shot into the mountains and Smuggler's Pass. Wiggy wouldn't lie, it was forty miles of tough driving on steep narrow roads through land God forgot. He didn't go near critty on such trips, had to have his wits about him cause any mistake could result in a blown tire or a busted axle and then they'd be up shit's creek without a paddle.

Chugging up a steep grade, Wiggy saw headlights behind him about a hundred yards, thinking border patrol cause they were on federal land, and the sheriff and local police didn't have jurisdiction, but crazier shit had been known to happen.

At the top of the hill, Wiggy saw blue-and-red LEDs and strobes flashing behind them, and floor-boarded it. He slid open the panel behind him and said, *"La Migra, La Migra,* chill." The van rocketed down the other side of the hill, fishtailing into a turn, brights lighting up a sign ahead that read:

DANGER
UNEXPLODED ORDNANCE
DO NOT ENTER

Wiggy cut the headlights and turned right onto the Aerial Gunnery Range, bouncing on rocks and ruts, coming to a stop behind an old camouflaged WWII tank missing its tractor treads. He didn't think the cops or border patrol would come out on the range. It was too dangerous. No one knew when an F35 was gonna come screaming overhead, lighting up the sky.

He opened the rear doors, put his finger over his mouth to shush the wets, told them to chill, they weren't there yet. A few nodded like they understood. Wiggy told them they wanted to go to the bathroom, have at it but do it quiet.

Twenty minutes later they went through Smuggler's Pass, and twenty minutes after that they turned onto Interstate 10 heading for LA.

SEVENTEEN

Mr. Boy said, "How you say the name of that town again?"

"Tucumcari," Rindo said from the back seat.

"That's a funny name," Mr. Boy said. "Tuconwhat?"

"Tucumcari."

Mr. Boy smiled. He held the Escalade's steering wheel with both hands, looking at a mountain range ahead and brown, flat land on both sides of the road. "Why they call it that? What do it mean?"

"It's a Spanish word," Rindo said. "Means stop asking dumb fucking questions."

Mr. Boy laughed. "Does not." He looked in the rearview mirror, saw a car back a ways coming up on them, and then he saw the lights on the roof. "Got a cop tagging." Mr. Boy always got scared he saw a police car even when he ain't done nothing.

He saw Rindo turn, look out the back window. "How fast you doing?"

"Seventy, just like you tole me."

"Be cool," Rindo said. "Cop's got no reason to stop us."

"Motherfuckers don't need no reason," Thunderbird said, opening his eyes in the front seat.

Mr. Boy said, "Why's he following us?"

"He's not following us," Rindo said. "He's just behind us."

"What's the difference?" Mr. Boy could feel sweat on his face and wiped it with his hand. The .45 was under the seat. All he had to do was reach and pick it up. He eyed the mirror, cop was hanging back, but still there. "Cop pull us over, what we gonna do?"

"Be cool till we can't." Rindo was calm and relaxed.

Mr. Boy tried to keep it together but it was hard watching the police behind them. He waited till he couldn't wait anymore and said, "Dude still there."

"Forget about him," Rindo said.

"Yeah," Thunderbird said. "Why you bitching out?"

"Ain't bitching out, skinny motherfucker. Make you my bitch." Now the dude was getting closer to them. Mr. Boy thought he was gonna see flashing lights. But the cop took a lane, blew by them, and he felt the tightness in his body ease up.

Thunderbird cracked the window a couple inches and lit a joint.

•••

IT WAS LATE AFTERNOON when they got to Las Cruces. Rindo wanted to get something to eat, stop for the night. He rented two rooms at the Townhouse Motel on West Picacho. They'd been in the car twenty-four straight hours. Tucson was only 275 more miles, but he couldn't do it. Had to get away from his homies for a while, take a shower, make a few calls.

An hour later they drove into town, looking for a place to have a meal. Rindo picked one that served Mexican food. This close to the border, what else you gonna get? Mr. Boy parked the Escalade and they walked half a block to the restaurant. There was a festiveness about the city, mariachis playing on the street corner and people everywhere, and it was hot.

At the table, Rindo ordered tequila, Thunderbird a double margarita, and Mr. Boy a Coke. For dinner, Mr. Boy put away six burritos, six tacos, two orders of beans and rice, and had guacamole and salsa dripping down his chin. "Get enough?" Rindo said. "You could feed a village on that."

After four doubles, Thunderbird was fucked up and tried to pick up the waitress, a cute little Mexican girl looked like she was still in middle school. T-Bird liked them young.

"Hey there, what's your name?" Thunderbird said, smiling with mouthful of chiles rellenos.

"Maria."

"What time you get off, *Maria*?" Thunderbird trying to pronounce her name like she did.

"Eleven."

She was shy and innocent, didn't know what T-Bird was asking, what he wanted.

"Wanna hang out? You can come to the motel. We can have some fun." Thunderbird grinned and touched the girl's arm, and now she flinched and moved away from the table.

Rindo said, "What're you doing? You out of your fucking mind?"

Thunderbird said, "What I do?"

Now a serious-looking Mexican dude about forty came across the restaurant to the table, his dark eyes fixed on T-Bird. "This girl you proposition is sixteen years old."

"I didn't proposition anyone."

"Whatever you call it, you frightened her. Maria is not going to see you or anyone. She is going home."

Thunderbird said, "What're you, her father?"

"I am her uncle and the owner of the restaurant." His tone was stern, unforgiving.

"You probably want her for yourself, don't you? That young trim's where it's at."

"Listen to me," the man said, trying to hold back his temper. "Leave your money on the table and walk out the door, or I call the police."

"We not finished yet," Thunderbird said.

"Yes, I believe you are."

"*Pido disculpas por mi amigo*," Rindo said. "*Esta borracho*. Give me the bill and I'll take care of it."

The owner walked away from the table to where the girl was standing by the bar.

Mr. Boy said. "What you say to him?"

Rindo gave Thunderbird a hard look. "You out of your mind? We're trying not to attract attention. That means you don't put the moves on sixteen-year-old girls. You want the police to come?"

"I's just being friendly," Thunderbird said. "What's the problem?"

The manager came back to the table and handed the bill to Rindo, who stood and said, *"Muchas gracias. No nos verás de nuevo."*

"I hope not," the manager said. "I hope for your sake I do not see you again."

When they came out of the restaurant, Jose felt the heat and heard the mariachis playing. He looked left toward the Escalade and saw two blue Las Cruces police cars double-parked next to the big SUV. "Hey, you see what's going down?"

Thunderbird said, "What the fuck."

Rindo heard a siren. Another police car sped onto the scene, lights flashing. The doors of the Escalade were open, cops checking the inside. There were crowds of people on both sides of the street, watching the action.

He led them around the block, standing next to a restaurant storefront, trying to figure out what to do when he saw an old Benz 500 SEL parked in front of them, an old man behind the wheel. "Get the keys, put him in the back seat," he said to Mr. Boy.

Rindo drove out the center of Las Cruces, looking down the long hood at the three-point star, thinking about fate, thinking Thunderbird didn't hit on the waitress, they would have come out the restaurant fifteen, twenty minutes later, and he believed they might either be dead or in custody. But it was more than that. He had escaped three times and now it was clear to him: he was destined for something important. And then there was the money. He was going to leave the banker boxes of cash—about three million—in the car, but at the last minute decided to stash it in his room.

Rindo's brain shifted gears. How did Las Cruces PD get on to them? There was only one explanation that made sense: Joey Yalda had given him up. It couldn't've been anyone else. Rindo had never really believed in the man and should have trusted his instincts instead of the dude. He would settle that one another time.

In the back seat, the scared old man was talking. "What's this about? Where are you taking me? I told you my wife is sick, I have to pick up her medicine."

"There, there," Mr. Boy said, stroking the old man's gray head with his big hand like Grandpa was a pet. "It gonna be okay."

At the motel, Rindo told them their pictures were probably gonna be on the late news and they had five minutes to get their things and clear out.

•••

THEY ARRIVED IN TUCSON, hot and tired at 11:10 p.m. The house was secluded in the foothills of the Tucson Mountains, nearest neighbor was a quarter mile away. Rindo took a gravel path that wound through the brown, dusty hills dotted with saguaro and cholla. He saw the dark shape of the house above them and continued to climb, the old Benz holding its own on the steep rough grade.

Rindo parked in the garage next to the Range Rover, got out, turned the light on, and popped the trunk. Shook the old man, curled up on the mat, didn't get a reaction. He turned him over, saw his eyes were open.

Mr. Boy, standing behind him said, "Something wrong with him?"

"Yeah," Rindo said, "he's gone."

"Gone where?" Mr. Boy frowned.

"Wherever you go when you dead."

"He was a nice old man. I think he up in heaven." Mr. Boy walked out of the garage and looked up at the black star-filled sky, and then back at him. "What about his wife? We have to tell her."

It was still over a hundred degrees and Rindo could feel sweat dripping down his face as he pulled Visqueen off the shelf, unrolled a long piece, wrapped it around the old man, and taped the seams.

"This ain't right. He didn't do nothing to us."

Rindo let Mr. Boy speak his mind and said, "We didn't kill him. He died of old age. It was going to happen anyway."

Mr. Boy looked confused. "How do you know?"

EIGHTEEN

LATE AFTERNOON, RAYLAN LANDED in Tucson, rented a Kia Sorento (a car he'd never heard of), drove to his hotel, checked in, and dropped off his bag. He had a meeting with Victor Hernandez, the marshal in charge of the Tucson office in the morning.

Now he was going to meet Nora Sanchez at a restaurant on Cushing Street close to the Federal Courthouse where the Marshals Service operated, and not far from the FBI field office.

Raylan got there first, sat at the bar, and ordered a beer. It was dark and cool and it felt good to get out of the heat. He saw her come in and look around. Raylan waved.

Nora walked over and sat next to him. She was better-looking than he remembered, or maybe it was because he had been thinking about her and was curious to see if she was friendlier and more relaxed on her home turf.

Nora's face was made up and she wore a blazer over a white blouse, and he could see her shape, the swell of her breasts, her flat stomach and narrow hips.

Instead of opening with pleasantries, "Raylan, how are you? Good to see you," she said, "What's the story on Jose Rindo? No one can seem to hold him. How does he keep escaping?"

"He's determined, but he's also lucky. What can I get you?"

"I'll get it." Nora raised her hand, got the bartender's attention, and ordered a glass of chardonnay.

"You don't let anyone help you, huh?"

"I'm used to doing things on my own." Nora smiled. "How do you like Tucson?"

"It's hot. I don't know how you do it."

"Same way you handle winter. You get used to it."

The bartender put a glass of wine in front of her. Nora picked it up and took a sip.

Raylan said, "You have any idea where Rindo might be?"

"If I did, I would have him in custody. Why do you think he's here?"

"We know he was coming this way. Acting on a BOLO, Las Cruces Police found the Cadillac Escalade Rindo and two accomplices were traveling in. You didn't see it?"

"When was that?"

"Yesterday."

"I was in court all day. And since early this morning I've been doing surveillance."

Raylan unfolded the wanted posters on Demarco Hall and Melvin Gales, Jr. and handed them to her.

She studied their faces and read their sheets.

"Why's Jose Rindo hanging with these cocolos?"

"Rindo's father was black, but he got his mother's Hispanic looks. Grew up with these two, went to school with them." Raylan tilted his beer bottle and took the last sip. "Anyway, back in Las Cruces, Jose Rindo rented a couple rooms at a local motel, manager positively ID'd all three of them. Said they arrived in an Escalade, took off and came back an hour or so later in an old Mercedes. Las Cruces PD believe they carjacked an elderly resident. The man and his 1995 Mercedes-Benz have disappeared."

"Why would he come back here, knowing we're looking for him?"

"It's one of his staging areas. Rindo thinks he's invisible, can get around without being seen. Law enforcement gets onto him, he moves to Mexico."

"So how do we find him?"

"He has a girlfriend lives in the Catalina foothills."

"What does she do?"

"She's a student, junior at Arizona." Raylan held up his empty beer bottle and the bartender nodded.

Nora sipped her wine.

"You want to call on her, see what she knows? Or just keep an eye on her?

"Find the hole, you'll find the pole."

Nora glanced at him and frowned. "That's disgusting."

"But true—the way it is. Fugitive on the run, there are three things he needs: shelter, food, and sex. No matter how dumb it is, how obvious it is, the guy calls his girlfriend, his baby momma, or his wife cause he hasn't had any for a long time. And we're usually there waiting for him. For a man hunter, that's square one. We cuff him, he says, 'How'd you find me?' Like it's some big mystery. The guy's a crackhead, he's gonna buy crack. He's a drunk, he's gonna buy booze."

Nora sipped her wine. "Tell me about the girlfriend."

"Her name's Deanna Lyons. She's an only child from a wealthy Boston family. Six months ago she was busted for possession. Her parents got her a big-time lawyer, and now she's on probation. Deanna's a rich-girl rebel. You can imagine why she's with Rindo— free cocaine or heroin—and the allure of hanging with a bad boy drug dealer her parents would never approve of."

"Seems to have everything but chooses to do things the hard way." Nora stroked the stem of her wine glass. "I'm going to go home, freshen up. I'll pick you up about eight thirty. Where are you staying?"

"Congress Hotel." Raylan drank his beer. "Call me when you're on your way. I'll get the check."

"No, you won't." Nora got up, reached in her bag, brought a wallet out, and left a ten on the bar.

"What is it with you? You won't let me buy—"

"I'll see you later," she said, cutting him off. Nora got up and walked out of the bar.

•••

RAYLAN WAS SWEATING, STANDING in front of the hotel at 8:40 p.m., still thinking about Nora when she pulled up in a white Chevy sedan. He got in the car next to her, felt the chill of air-conditioning. Raylan could see the outline of the soft vest under her blouse, Glock holstered on her right hip. Nora smiled and handed him a bottled water. "You're going to need it."

Raylan wanted to say, *"What do I owe you?"* See if she had a sense of humor. He hadn't seen any evidence of it yet, but instead he said, "This allowed, giving FBI water to assisting federal agents?"

Nora smiled. "Okay, I'm sorry. I should've let you buy me a drink. Thank you. It's all the Bureau rules. You wouldn't believe it. You can't do anything."

"Are you naturally uptight, or do I bring it out of you?"

"That's what you say to the person you're doing surveillance with? Aren't you the diplomat." Nora paused. "You're telling me you think I'm tense and angry?"

"I wouldn't put it that way exactly, but you're close."

"Are you finished?"

"I don't know. We'll have to see how it goes." Raylan managed a grin.

She gave him a sour look, slid the shifter into gear, and they pulled out of the lot. Driving through the city, Raylan glanced at Nora occasionally, her body rigid, delicate hands wrapped around the curve of the steering wheel at ten and two like she'd just finished driver's training.

Being with her again in a car reminded him of their trip to Columbus—at odds with each other from the start. She kept her eyes straight ahead. Neither of them said anything till they were driving into the foothills of the Catalinas. Raylan didn't know what to make of Nora. He couldn't decide if she had something against him personally, or if it was an FBI superiority complex.

There were lights on in the houses scattered through the hills. They were on a steep incline when Nora hit the brakes and pulled over to the side of the road. "She lives right up there." Nora pointed. "We're going to have to walk."

Standing on the hilltop, Raylan stared at Tucson, a long horizontal strip of light that shimmered and pulsed in the valley below them. He liked the look of the city a lot better at night.

They climbed down a steep stretch of hillside and hid behind an outcropping of rocks with a view of the back of the house, pool area all lit up about fifty yards away. It was cooler up there and it reminded Raylan of the brown fracked hills of Kentucky that had been stripped of vegetation.

Nora had her binoculars out and was sweeping them across the back of the house, clean, modern design with a lot of glass. Raylan said, "See anything?"

"She's in there with someone, but I can't see who it is. They're too far away. But if we move closer there's no place to take cover. And anyone looking outside would be able to see us."

"I think we should walk up the road to the house. If Rindo's there, arrest him. He's not, we call it a night."

At the car, Raylan said, "Let's drive up. We take Rindo down, we're gonna need a way to bring him in."

"I was thinking we'd call the Tucson PD."

"Let some inexperienced cop try to handle this fugitive that's escaped three times?" He was surprised she didn't see it that way.

Nora started the car. "Aren't you getting a little ahead of yourself? We don't even know if he's there."

"But we better be prepared if he is."

She parked across the road from Deanna Lyons's house. There was a car in the gated driveway.

Raylan said, "You gonna run the tag?"

"If I could see it."

He thought she was being lazy. He got out, crossed the road, stood at the locked gate, and read the license number. Back at the car, he said, "It's a Jag sedan, Arizona plate: seven one seven RWN."

Nora booted up her computer, typed in the information, waited and said, "It's registered to Richard Gomez, Four Three Oh Five

North Larrea Lane, Tucson, Arizona. DOB: May seventeenth, 1987. Evidently, Gomez is clean, never been arrested."

Raylan walked down the stone stairway on the side of the house to the pool area. He was a little uneasy with Nora behind him, a Glock in her hand. She wasn't first on the list of people he'd want backing him on a fugitive takedown. He stopped at the bottom of the stairs, heard voices. Raylan looked around the corner, through the wall of glass into the house. He could see a blonde sitting close to a dark-haired guy on a sectional couch, watching a movie on a giant flat-screen. He turned, whispered, "It isn't Rindo. Have a look."

She started up the stairs and he followed her to the car. "I think they've got something going on. You see how close they were?"

"Gomez is gonna be in for a surprise when Rindo finds out. I don't think he's the type that likes to share his women. Just a guess, knowing what I do about him. Sooner or later Rindo's gonna want to see this girl, and when he does, I'd like to be there."

NINETEEN

Raylan was having breakfast in the hotel restaurant, huevos rancheros and black coffee, when his phone rang. He slid it out of his shirt pocket, checked the caller ID, and said, "You're the last person I expected to hear from. How're you feeling?"

"I'm bored out of my mind," Bobby Torres said. "Discharged from the hospital a couple days ago."

"Nancy's got to be happy."

"She didn't see enough of me and now she's seeing too much." Bobby let out a breath like he was in pain.

"You okay?"

"Yeah. How's it going?"

"I'm in Tucson working with Special Agent Sanchez again."

"I heard. She any more agreeable?"

"Not that I've noticed."

"Anything new on her ex-partner, Tyner?"

"Nothing yet, but I'll get to it."

"In my spare time I've been following Rindo on Facebook. I know you don't believe in social media."

"It's not that I don't believe in it, it doesn't interest me."

"You were born a hundred and fifty years too late. Anyway, I just sent you a shot of Rindo posing in a desert location with mountains in the background. Might help you find him."

"Why do you suppose Rindo's sending out clues to his whereabouts?"

"He thinks highly of himself and thinks we're a bunch of dumbasses.

"I'll stay on it and send more when I can."

"I appreciate your help, but you're supposed to be taking it easy."

"Don't worry about me. We've got to find this guy."

•••

THIRTY MINUTES LATER, RAYLAN was in the chief's office studying framed photos of Victor Hernandez on the wall while he was on the phone. There was a shot of him in camouflage holding an AR-15 when he was with special ops, and a shot of him in a helicopter, transporting two restrained, blindfolded Sinaloa capos.

The chief hung up the phone, shook hands with Raylan, and offered him a seat in his light-filled corner office in the federal building. Victor reminded him of an older, more compact version of Bobby. He sat behind a spotless desk, muscles bunched in a white dress shirt. At forty-nine, Victor looked like he should still be out hunting fugitives.

"We're up to speed on Jose Rindo. We know about the Cadillac Escalade the PD found in Las Cruces, and Maynard Summers, the senior citizen that was carjacked, his whereabouts and that of his 1995 Mercedes still unknown. I want to assure you, Deputy Marshal Givens, you have the full support of the district. Anything you need, just let me know."

"A UAV and an AR-15 would be helpful."

"I'll introduce you to Rudy Llanes in the gun vault, he'll fix you up."

Victor Hernandez paused, folded his hands in a pious gesture. "I don't recall ever seeing a case like this. Man escapes three times, he's still at large. Where the hell's he at?"

"You see this?" Raylan took out his phone and showed him the Facebook picture. "Looks like it was shot somewhere in the foothills outside the city. Rindo's saying, 'here I am, come and find me.'"

"You need backup, the fugitive task force is at your disposal." Victor Hernandez paused again. "Only complication, aside from Rindo himself, is the FBI's involvement. They do things their way, we do things our way. I understand you're acquainted with Special Agent Sanchez. Can she cut it?"

"I wasn't sure till we were ambushed transporting Rindo from Columbus to Detroit. She held her own with an eight seventy, allowing us to get away with the prisoner." Raylan didn't tell Victor his concerns about Nora. Why complicate the situation? He'd work with her and hope for the best.

"You find out his location, we'll get the team over there, take him down."

•••

RAYLAN HAD AN HOUR till Nora was gonna pick him up. He drove to a western apparel store on Campbell Street, bought a white Ariat shirt with snap pearl buttons, and tried on a black Stetson. Looking at himself in the mirror, he fit the hat, adjusting it on his head, pulling the brim down just over his eyes. The salesman, a bowlegged old coot, looked like he'd spent a lifetime on horseback, said, "Sir, where're you from, you don't mind my asking?"

"Harlan County, Kentucky."

"Well I'll tell you something, you sure know how to wear a hat."

•••

RAYLAN WAITED, STANDING ON the courthouse steps, the UAV at his feet, an AR-15 slung over his shoulder, working the brim of the Stetson the way you do with a new hat. He could feel the morning sun already baking him and it wasn't yet 10:00 a.m. Nora pulled up a couple minutes later. Raylan picked up the vest and walked down the steps to the car, opened the rear door, set the AR on the seat and the vest on the floor. He got in and tipped the brim of the Stetson.

"You look familiar except for the hat. At first I thought you were an out-of-work cowboy. The UAV looked like a bedroll. When did you get the hat?"

"How do you like it?"

"It's black. What're you, a bad guy now, or just a bad ass?"

"You seen this?" Raylan had his phone out, showing her a shot of the fugitive standing next to a fifteen-foot-tall saguaro.

"What is it?"

"Rindo's Facebook page."

"I didn't know he had one."

"This is his new profile picture. Bobby Torres, who you met, found it and sent it to me. Can you tell where this is?"

"Seriously? You think we're going to find the location based on this?" Nora held him in her gaze, dark curly hair framing her face. "You know how many places this could be?"

He handed her the phone. "Look in the left corner of the picture. What is that?"

Nora put on her readers, studied the image. "It looks like a trash can."

"What does that tell you?"

"It's a hiking trail. Could be Catalina State Park, the Tortolita Mountains, Saguaro National Park, or any number of other places. But Rindo wants us to know he's in Tucson. What I don't understand is why."

"He's escaped three times. I've got to believe that figures into it."

Raylan turned off the phone, slid it in his shirt pocket. "All right, what's your plan?"

"You mean our plan, don't you?"

Raylan didn't think of them as a team, but if she did, it was a step in the right direction. Nora put the car in gear and they took off, heading through Tucson to the Catalinas. There was a haze that hung over the city like a dark cloud.

"Follow Ms. Lyons is what I thought we were going to do. Unless you have another idea?"

"No, I think that's a good place to start."

•••

THERE WAS A POOL maintenance truck in the driveway when they drove past the house. The garage door was open. There was a convertible inside. Nora drove higher into the hills, turned around and parked off the road on a flat graded lot with a For Sale sign.

It was 10:33 a.m., and already ninety-two degrees. Raylan lowered the window and felt the heat. He picked up Nora's binoculars and rested his elbows on the door sill. He looked down at the house, didn't see anyone, and turned to Nora. "I'm gonna take a closer look."

"You're going to need this." Nora handed him a cold bottle of water.

"That's two I owe you."

"Are you keeping score?"

Raylan stepped out of the car and crossed the road. He put the binoculars around his neck and climbed down the hill, sliding in his boots. He ducked behind a rock formation with an unobstructed view of the house and pool area about fifty yards away. He could see the pool man crouching near the diving board, testing the water.

Deanna Lyons appeared in a light blue bikini, wrapping an orange towel around her waist that hung to her ankles. She talked to him for a couple minutes. Then he grabbed his equipment and started up the stairs.

Deanna spread the towel on a lounge chair and sat, rubbing suntan lotion on her arms and legs. At the top of the stairs, the pool man stopped, looking over his shoulder, checking her out.

Raylan was doing the same thing from his perch on the side of the hill. When the pool man disappeared, Deanna took off her top, and now Raylan had the binoculars up and was holding on her perfect breasts. He continued down her flat, brown stomach and the curves of her hips to her long tan legs and feet with orange toenails. She had a body all right.

"Hey, what're you doing?"

Raylan looked up at Nora and felt like a teenager busted by his mother looking at a *Playboy* centerfold. Deanna glanced in Nora's direction, got up, covered herself with the towel, and went inside.

In the car, Raylan said, "She saw you."

"So I'm looking at the lot across the street. What were you looking at?"

Raylan didn't say anything.

"She didn't have any clothes on."

"I noticed."

"I'll bet you did."

Deanna, in a convertible with the top down, backed out of the driveway.

Now they were speeding after her, Raylan seeing glimpses of the car as it snaked through the hills and through the city to the Tucson Mall.

"I want to go with you," Nora said.

"She knows what you look like. I hope she's telling herself you're a realtor trying to sell that property up the road, but if she sees you again it's all over."

It was crowded in the mall, so he didn't worry about Deanna Lyons making him. Her first stop was Arizona Watch and Jewelry on the lower level. Deanna, in a white T-shirt and black Capris, took the stairs and Raylan hung back, giving her time and distance. She came out of the store looking at her watch, moving along the concourse to a Starbucks and going inside.

Raylan watched a couple of teenage girls on their cell phones, texting. He'd never seen anyone move their fingers that fast. He had his back to Deanna when she walked out of the coffee shop but could see her reflection in the store window in front of him. He turned and followed her up the stairs to the second level.

She moved along the crowded concourse, taking her time, looking in store windows, sipping coffee. Her next stop was Victoria's Secret. Raylan was standing a couple stores away when Nora called. "Where are you?"

"Outside Victoria'a Secret," Raylan said, moving toward the front of the store.

"What's she doing?"

"I imagine buying something. I'm going in. You need anything?" Silence on the other end. "How about a limited edition cutout corset?" Raylan said, reading the display in the window. "That sound like you?"

Now Raylan looked through the doorway, saw Deanna Lyons at the counter, handing a credit card to the sales girl. He turned off the phone, walked in the store, looking at tiny skimpy underwear on hangers. A girl's voice behind him said, "Sir, may I help you?"

He turned, "Just looking."

"Is this a special occasion?" The salesgirl was cute and young and could see he was out of his element.

"I'll know when I see it."

Deanna Lyons was moving away from the counter, coming toward him now, carrying a shopping bag, her phone out, punching keys, sending a text maybe or an email.

Raylan, feeling like a fool, moved to the left behind a display of Nude Add-2-Cups Push-up Bras.

The sales girl said, "Do you know what size she is?"

Deanna walked out of the store. Raylan followed along the concourse to the stairs. He was half way to the lower level when Nora called again. "Where is she?

"Going into a store."

"Which one?"

He looked at the sign. "Forever Twenty-One."

"Stay with her."

Raylan took off, ran in the store, and stopped. Deanna, her back to him, was moving along the main aisle but then disappeared behind a grouping of mannequins.

She was sitting in the shoe department as he walked by and kept going. He went to the far end of the store, and when he came back she was gone. He moved as fast as he could without running, went back in the mall. Sunlight was streaming through a wall of windows at the entrance. Raylan saw a quick glimpse of her going through the door.

He felt the searing midday heat as he went outside. Deanna, carrying a pink striped shopping bag, cell phone pressed to her ear, was moving across the parking lot, and then standing next to a white SUV.

Nora pulled up. Raylan got in the car. "Where is she?" He pointed to the SUV that was moving now. Nora floored it, speeding through the lot, and was half a dozen car lengths behind a white Range Rover when they turned onto West Metmore Road. "I want to run the plate."

"Let's give them some room, see what they do. Why rush it?" He could see Nora was tense, wound up, but he couldn't blame her.

It was always stressful in a situation like this: trying to speed and not look like it, trying to stay close to suspects without letting them see you.

Annoyed, Nora said, "What was that you were saying about Victoria's Secret?"

"I followed her in the store—that actually happened. The rest of it, I was having fun with you."

"Do you think I shop there?"

"I don't know. I've never seen you in your undergarments."

"And you're not going to." Nora passed a car, glanced at him and frowned. "Undergarments, are you kidding? That's seriously what you call them?"

"Those were the words my momma used for female panties, brassieres, and such. She's since passed, or I'd call and let you talk to her."

Nora looked embarrassed now and said, "I'm sorry."

"For what?"

"Your mother passed away." She didn't want to look at him, kept her eyes on the road. "You're..." But she didn't finish the thought.

"I'm what, what were you gonna say?"

"*Pieza de trabajo.*"

"I don't know what that means but the way you said it, it can't be good."

TWENTY

First thing, Mr. Boy said, "Seen anyone follow you? He want me to ask."

Deanna rewound. There was the real estate lady up the hill but she didn't count. There was the dude in a cowboy hat outside Victoria's Secret on his cell. That one just looked lost. There wasn't anyone else Deanna remembered, and she'd been paying attention. She could see Mr. Boy's face in the rearview, looking at her in the back seat. Did he want her like most guys, was it that kind of look? She couldn't tell.

Every time she saw him he was bigger: shoulders two feet wide, head the size of a beach ball, but he had that high Michael Jackson voice that didn't fit. And he acted like a little kid. She could see him smiling in the mirror, checking her out again. "Yo, so what's up?"

"Nothing much," Deanna said. "How's everything in Detroit?"

"Oh, you know, it's cool."

"You like Arizona?"

"It's like the heat's on. I wish somebody'd turn it off."

Even in the air-conditioning he had sweat running down his face. "You get used to it."

Mr. Boy smiled now, showing tiny teeth that had gaps between some of them and deep pink gums. "I don't know, he tell me I gotta shower two times a day. What's up with that?"

"How is he?"

"Crazy, you know, but I never said that, right?"

She shook her head. "You never said anything."

Mr. Boy smiled again.

Most of the time Deanna liked the situation. Liked living in the house. Beat the apartment her parents rented for her. Liked the blow—as much as she wanted. That was the real draw. Liked spending time with Jose at first. He was a gangsta. There was this excitement, this element of danger. But that had worn off, and now he was boring, kinda dumb, too. It was tough spending time with him, walking on eggshells, waiting for him to freak out, go ballistic about something that didn't matter. The worst though was having to be available when he was in town.

It was tougher now, and more complicated since she had been seeing Richard, this normal, low-key guy. Richard, of course, knew nothing of her arrangement. At first she was afraid to get involved with him. But it happened so effortlessly. They'd met at a coffee shop. He stood behind her in line and they started talking. As it turned out, his company had built the house she was living in.

Richard was smart, good-looking, fun to be with. They'd hit it off and now Deanna was worried that Rindo would find out and go schizo. She was going tell Jose she didn't want to see him anymore. All she had to do was figure out what to say.

"A car been following us since we leave the mall." Mr. Boy's face was serious now, his tiny teeth and big gums filling the rearview mirror. He reached under the seat and brought up a gun.

"Do you know who it is?"

Mr. Boy shook his head.

"Why do you have a gun?"

"Jose say I's a gangsta, and gangstas pack."

"What're you going to do with it?"

"Shoot the bad guys."

Deanna didn't know how to break it to him: he was one of the bad guys.

•••

"I THINK THEY MADE US," Nora said.

The Range Rover pulled into a little shopping area on El Camino del Cerro, cruised to the far end of the lot and backed into a space. Nora kept going, made a U-turn, passed the shopping area going the opposite way, turned left into a gas station, and now they were behind the SUV. They could keep an eye on it without being seen.

Nora turned in her seat. "Think someone is going to pick her up? That someone being Jose Rindo?"

"You were him, would you take the risk?"

"You're asking me to get in Rindo's head?"

"That's how you do it."

Nora unscrewed the cap and took a drink of water. "No, he has people working for him that will take the risk." Now Nora brought the binoculars to her eyes. "The plate number is NRX zero zero five. Arizona." She punched the number in her computer, waited for it to process the information.

"It's registered to VIP Limousine Company," Raylan said. "Detroit, Michigan."

"My God, you're right. How do you know that?"

"Rindo has or had some kind of deal with the owner, guy named Joey Yalda. VIP provides cars that can't be traced in exchange for money or drugs, or both. There was the Escalade in Las Cruces and a BMW in Ohio."

•••

MR. BOY TOOK OUT his phone, dialed, and heard Rindo say, "The fuck you at?"

Just the sound of his voice made her heart start to race. Mr. Boy mopped sweat off his face with his bare arm. Clearly agitated, he did his best to explain what was happening and where they were, but Rindo, the bully, kept interrupting, kept yelling at him. "Put Deanna on."

Mr. Boy made a face, reached back, and handed the phone to her.

"How you doing, baby?" Rindo said in a breathy voice. "I've missed you. Gonna show you how much."

"I'm fine." She could hear him do a one-and-one, snorting hard.

"Miss me?"

"What do you think?"

"I hope so." Rindo paused. "See anyone following you?"

"No, but I haven't been looking."

"See anyone now?"

"I see a lot of people. Most of them pushing grocery carts, buying food and shit. Are they, like, undercover law enforcement? That what you're asking?"

"Hey, listen, I have a surprise for you," Rindo said, changing the subject, dude could only keep his mind on something for a few seconds when he was high.

Deanna tried to imagine what it was, picturing jewelry, diamonds. He did give her expensive gifts, and she liked that part of the relationship. "I have something for you too." What she bought at Victoria'a Secret was for him, not her. It was strange, a man needing a sexy outfit to get turned on.

"You gonna tell me?" Rindo sounded high but excited.

"If I tell you, it won't be a surprise."

"Okay, I see you soon. Give him the phone." She handed it back to Mr. Boy. "All right, drive to the place. You know what I'm talking about?"

"Uh-huh."

"See anyone following you, keep going. No one's on you, park."

"Where?"

"You listening? Where I just told you. Understand? See anyone, chill till they leave. Feel me?"

Mr. Boy nodded. "Uh-huh."

"Bring my bitch to me, negro."

She knew Rindo was fucked up, giving Mr. Boy this much responsibility. But it might be a blessing. *Jose gets busted, they got nothing on me.*

Mr. Boy drove out of the parking lot and turned on the main road. Deanna still wasn't sure what was happening. "Where we going?"

•••

NORA FOLLOWED THE RANGE Rover out of the city into the desert, heading for a wall of high dark mountains in the distance. They drove for several miles and Raylan watched the SUV turn and drive down a one-way lane into a small paved parking area in the middle of nowhere. "What's this?"

"Gates Pass. It's a trailhead. People come here to hike, and at night to watch the sunset."

"You think Deanna and Melvin are going hiking?"

Nora shook her head. "No, Mr. Smart Ass. I think someone's coming to pick them up."

The paved lane went uphill to another larger parking area. Raylan said, "Wait here, I'll go check it out." He got out of the car, adjusted the Stetson, brim low over his eyes, and walked up the hill to an adobe structure where the restrooms were. He stood with his back against the wall, peeked around the corner, and saw a dozen cars including the Range Rover parked in the lot.

Now a minivan arrived and pulled into a space. The side door slid open and four kids jumped out and ran ahead of their parents uphill to the trail. Raylan walked up the paved lane to the parking area, watching a couple of young guys with backpacks put their gear in the bed of an old pickup truck. He was still a hundred feet from the Range Rover when a Jeep that was parked next to it backed out and drove up to the highway.

Raylan drew the Glock, approaching the Range Rover from behind, then coming up on the right side. As he got close, he could see there was no one in it. He had his phone out calling Nora, heard her voice and then static. "Jesus, get up here. They're in the Jeep." He didn't hear anything. "You there?"

Raylan disconnected and tried her again, same result. He ran down to the lower parking area. Nora's car was gone. He ran up to the highway, looking left then right, but didn't see her. He tried calling her again. It went to voicemail. "They're in the Jeep, you see it? Where the hell are you?"

•••

MR. BOY GOT OUT of the Range Rover. Deanna saw him crouching next to the Jeep, running his hand over the top of the left front tire, found the key, opened the door and waved her over. She sat in front this time and put the Victoria's Secret bag on the floor at her feet.

Mr. Boy's huge body was crammed in the seat like he was driving a toy car. He went out to the main road and turned left heading back to the city. Jesus, now where was he going?

He'd only been outside for a minute and there were wide arcs of sweat in his armpits and around the front of the tank top where the gold medallion hung on a thick gold chain. Man his size shouldn't have been wearing a tight-fitting top that bulged around his stomach, or shorts that went below his knees, black socks and black athletic shoes. Deanna could see herself taking him back to the mall, buying him new everything. A "makeover" didn't quite explain what he needed.

Mr. Boy glanced at her. "Why you looking at me?"

"Where do you shop?"

"Huh?"

"Where do you buy your clothes?"

He seemed confused now. "A store." It sounded like a question.

"I mean your style."

"I don't know." He didn't know cause he didn't have any.

"I'm going to help you." Deanna could see he didn't understand, and decided to let it go, give it a rest.

The house they were going to had to be somewhere in the Tucson Mountains. Deanna had never been there, and like most things about Rindo, it was a secret. He wouldn't tell her where it was. They drove into the foothills. At first there were houses scattered around, but now it was desolate, desert on both sides of the car, a road going nowhere. She wondered if he was lost.

Deanna didn't want to say anything, embarrass him, but finally had to. "Just checking now—you sure this is the right way?"

"Uh-huh." Mr. Boy nodded, showing his baby teeth, like dolphin teeth, and that gummy smile. "I show you."

He turned right on a narrow path barely wide enough for a car that rose into the hills. It was a bumpy ride. There were stands of acacia and sycamore and giant old saguaro up ahead on the mountainside. Then she saw a roofline behind the trees. It was a house and looked like part of the scenery, its muted gray-brown and terra-cotta accents blending in with the background.

When they drove into the yard, Rindo came out the front door in shorts, sunglasses, and sandals, no shirt, sweat glistening on his hairless chest, bald shiny head reflecting off the high hot sun. Deanna got out of the Jeep with the Victoria's Secret bag and kissed him on the cheek. She didn't want to get too close, he smelled.

"That all I get?"

"Absence makes the heart grow fonder."

Now his spaced-out gaze was fixed on the bag. "What's that?"

"Little present. I'll put it on for you later."

Rindo turned, glanced at Mr. Boy moving toward them. "The fuck took so long? I talk to you like thirty minutes ago."

"We were being cautious," Deanna said, trying to keep Rindo calm. "You can't be too careful." She looked down the mountain at the city spread out under the smoggy haze.

"Yeah…can't be too careful," Mr. Boy said.

Deanna said, "Hey, you said you have a surprise for me."

"You want it now?"

"You know how much I like surprises."

Thunderbird came out the front door smoking a joint, hand over his eyes, blocking the sun like he was saluting them. "Want a hit?" he said, coming toward her, reaching out with the blunt. "It's some bomb shit called Master Yoda. Smoke it, the Force be with you."

Deanna shook her head.

"Girl, what's up?"

Thunderbird creeped her out. She moved closer to Rindo and followed him across the gravel parking area to the garage.

"Okay, ready?"

Now she was thinking he bought her a car. What was it, a Benz, BMW? Deanna couldn't stop smiling. Rindo pressed the remote and the door started to go up. There was an old car on the left side. Was that it? Then she saw something else but didn't know what it was until the door was up all the way and the afternoon sun filled the space with light. It was Richard hanging from the rafters, but alive, eyes wild, duct tape over his mouth, trying to talk, making unintelligible sounds.

Deanna felt like the wind had been knocked out of her, felt dizzy, tried to say something, but nothing came out.

"You should see your face." Rindo turned to Thunderbird. "Ever see someone more surprised?"

Thunderbird was squinting, his stoned eyes almost closed. He pressed the remote and the door started down.

"He's just a friend. He didn't do anything."

Rindo said, "What you worried about?"

"Let him go."

"You tell him my business?"

"I don't know anything about your business."

"I think the man's police."

"His name is Richard Gomez. He's normal—"

"What and I'm not?" Rindo said, cutting her off.

"Will you let me finish? He doesn't sell drugs or carry a gun, he's a builder."

"I think it's a cover."

"No, it's the truth."

"You want to help him?" He glanced at the Victoria's Secret bag. "Put that on, show me how much."

"Promise you won't hurt him."

"First, let's see what you do for me."

TWENTY-ONE

RAYLAN WAS LEANING WITH his back against the stone wall of the Ramada when he saw Nora's Chevy. He'd been waiting forty-five minutes and was starting to wonder. He got in the car and she said, "Listen, I'm sorry. I didn't mean to leave you here. I saw the Jeep pull out and had a feeling. Turned around, went out the entrance and followed them. I tried to call but couldn't get through. Service is spotty out here. I got close enough to glass the plate. It's registered to—this'll surprise you—VIP Limousines, Detroit, Michigan."

"So, where are they?"

"That way about fifteen miles." Nora pointed northwest at the Tucson Mountains. "Go into the foothills, drive till you don't see any houses and keep going."

Nora turned onto an arrow-straight desert road and gunned it. Raylan watching the speedometer needle climb to eighty and level off. They cruised like this for some time, Raylan studying the desert landscape, seeing the bleak beauty of it for the first time. And then, without warning, Nora hit the brakes. He jerked forward and the seatbelt tightened across his chest. She pulled over on the side of the road. "It's back there," she said, turning in her seat, looking at something behind them.

"What is? I didn't see anything."

"Where they turned."

"We should call for backup," Raylan said. "It's too big an area to cover with two of us."

"Phones don't work out here, remember?" Nora sipped her water. "Gang of armed men show up, we're going to lose the element of surprise."

"Regroup, come back tomorrow."

"Rindo might not be here tomorrow."

"What's going on? This doesn't sound like you. I think you're doing it for the wrong reason, avenging your friend's death and risking your own, not to mention mine."

"I thought you were tough."

"Being tough has nothing to do with it." He paused, surprised by Nora's aggressive attitude. "What's stopping me are the unknowns. Where's the house? What's the floor plan? How many armed men are on the property? What kinds of weapons do they have?" He couldn't tell her one of his main concerns was bringing her, an inexperienced agent, to a gunfight.

"All right, but we're here. I'm going to have a look. You can come or not, it's up to you." Nora got out of the car and opened the trunk.

It was a bad deal, but he couldn't let her go alone. Raylan, standing next to the car, lifted the UAV over his head and adjusted the straps. "Okay, but you've got to promise me to be cool."

"I don't have to promise you anything." Nora held the shotgun in one hand, stock on her hip, closed the trunk, and glanced at him.

"That's the way it's gonna be, huh?" He cradled the AR-15 over his right forearm.

"That's the way it is." Nora took off, walking back along the road the way they'd come to a gravel path barely wide enough for a car that went toward two distant peaks. The terrain on both sides was scattered with brush and cactus and rose up to heavy walls of granite.

"Somebody drives in or out, we're gonna be standing here in the open."

"You have a better idea?"

Raylan, holding the rifle with both hands across his body, started up the hill, stopped, looked back at Nora. "You coming?"

It took twenty minutes to hike to the top of the rise, Raylan, crouching looking at the other side. The sun was hanging on the mountaintops in the distance. He aimed binoculars at the house below them in the foothills. The Jeep he'd seen earlier was parked in the yard. There was a black dude with a gun stuck in his waistband, standing nearby.

Nora sat next to him on a rock formation, drinking water, black smudges on her sweaty cheeks where the mascara had run. He handed her the binoculars. "I think we've come to the right place. Guy down there smoking a joint looks like Demarco Hall."

•••

MR. BOY WAS LOOKING through the telescope watching a furry little dude he thought was a gopher climbing around the hill behind the house. The gopher'd disappear in the green plants and come out, stand on his back legs eating an insect. It was fun to watch. He wished he could live in Arizona all the time. He loved the birds and animals and the cactus. Jose told him the names of some of them.

His job was to make sure nobody snuck up on them. Mostly, though, he looked at things. There were lizards, snakes, and coyotes. One time he saw a tarantula. He thought it was okay. Didn't know why everybody was scared of them. They minded their business. There were all kinds of pretty birds, too. Mr. Boy wished he could feed them. He made birdcalls trying to talk to them. And they made noises talking back. He told Jose that and Jose said, "What'd you do, hit T-Bird's one-toke?"

Just before it got dark, he would see bats flying around making little beeping noises. And then at night there were more stars than he'd ever seen in his life, like gazillions of them.

He turned the telescope trying to follow the gopher. It was tough cause the little dude was quick. He wished he were a gopher—not a big fat guy. Being a gopher looked like fun, running around hunting insects, doing anything he wanted. Mr. Boy lost the gopher again, tilted the telescope up a little and saw cowboy boots and it freaked him. The man in the boots held a rifle and wore a cowboy hat. At first he thought maybe the man was a hunter till he noticed the bulletproof vest. Why would a hunter wear that? There was a girl next to him, sitting on some rocks, looking through binoculars, a shotgun across her legs.

He went and told Thunderbird about the two people, T-Bird as usual high on Master Yoda, with little slits for eyes. T-Bird just looked at him but didn't say anything.

Now Mr. Boy was staring at the bedroom door, hesitating before he knocked. Earlier Jose had said, "When I'm in the room with her and the door's closed, stay the fuck away. It means I'm knocking off a piece of ass. Don't bother me less it's an emergency."

He heard Deanna making strange noises that sounded like Jose was hurting her. He knocked a couple times and waited, knocked again and heard him say, "The fuck did I tell you?"

Mr. Boy opened the door. "We got a problem."

Jose was naked on his back on the bed and Deanna was naked sitting on him. She brought her hands up to cover her tits.

He said, "What're you doing in here?"

"Two people up on the hill with guns. You better come see."

Jose stood looking through the telescope for a couple minutes and turned to him. "It's the marshal from Detroit and the FBI agent. See anyone else? They usually bring a team."

"No, no one." Jose wasn't wearing a shirt and smelled like Deanna's perfume.

"How do you think they found me?"

He didn't know. Jose was angry, could see it on his face, hear it in his voice.

"Think maybe they followed you?"

"I switch cars like you tole me."

"See anyone? Anyone else at the trailhead?"

"Just a family and some young dude hikers." Oh yeah and there was another one, could've been the man in the cowboy hat. He didn't tell Jose that. He was sweating and all nervous now, felt like he'd done something wrong.

"What did I tell you?"

"I don't remember."

"See someone, chill till they leave. Recall me saying that?"

"Sort of." They had to get out of there, but Jose didn't seem like he was in much of a hurry. "What do you think we're gonna do?"

•••

THE SUN WAS SETTING over the mountains. Raylan crouched next to a big cactus, watching the house, an adobe structure surrounded by trees and foliage. He gripped the AR, eyes taking in the scene, taking his time. The air was still. He could feel his sweat-soaked shirt heavy under the vest. Nora, crouching to his left, held the shotgun across her body. She took a bandana out of a vest pocket, dabbed her wet face, rolled it in the shape of a headband, and tied it across her forehead like a tennis player.

"I'm going to check it out. Cover me, will you?" It was almost dark when he went down the hill and walked along the back of the house looking in windows but not seeing anyone.

He signaled Nora and she came down and joined him and they moved along the side of the house to the front, Raylan leading the way, the AR-15 on full automatic. The Jeep he'd seen parked there earlier was gone and he had to believe Rindo and his posse were too.

Nora looked through binoculars, scanning the desert below the house and confirmed it. "There they are." She handed him the binoculars. He saw the Jeep going downhill, bouncing on the rutted, rock-strewn terrain.

The front door was unlocked. Raylan went primary into the house, two hands on the Glock, barrel pointed at the ceiling, believing in the possibility there could be someone armed and dangerous still inside. He could feel Nora behind him, crowding him crossing the threshold, and then she was next to him, barrel of the shotgun pointed straight ahead, finger on the trigger.

He went through the living room, down a short hallway to the back bedroom. Deanna Lyons was on the floor on the other side of the bed. She'd been shot in the head. Raylan wondered what she'd done. But in Rindo's paranoid world he didn't think it took much.

"*Dios mío.*" Nora saw the body and lowered the shotgun. She put a hand over her mouth and looked away. After a time, Nora, more composed, said, "We saw this poor girl alive this morning. That someone could do this to another human being…"

Raylan felt the same way, but in his line of work it was part of the job.

They found a second body in the garage. A man, rope around his neck, was hanging from the rafters, duct tape over his mouth, hands tied behind his back. Nora walked out and waited on the gravel drive in front of the house.

In the space next to the dead man was an old Mercedes-Benz sedan. Raylan sat in the front passenger seat and opened the glove box. The car was registered to Maynard Summers, the old man that had been carjacked and kidnapped in Las Cruces. Where was the body?

Raylan checked the trunk, it was empty. He closed the garage door and approached Nora. "You okay?"

She frowned and said, "No, I'm not okay. I'm not close to being okay. We have to find this guy."

"We will." Raylan paused. "I get the feeling you're not used to being at a crime scene, not used to the seeing grisly remains. It can be disturbing."

"I'm not used to it and I hope I never am." Nora let out a breath like she was releasing pressure. "You don't seem affected by it one way or the other, which I have to tell you is in its own way disturbing."

"I've been to my share of these. The key is to not get emotionally involved. Don't let it get in your head."

TWENTY-TWO

IGNACIO, AN OLD FRIEND Rindo could trust, met them at the shop in South Tucson. Two of Nacho's men wiped the Jeep's interior with bleach-soaked rags and parked it on the street near the Federal Courthouse. Let the marshals find it in the morning, scratch their heads.

Nacho had a friend worked at the secretary of state, got Jose Rindo an official Arizona driver's license in the name Carlos Vela, a good name and easy to remember. Nacho also got him a 2014 Chevy Suburban with four-wheel drive, and a registration for the vehicle that matched the name on the license. The ID had been arranged after Rindo escaped from the sheriff's transport van. With the new identity, he could go to Mexico and come back whenever he wanted.

"What do I owe you?" Rindo said when they were alone in Nacho's office.

"Thirty thousand."

"You sure that's enough to cover everything?"

"Feeling generous, you can give me more."

Rindo took four banded stacks of hundreds, forty thousand, out of the banker box, and put the money on the desk. "How's this?"

"*Muchas gracias*. Let me know you need anything else." Nacho looked like something was on his mind. "Listen, is not my business, but as a friend I have to tell you. I see your pictures on the TV. You travel with those two, people are gonna notice. Sooner or later the police are gonna find you. By yourself, alone, you can blend in. I was you, I leave them in Tucson, get on the freeway don't look back."

He knew Nacho was right, but it wasn't that easy, and he didn't feel the need to explain himself. "I'm leaving, but first I have to make a stop."

"Let me guess, Pecoso owe you money. Some things never change."

"You want back in?"

"Not if I want to stay married." Nacho gave him a pained look. "You know how Maria feels."

"I would say you can find another woman, but the way you are I don't know it's possible." Nacho and Maria had been together since they were young children in Mexicali. "Consider it, will you?" Although he knew it was never gonna happen.

•••

RINDO WALKED AROUND TO the back of the house. There were landscape lights on around the pool and ramada, and a black aluminum fence around the perimeter of the property. He could see lights from neighboring houses scattered in the hills and the dark shape of the Santa Ritas to the south. Pecoso was on the veranda next to the pool, smoking, seeing the red glow of a cigar, catching the faint smell in the hot still air.

He opened the gate and moved toward the house, lights on inside, Pecoso's woman in the kitchen, washing dishes. Rindo saw the skinny silhouette of Thunderbird coming through the gate on the other side of the yard.

Pecoso must have seen him too. He got to his feet and said, "How you doing, man?" Glancing at T-Bird and then Rindo. "I'm looking at you, but I don't believe it. Where the big dude? I only see two of the amigos."

Rindo said, "Where's the money? What the Martinezes brought back was five pounds light. You think I don't notice?" Pecoso had done it before, half a pound here, half a pound there, trying to see if he could get away with it.

"I give you what I have."

"You owe me a hundred grand."

"I hear you in jail, man. I was holding it for you."

"Well now I'm out."

"I don't know for how long. I see you all over the news, the three amigos, man. Everyone looking for you: police, FBI, DEA, the US Marshals. They want you bad. There's even a reward." Pecoso was grinning, enjoying himself.

"You want to collect it, is that what you saying?"

"Why would I turn you in?"

He could think of few reasons—all of them relating to money.

They walked in the house through the French doors into the dining room. Rindo glanced left into the kitchen. "Where is your woman?"

"She has nothing to do with this," Pecoso said.

"She's with you," he said, "she's involved."

"Wait here, I get your money."

"Go with him," he whispered to Thunderbird. "You see a gun, shoot him."

Rindo went in the bedroom, heard the whispering voice of the woman speaking Spanish behind the closed bathroom door. He tried the handle, it was locked. "Open it." He could hear her talking and put his shoulder into the wood, and on the third try the molding shattered and the door opened all the way banging into the wall. The woman turned off the phone and backed away from him.

"*Que usted habla?*"

Her eyes held on him but she didn't answer.

He moved toward her, took the cell out of her hand, looked at the last call on the phone log, and pressed the number. A man's voice said, "*Estamos en nuestro camino.*"

Rindo disconnected. "Who is on their way?" he said to the woman. She didn't answer and he drew the Beretta from behind his back and aimed it at her chest. "I am gonna ask you one more time, and you don't answer I'm gonna shoot you. *Comprende?*"

The woman nodded.

"Who's coming?"

"Friends. You better go, *rapido*," she said in a threatening tone. "They bring many guns."

He tossed the woman's phone in the toilet, grabbed a wrist, and pulled her into the dining room and sat her at the table. "Where is Pecoso? *Donde esta Pecoso?*"

"*No se.*"

•••

MR. BOY LIKED THE Suburban cause it was big and he fit good, could move a little without feeling like he was trapped. He opened the window looking at the big black sky. Man, all the stars, the points of light and shit, but not as many as were at the house in the mountains. Why was that? Was the same sky. He turned on the radio, listening to Lil Wayne doing "Krazy." He liked the jam, knew the words, started singing:

> *Tell me something I don't know, I'm flexing on em like torsos*
> *These niggas slipping like bar soap, these niggas listening use Morse Code*

He heard something. Wait a minute, what was that? Sounded like a gun. He turned down the radio. Now it was quiet. Was he hearing things? No, man, he heard it. Was sure of that. He didn't know what to do. Was thinking about what Jose said: "You the guard, stay in the car, keep watch. Any motherfuckers show up with guns, take em out. You got it?"

Mr. Boy felt under the seat, brought up the .45, racked it. He heard another shot and was sure it was coming from the house. He got out the Suburban, moved to the front door, looking in the windows but didn't see anyone. Tried the door, it was locked. He walked around to the back. There was a swimming pool and a waterfall. No one out there. He went inside. There was a girl coming out of the kitchen with a big knife in her hand. She looked at him, saw the gun, and put the knife on the table.

"Yo, where Jose at?"

TWENTY-THREE

"WHY DIDN'T YOU CALL for back up?" Victor Hernandez looked like he was flexing his upper body, sitting behind the spotless desk in a crisp white shirt and striped tie.

"Chief, you know how these things can go in the best of circumstances. Throw a paranoid drug dealer, murderer, and an FBI agent with her own agenda into the mix, you might as well throw out the playbook."

"How long you been with the marshals?"

"Twenty-five years."

"So you're familiar with protocol." Victor Hernandez held on him with his solemn gaze. "But I understand you like to do things your way."

Jose Rindo was a high-value fugitive and Victor wanted the Tucson office to get some credit for the bust—that's what this was about.

"Chief, I'm not exactly sure what doing things my way means, but let me tell you what happened and you can decide if I went off the rails." Raylan sipped his coffee. "We started yesterday, sitting code at the house where the girlfriend, Deanna Lyons was staying, ten thirty-three a.m. Positive ID on S-four. Ms. Lyons left in a car at approximately ten fifty-seven. We followed her to the Tucson Mall. I went inside, and Agent Sanchez," he almost said Nora, "waited in the car." Raylan paused, thinking he was talking too fast and sounded defensive.

Chief Hernandez said, "The girlfriend meet anyone? Talk to anyone?"

"Other than sales people, I didn't see anyone. Ms. Lyons did her shopping, went outside, and got in a white Range Rover."

"Did you see who was driving?"

"Not then, but I did later."

"Why didn't you call it in?"

"We didn't know if we had something or not. She could've been meeting a friend for lunch. We followed the Range Rover out of the city and into the desert. They stopped at Gates Pass and parked. I didn't see them switch cars, get into a Jeep and drive out. But Agent Sanchez did and followed them to a secluded house in the Tucson Mountains. We didn't know what was going on. And when we did it was too late. It was a judgment call. I was with an FBI agent who was going to arrest Jose Rindo with or without me."

"If you'd done it right, we'd have him in custody instead of starting over."

Maybe, maybe not, Raylan wanted to say. "This is the kind of thing you can second guess, tear apart if you want. But when you're out there, you rely on instinct."

Victor Hernandez sipped his coffee and fixed his attention on Raylan. "What'd you do after you found the bodies?"

"Agent Sanchez drove down the mountain to a spot where she could get phone reception and contacted the PD. I secured the crime scene."

"From what, a pack of javelinas?" Victor grinned, trying some desert humor on him.

Raylan said, "Who's Richard Gomez, the guy they hanged in the garage?"

"He's a local builder. Seems to be a hardworking, taxpaying citizen, or was. Thirty-eight, married, couple of kids. Never been in trouble."

"Looking for motive? I think Deanna Lyons had a romantic relationship with him. You can imagine Rindo finding out about it."

"Which I guess is what happened."

"You're one of Rindo's girlfriends, don't plan on living to old age," Raylan said. "He had another one killed in the suburbs outside Detroit."

"What did she do?"

"Hooked up with the wrong guy."

"Police found the wrong guy's Jeep Grand Cherokee parked on Congress a block from the courthouse. Tucson PD, acting on a BOLO, spotted it. The assumption was it might be filled with explosives. Reminded me of that wacko in Oklahoma City, detonated the bomb that blew up the federal building. What was his name?"

"Timothy McVeigh."

"That's right. They executed him, if I'm not mistaken." Chief Hernandez paused. "But this Rindo character's just daring us, isn't he?"

"When a guy thinks he's invincible, he'll do anything."

"Okay, you're the so-called expert. Where's he at, or where's he going?"

"Let me show you something." Bobby Torres had sent him another photo Rindo had posted on Facebook. Raylan took out his phone, clicked on Bobby's email, and handed the phone to Victor. It was a shot of Jose posing with a steel gate behind him. "Know where this is?"

"Yuma Territorial Prison. It's a museum now."

"As I said before, Rindo thinks he can do anything, get away with it. Takes a selfie in front of the stockade, saying, 'You can't catch me, you can't hold me.'"

"I can understand his confidence," Chief Hernandez said. "Man's escaped three times. We had him cornered, he got away again."

Raylan didn't agree with him but wasn't going to protest. What good would it do?

"So where's he going?"

"I had to guess, I'd say Mexico eventually, with stops in El Centro, maybe, or San Diego, checking on his business interests." Raylan finished the coffee. "What about Maynard Summers?"

Victor gave him a blank look.

"The old man who was carjacked in Las Cruces. His Mercedes was in the garage at Rindo's house."

"Haven't found him yet. I wouldn't be too optimistic."

Victor Hernandez's phone rang. He picked it up and said, "What do you need?" He listened for a couple minutes, opened his desk drawer, took out a pen and a notepad, wrote on it, ripped off the sheet, and handed it to Raylan. "Something you better see before you leave town."

TWENTY-FOUR

THE CORONER'S VAN WAS parked on the gravel drive behind two Tucson PD marked units. Two uniformed patrolmen stood near a body covered with a bloodstained sheet in front of the house. Raylan and Nora approached, showed their IDs.

There were three tagged shell casings on the ground fifteen feet from the body that suggested the shooter had come from behind. That hunch was confirmed as Raylan crouched next to the body, lifted a corner of the sheet to see a Latino gangbanger, mid-twenties, with exit wounds in his chest.

Inside they met a stocky homicide investigator named Jerry Fritz, sunglasses angled in his wavy brown hair. "Four dead, eight shots fired. Looks like a turf war. Got a witness, girl named Helen Mendoza," Jerry said in detective shorthand. "I found her hiding in a bedroom closet, scared out of her wits."

Raylan said, "Who is she?"

"Pecoso's girlfriend," Jerry Fritz said, "the hombre that lives here, or should I say lived?"

Raylan thought the name sounded familiar.

Nora said, "Where is she?"

"Right through there." Jerry Fritz pointed to a hallway.

Raylan walked that way, Nora behind him, glanced left into a bedroom, and saw a dark-haired Latina sitting cross-legged on the bed, staring off into space. She didn't seem to notice them. They went back into the living room. "I want to talk to her," Nora said.

"Good luck," Jerry Fritz said, straightening his tie that had food stains on it. "I couldn't get the time of day."

"You're not a woman."

Nora went in to see the girl and Jerry Fritz led Raylan through the house into a room that looked like an office with a desk and bookshelves. There was a big old Mosler floor safe against the far wall, and next to it was the body of a Latin male, shot in the chest.

"The man himself," Jerry Fritz said, "or what's left of him."

Pecoso had a freckled face and red hair. Raylan remembered Bobby mentioning him. Pecoso had met Eladio and Irena Martinez, had taken a suitcase filled with money from them when they arrived in Tucson, and gave them a suitcase filled with heroin to take back to Detroit.

There were two more bodies out by the pool, heavily tatted young Latinos like the one in front, dead from an assortment of gunshot wounds. "Pecoso worked with Jose Rindo, the fugitive we're after," Raylan said. "Looks like the three dead gangbangers came to put him out of business."

"But according to Helen Mendoza that's not what happened," Nora said. "Rindo came here claiming Pecoso owed him money. Helen called her brother, told him she needed help. That's why she looks like she's in shock. Can't believe she caused her brother's death." Nora paused. "It was Rindo and two of his homies from Detroit—Demarco Hall and Melvin Gales, Jr. Evidently Melvin was hit a couple times."

Jerry Fritz said, "You know who Ms. Mendoza's talking about? This make sense?"

"That's why we're here," Raylan said.

Nora said, "I think we should be checking Tucson hospitals and clinics."

Raylan said, "You think Rindo took a man with fugitive warrants to a hospital?"

"If it was the only way to keep him alive," Nora said.

Raylan didn't buy it. "Let's ask Helen."

Nora, arm around Helen Mendoza, escorted her into the room in the same trancelike state she was in earlier.

"I'm Deputy US Marshal Raylan Givens." The girl didn't look at him, staring at something across the room. "I understand Pecoso and your brother were murdered by Jose Rindo and his men. You have my condolences."

Helen came out of her trance. "I don't want your condolences. I want to know what are you gonna do about it."

"Find Rindo, put him away," Raylan said.

Helen said, "Why don't you save yourself the trouble and shoot him?"

"That's a possibility," Raylan said, "depending on what happens when we find him. And that's what we're hoping you can help us with. Where would he take a wounded man? Rindo have any friends in Tucson?"

"Nacho's the only one I know of," Helen said, "but they don't work together anymore."

Nora said, "Are you talking about Ignacio Perez?"

Helen nodded.

Raylan said, "Where can we find him?"

•••

IN THE CAR ON their way to South Tucson, Nora said, "When Special Agent Tyner was murdered, I talked to Nacho, asked him who he thought was involved. He said he had no idea."

"You believe him?"

"I said, 'give me a name or I'm going to implicate you.' He said, 'I wasn't there, you have no proof.' I said, 'Your fingerprints are all over the house. You're going away for a long time, tell your wife goodbye.'"

Raylan said, "What did you have on him?"

"Nothing. But I knew he knew."

Raylan didn't expect this from straight-arrow Nora Sanchez, so concerned about Bureau rules she wouldn't let him buy her a drink. "This is how the FBI does it, huh? I'm surprised."

"You don't bullshit suspects to get what you want?"

"Sure, I do."

"Then what's the problem?"

Raylan said, "Why do you think there's a problem?"

They were on South Tenth Street in light traffic. Nora made a couple turns. "You want to hear the rest of it or not?"

Why was she confiding in him? This wasn't like her. "I don't know—I might get the wrong impression of you."

"I think you already have." Nora took a beat. "Nacho said, 'I give you a name, tell you anything, it's gonna come back to me. I'd rather take my chances in prison.'"

"He's the one gave up Rindo, huh?"

"Rather that than face his wife," Nora said, "who I understand is a real ballbuster."

"That's odd, isn't it, a Latino allowing that to happen?"

"So you're a chauvinist too? I guess I'm not surprised, alpha male, tough-guy marshal. What else would you be?"

Nora parked across the street from a sprawling repair shop with eight bays and a sign that read: Nacho's Auto Restoration. They walked into the small cluttered office and Nora said, "Remember me?"

Ignacio Perez looked up from the desk, surprise on his face at first and then concern as he seemed to recognize Special Agent Sanchez.

"You want to buy a car, that why you here? I can't believe you come back to hassle me after the last time, after I risk my life to help you."

Nora said, "What have you done for me lately?" Her dark eyes bored into him. "Where's Rindo?"

"What did I do this time? What laws are you gonna say I broke?"

"I don't know. Maybe you were involved in that shooting in the Santa Rita foothills. Four men are dead. We know Rindo was there. We know one of his men was shot."

"What does this have to do with me? You see what I do, I restore cars. I'm not involved in any way with drugs. You know this is true, but you keep fucking with me. You think Jose Rindo is here? Go look for yourself."

"Maybe he's at your house," Nora said. "We stop by, talk to your wife, see what she has to say about it."

Nacho's eyes moved to Raylan now and held on him. "Hey, man, who are you, her boy or what?"

"I'm Deputy US Marshal Raylan Givens."

Nacho looked puzzled or amused. "She the boss?"

"She thinks so. That's all it takes."

Nacho grinned. "Man, I hear you. Why don't we handle this man to man, have a glass of tequila, come to an understanding, let her go shopping or something."

Raylan stared at Nora waiting for a reaction. "Not a bad idea, what do you think?"

She glared at him, "Let's see how good you are," got up and walked out of the room.

"I think you offend her," Nacho said.

"It's not hard, let me tell you."

"I can see it. Woman with that much anger, she need to get laid, you know?" He shook his head. "Direct that aggression in a positive way."

"Maybe you should counsel her," Raylan said.

"Or take her to a motel." Nacho paused. "Better you take her. My wife finds out she cut off my *pene*." He made a face.

"Where's Rindo?"

"You want to go back to that?"

"I better, or the FBI agent will cut off mine."

Nacho smiled. "You seem reasonable. I can talk to you."

"Then talk. Where is he?"

"First, a drink." Nacho got up and moved to the file cabinet behind his desk, opened the top drawer, and came back with a bottle of tequila and two short glasses. Nacho filled them and handed one to Raylan, raised his, and said, "*A su salud*," draining the tequila.

Raylan drank, feeling the hot rush of liquid in his throat. Nacho picked up the bottle and tipped it toward Raylan's glass. "*Otro?*"

Raylan shook his head.

"Jose call and stop here after the *disparo*, the incident. The big man was shot in the leg and up here." Nacho patted the left side of his upper chest. "He was crying, and Jose try to calm him. I give them bandages and *desinfectante* we have in the shop. That is all. Jose take him and go."

"What's he driving? I know you gave him a car."

Nacho stared at him, holding back, considering what he was going to say. "I want to see my daughter get married and grow old with my wife. I cross Jose Rindo, friend or not, he send someone..." He didn't finish but the implication was clear.

"This shouldn't be your problem, but it is. Help a fugitive, you're involved. I can't ignore it, walk away. You know how it works." Raylan's hard stare held on him. "Tell me where he's going."

"Mexico."

"With stops in El Centro maybe or San Diego."

"You know, why ask me?" Nacho poured more tequila in his glass and drank it. The good-natured grin was gone. He was worried now.

"I need details, names, addresses."

"I have not been in the business for a long time. Anymore, I don't know the players. I don't want to know."

"Give me something, or I'll bring the FBI agent back in."

"There was a man name Pelon in El Centro, but that was many years ago. Is he still involved? I have no idea."

Raylan didn't believe him. He said, "Rindo didn't tell his old friend what he was gonna do?"

"I have no contact with him for three years."

"What is he driving?"

"He came here in a car, I think was a Ford sedan."

"You see the tag?"

"Why would I look at the tag?"

•••

"YOU PLAYED IT WELL," Raylan said when he got in the car, gaze fixed on Nora. "You're a good actress."

"How do you know I was acting?" She seemed tense, but then what else was new?

"Well, either way it worked."

"You and Nacho seem to look at life from the same point of view. I think you could be friends." Nora sipped her water.

"That's the idea, what you do. Get the suspect relaxed, talk to him like a friend."

Nora pulled away from the curb. "Opposite of the way I do it, is that what you're saying?" She was on the muscle again.

"You have your way and I have mine."

"But yours is better, you think."

"Maybe in this situation, we'll see if what he told me pans out. Other times, other situations, intimidation might work better."

Nora's body seemed to tighten. She kept her eyes straight ahead. "Where're we going?"

TWENTY-FIVE

Rindo held the big Suburban steady, driving five under on the freeway leaving Tucson behind. He could feel the adrenaline still geezing through him from the gunfight at Pecoso's. He heard the gunshot and ran into the man's office, and there was Pecoso on the floor, a bullet hole in his chest, alive but not for long judging by the amount of blood. Thunderbird, easy to underestimate, was standing over him, holding a gun. "Motherfucker pulled, but not fast enough."

The safe door was open and Rindo could see it was filled with money. He found a plastic garbage bag in the kitchen under the sink, went back to the office, told T-Bird to check on Mr. Boy and cleaned out the safe.

There was a sliding door that led to the pool area. Rindo opened it and went outside. Two gangbangers, young tatted up dudes were pointing MAC 10s at him.

"Where Pecoso at?" the one with blue teardrop tats under his eyes said.

"Inside."

"What's in the bag?"

"Money, you want it? Help yourself." Rindo opened the top and dumped banded stacks of cash on the stamped concrete pool deck. The bangers took their eyes off him, going for the money. He reached behind his back, pulled the Beretta, and shot them.

Thunderbird, riding the jet stream of Master Yoda and hearing some beat in his head, was leaning forward with his long arms, fingers drumming on the dash like it was a bongo.

"Hey, that's enough," Rindo said.

Thunderbird stopped, sat back. Now Rindo could hear Mr. Boy moaning in back. It was more annoying than the drumming, and it would be another forty minutes till they got to Yuma. "Try not making any noise, okay? Think you can do that?" The rear seats were folded down. Mr. Boy was on his back taking up most of the cargo area, big head propped up on pillows Rindo had taken from the couch in Nacho's office.

"It hurts. My leg's burning, so's my chest. I needs a doctor."

"I take you to a doctor, they gonna call the police. Police are gonna run you through the system, find out you're a fugitive, an accessory to murder. You want that?"

"No, I just want it to stop hurting."

The moaning kept on. Rindo, with his knees under the steering wheel, going seventy, ripped a Kleenex in half and rolled the halves into little balls and stuffed them in his ears, and now he could barely hear anything.

In Yuma, he checked in the Hacienda Motel, got them a corner room with twin beds as far away from other people as he could get. Helped the big man get in a lukewarm tub, blood from the wounds turning the water red. Both gunshots had gone through Mr. Boy. That was the good news. Now he had to figure out how to stop the bleeding.

Rindo dabbed the bullet holes with gauze Nacho had given him. Mr. Boy's eyes were closed and his face was all scrunched up, breathing through his mouth, trying to keep it together. He took the vial of blow out of his pocket, unscrewed the cap, and did a one-and-one. Felt the numbness in his nostrils and the rush in his brain, went from tired and stressed to everything cool again.

He sprinkled a spoonful of blow into the bullet wound in the big boy's leg, wrapped that big thigh—like wrapping a tree trunk—with gauze and tape.

Couple minutes later Mr. Boy opened his eyes, said, "Hey, what you do?"

"How's that feel, motherfucker?" Only question, how long was it gonna last? Rindo applied the same special anesthetic to Mr. Boy's shoulder, and now the big baby was smiling, showing those scary little horror film teeth.

Before he screwed the cap back on, Rindo did a bump. Whoa. Took a couple seconds and now he was flying. He helped Mr. Boy up and handed him a bath towel. Let the motherfucker dry his own self.

In the bedroom, T-Bird was asleep on one of the twins, mouth open, snoring. He pulled the comforter off the other bed and spread it on the floor, hoping to get a few hours' sleep.

TWENTY-SIX

His phone rang as Nora parked in front of the motel. Four Yuma patrolmen stood outside the room, talking and smoking.

Bobby said, "Get the photo I sent?"

"Yeah," Raylan said, getting out of the car. "We're in Yuma but a few steps behind him."

A couple people from adjoining rooms opened their doors to see what was going on.

"How're you feeling?"

"Whatever you do, don't get shot and put on medical leave."

"I'll try to remember that. Got time to help me with something?"

"Man, all I've got is time," Bobby said. "What's up?"

"I need background on a guy named Pelon. Lives in El Centro, or did, connected to Rindo, or was."

"See what I can do. Hey, how's it working out with Special Agent Sanchez?"

"She has a problem with authority."

"Sounds familiar."

"You're enjoying this, aren't you?"

When Raylan and Nora walked into room number twelve, the night manager, C. L. Boyd said, "Looks like someone gutted a whitetail in the bathtub, took the carcass."

Nora unfolded Rindo's wanted poster and handed it to Boyd. "Is this the man you rented the room to?"

"I think so, pretty sure it's him."

"What name did he use to check in?"

"I don't remember, but it's wrote down on the ledger." Boyd scratched his head and ran a hand through his wild rooster hairdo.

Nora said, "You didn't ask to see his ID?"

"No, ma'am," C. L. Boyd shrugged. "It was late. I could see he was tired."

"What does that have to do with asking for identification?" Nora paused. "Was the man bleeding?"

"Ma'am?"

"You see that blood on the bedsheet?"

Boyd nodded and rubbed his jaw with nicotine-stained fingers.

"Then let me ask you again. Was the man who checked in bleeding?"

Boyd shook his head. "Not that I noticed."

Nora said, "What was he driving?"

"Looked like a big SUV, Suburban would be my guess."

Nora said, "You didn't write down the license number?"

"No, ma'am. The customer's supposed to do that."

"You don't keep track of what vehicles are in your parking lot? Management didn't tell you that was one of your duties?"

C. L. Boyd wasn't expecting that either. Poor guy stared at the floor.

Nora said, "Anyone else in the car?"

"I don't know. I didn't see anyone."

"Well if the man you rented the room to wasn't bleeding, it had to be someone else in the car who was. Does that seem logical?"

"I guess."

"You guess? Look at the bed. Take another look in the bathroom."

"Listen, that's all I got to say. Told you all I know. I'm going home now."

"You've been a big help, Mr. Boyd," Nora said. "I don't know how to thank you."

Boyd had a cigarette in his mouth before he walked through the door and lit it as soon as he walked out.

Raylan gave Nora a hard look. "What're you doing, taking out your aggressions on that poor fool? Jesus."

"Was I too hard on him?"

"I think you're too hard on everyone."

Nora gave him a dirty look, and boy was she good at it. "What should I have done, made friends with him like you would have?" She was still pissed off from their last conversation. "Is it too much to ask someone to do their job? Had this idiot done his, we'd know what Jose Rindo was driving and be able to give out his license number. We might also know the condition of his occupant."

"You want to know the condition of his occupant? Look around."

"Tell me again, what did Ignacio Perez say?"

"Rindo's on his way to El Centro to see a guy named Pelon. Pelon is on the payroll, or was."

"Ignacio Perez is the last man who would tell you the truth, and you believe him?" Nora, hands on the steering wheel, glanced over. "But that's right, I forgot, you're friends, aren't you? Drink tequila together."

They were on Interstate 8, passing a sign for El Centro, forty-two miles. "Nacho told me about Pelon cause he's afraid of you, knows you can make trouble for him."

"Who's this coming from, him or you?"

"Who do you think?" Raylan was tired of her attitude. "Listen, you have a better idea? Let's hear it."

Nora didn't say anything, kept her eyes straight ahead.

"Maybe you're not cut out for this." Raylan went at her again. "You should go back to Tucson, do what you do. I'll call you when I have Rindo in custody. You can come talk to him."

She glared at him. "You'd like that, wouldn't you? You'd like to get rid of me."

"No, I'd like your help."

"Is that how you see it, I'm helping you?"

"We're working together but not very well, is how I see it."

"What do you suggest?"

"Relax, stop forcing it."

"Do me a favor, don't give me any more advice, okay?"

With that, Raylan had had enough. "I'll tell you what, just drop me off at the federal courthouse in El Centro. You're on your own. Find Rindo any way you like."

"I can drop you off right here. It would be my pleasure."

Raylan ignored her, looked out the side window at the desert terrain that hadn't seemed to change much since they'd left Tucson.

Half an hour later, Nora got off the highway at El Centro, the Imperial Avenue exit. They drove into a town of strip malls and fast food restaurants. In the distance were the flat green fields of the Imperial Valley, day laborers bent over picking crops.

Nora found the courthouse, parked in the lot, turned in her seat and said, "Here you are." That was the friendliest thing she'd said in quite a while.

"Good luck," Raylan said. He got out of the car and felt a wave of heat. Nora popped the trunk and he grabbed his bag and was pitted out by the time he got to the building. Raylan thought it was odd she didn't say anything, try to talk him out of it. He'd have to call Chief Broyles at some point, explain what had happened. What had? He'd hit the wall, run out of patience.

Nothing he could do about it now.

TWENTY-SEVEN

A T 4:30 P.M., NORA watched them come out of the building, Raylan carrying his suitcase, walking with a tall guy, who had the bearing of a lawman and wore a Glock on his hip. They got into an SUV. It was 127 degrees outside. She had been sitting in the car with the engine running for two and a half hours. Nora had calmed down since her latest disagreement with Raylan and felt bad about it, knew he was more right than wrong, that her stubbornness was getting in the way again, making the situation difficult for no reason.

Nora's colleagues in the office had referred to her at times as headstrong, contrary, and unreasonable—all of which were code for "Nora Sanchez is a bitch."

Now here she was in the federal courthouse parking lot in El Centro, California, embarrassed by how she'd acted, what she'd said, and had no idea how to resolve the situation without looking like a total fool.

She followed Raylan and the other guy down the street to the Budget Inn, watched Raylan get out with his bag and go in the office. The guy in the SUV drove away. Nora waited ten minutes, went into the hotel, and stood at the registration counter. "Did my partner, Deputy Marshal Raylan Givens, check in yet?"

"He sure did, just a few minutes ago," the woman said.

"I'd like a room next to his if possible."

The woman stared at her computer screen for what seemed like an eternity, Nora wondering how it could take this long. You look at the floor plan, see if there's a vacant room in the vicinity.

"We have a room available directly across the hall—one fourteen—that's eighty-nine fifty per night with tax." Nora handed the woman a MasterCard. She scanned it and handed it back. "How many nights?"

"I'm not sure."

"Let me know in the morning, if you will. Amenities include high-speed Internet access, outdoor pool, free parking—you know a lot of them charge you to park your car. You also get a complimentary breakfast, so bring an appetite," the woman said, smiling with pride. "Enjoy your stay, Ms. Sanchez."

The room was a dump. Nora didn't want to touch anything. She went to the window, opened the blinds, looked out at the parking lot and the hotel entrance. What was she doing here, and what was she going to do? Nora glanced at her watch. It was almost five. She could be back in Tucson by nine thirty. And then what? What would she tell her supervisor? Especially after Nora insisted—no, demanded—to be involved in the case.

What would she say, that she didn't get along with Deputy Marshal Givens? Nora didn't get along with anyone except her former partner, and he was dead. Maybe the anger she couldn't shake was guilt. Nora was there and didn't do anything. She'd played the scene over a thousand times and every time her conclusion was the same: there was nothing she could've done. But she could do something now.

Nora stood in front of the peephole and knocked on the door. She could hear a TV on in the room. She knocked again and the door opened. Raylan had a towel around his waist and he was dripping wet. "I leave something in the car?"

"I want to apologize," Nora said.

Raylan gave her a puzzled look.

"For being a pain in the ass." Down the hall, a maid was rolling a cart toward them. "Can we talk? I would prefer not to have the conversation standing here. But you probably want to get dressed first."

Raylan had a suite. Nora sat at the desk in the living room looking at his primary in a black holster, his marshal's star on a chain, two spare magazines, two pairs of handcuffs, loose change, his cell phone, and wallet. She picked up the wallet and opened it, looking at Raylan's Kentucky driver's license. He was younger in the photograph, but more handsome now. Nora heard the bathroom door open and put the wallet down. Raylan came in the room wearing Levi's and no shirt. He looked good, lean and muscular but not overly so, her idea of a sexy man.

"I saw you going through my wallet. What're you looking for?"

"I was checking out your license photo." Nora was embarrassed, like she had been caught prying into his personal life.

"Why?" He pulled a T-shirt out of the open suitcase on the bed and put it on.

She could see the comb lines in his wet hair.

"To see what you looked like."

Raylan squinted at her and said, "What do you care?"

"I know it doesn't make any sense." Nora felt stupid, decided not to say what she was going to say.

"Well, we do agree on something after all." Raylan grabbed the remote, turned off the TV, and glanced at her. "I accept your apology. Is there anything else?"

"I think we can work together."

"Based on what?"

"I know I've been hard to get along with."

"That's two things we agree on. Maybe there is hope."

"I'm willing to give it another try, how about you?"

Raylan seemed to consider her offer, eyes holding on her before he said, "Okay. You better check in."

"I'm right across the hall." Nora paused. "Tell me something, why'd you choose this place?"

"It's where the visiting marshals stay."

She almost said, "You're a classy group," but decided to try being nice.

•••

BOBBY HAD CALLED WHILE he was in the shower. Raylan was sitting at the desk when he hit speed dial and heard him say, "Where you at?"

"A hotel in El Centro."

"Got something to write with?"

"Hang on." Raylan grabbed a pen and pad from the drawer. "Okay."

"Pelon's name is Ramon Quintero. He's thirty-eight, married, no kids. Lives at Six Fifty-One West Hamilton Avenue."

Raylan said, "He do time?"

"Five years in the California State Prison in Centinela, called CEN."

"Let me guess," Raylan said. "He was busted for possession with intent. Was it heroin or coke?"

"Meth."

"Any known association with Jose Rindo?"

"Doesn't say, but that doesn't mean anything." Bobby let out a breath. "I'm not gonna ask you about the special agent." Now Bobby paused. "But how're you getting along?"

"I hope someday you get the opportunity to work with her."

•••

DEPUTY US MARSHAL OWEN BARNETT, a six-foot-four Alabaman called Big Country, picked them up a little before seven that evening. The big fella didn't seem too happy to have a special agent with the FBI in his back seat like she was watching him, critiquing his job performance.

There was something different about Nora since they'd talked. She was calm and friendly. Raylan thought he'd finally gotten through to her. And working together again meant he didn't have to call Chief Broyles, try to explain what happened, get involved in a lot of bureaucratic bullshit.

Nora said, "Owen, where're you from?"

"Monroeville, Alabama, originally. Head south out of Montgomery on Interstate Sixty-Five, take you an hour forty minutes. After graduating the academy, I worked in San Diego four years, met a girl from El Centro a few months ago, and, thinking she was the *one*, transferred here."

Raylan said, "How's it working for you?"

"Sherri and I broke up."

Poor guy, maybe the only person on earth who'd leave San Diego for this irrigated stretch of desert that smelled of manure and was below sea level.

"You've got deputy US marshals, border patrol, cops, and firemen living alongside each other," Big Country said. "It's called the blue ghetto."

Raylan said, "Every time I walk outside, El Centro smells a little different. I can't figure out what it is."

Big Country looked in the rearview mirror, maybe to see if Nora was paying attention. "Retired deputy works at the courthouse said EC smells like peat, ass, and piss." Big Country turned to Nora. "Sorry about that."

"You don't have to worry, Special Agent Sanchez is one of the guys. Isn't that right?" Raylan said, glancing over his shoulder at her.

"I think that's an accurate description," Nora said. "It's a strange smell. I've never smelled anything like it, the breeze bringing it in from the fields."

Big Country turned onto West Hamilton Avenue and crept along, finally parking behind a pickup truck. The houses were small, stucco or clapboard, single-story structures, and most had fences around the yards. A couple kids rode bikes on the sidewalk, and an elderly woman walked her golden retriever on a leash. It was a quiet neighborhood. The sun, still searing hot a little after seven in the evening, was hanging over the western horizon.

"Okay," Big Country said, "that's his house up there on the left, the green one with the pitched roof and white pillars that's seen better days."

Raylan could see a fence around the dirt yard, a pit bull sitting in the shade of the front porch and an old Chevy Malibu in the driveway. If Pelon were successful, you sure wouldn't know it looking at his possessions. "Ideally, I'd like to keep some distance between us, let him relax and take us right to where Rindo's at." Raylan took a beat. "What the hell kind of name is Pelon?"

"In Spanish," Nora said, "it's what you call someone who is either hairy or bald. In most cultures you would be offending the person. But in Mexico many of the nicknames are like that."

Pelon came out the front door, called the dog, and put him in the house. Now he went to his car, backed down the driveway, stopped, unlocked the gate, parked on the street, and locked the gate behind him.

Nora said, "What does he have in the house he's so concerned about, has to go to all that trouble locking up?"

Big Country said, "Maybe it's his woman. Pelon's worried someone will steal her."

Nora said, "Have you seen her? I think she's safe."

They followed Pelon to a 7-Eleven, waited, watched him come out with a grocery bag, carrying it against his chest, two hands under the load. Pelon drove to the La Siesta Motel on Adams Street near the freeway, got out of the car, put the bag on the ground behind the car, opened the trunk, and took out a duffle bag. Pelon carried the duffel and the grocery bag to a room and knocked on the door. It was almost dark.

Raylan had the binoculars up to his eyes when someone appeared at the window, pulling the drapes apart a few inches, looking in Pelon's direction. It was a longhaired guy, early twenties. The drapes closed, the door opened. Pelon went in.

Raylan said, "What's on the other side of the room?"

"There's a courtyard and swimming pool," Big Country said. "There could be people in the pool or hanging around, drinking a beer, smoking a doob, you know? I have to call this in."

"I wouldn't do that," Nora said. "We want to surprise them. The more troops we have, the more attention we're going to attract. We have to get in the room and arrest them. I'll be the maid, roll the cart up, knock on the door."

"They're not gonna let you in the room," Raylan said. "Someone's gonna meet you at the door, take what they need or not."

Nora seemed to accept that without issue. "Okay, how do we get in?"

"Deliver a pizza," Raylan said. "Or a bucket of chicken, whatever we can find."

"But they didn't order it," Nora said.

"My guess is they're high and hungry. Maybe they forgot they ordered. Get in the room, hand over the food, and then draw down on them."

Just then the motel room door opened.

"Hold on," Raylan said.

Pelon came out of the room carrying the duffel bag and put it in the trunk of the Malibu. They followed him back to his house.

Raylan's eyes met Nora's. "What do you want to do?"

"See who's in the motel room."

•••

RAYLAN HAD HIS GLOCK in his hand, back against the wall as Nora knocked on the door, balancing a large pizza on the palm of her left hand. The door opened a crack. A voice said, "What do you want?"

"I have your pizza," Nora said.

"We didn't order one."

"They told me room twelve. What am I supposed to do with it?"

"I don't know, man."

The door closed. Nora turned to Raylan and shrugged. "He's messed up."

"Try again," Raylan whispered. "Tell him he can have it."

Nora knocked and the door opened a couple inches. "The owner said give it to you. You want it? Come on, my hand's burning."

The door opened halfway. Nora stepped over the threshold and handed the pizza box to the longhaired kid with scabs on his face. Raylan followed her into the room, aiming his Glock at two other longhaired, guys with ponytails, early twenties, sitting on the queen-size bed, watching porn on a laptop. They were moving where they sat, rotating their heads and picking their scab-covered arms. They glanced at Raylan but didn't react. "US Marshal, keep your hands where I can see them." They turned back to the laptop on the night table like he wasn't there.

Now Big Country came through the poolside door, holding his Glock, taking in the scene. "Don't touch them, get that infection on you. You don't know what they've got: hepatitis, HIV, AIDS." He put on surgical gloves, cuffed the two meth heads on the bed, and sat them on the floor. They were moving their heads, stretching their jaws open, rocking back and forth, trying to pull their hands out of the cuffs. Big Country went over and cuffed the guy still holding the pizza and sat him by the other two.

Raylan focused on the bed, the spread covered with electronic parts, change, tools, empty vodka bottles and snack food wrappers. There was a dresser against the wall. He opened the top drawer. It was filled with ziplock bags of crystal meth.

Raylan stood over them. "Where's Jose Rindo?" The meth heads wouldn't look at him.

"They're so cranked they don't know their own names," Big Country said. "Wait till they start to detox."

After El Centro PD picked up the three dudes and took them to county lockup, Raylan said to Big Country, "I get the impression this isn't an isolated incident."

"You got that right. Jose Rindo is cooking in Mexicali, bringing it up here, hooking our young people."

"What is all this?" Raylan said, indicating the bed overflowing with junk. "I've never seen anything like it."

"They're tweekers," Big Country said. "They get high, start taking things apart. Tweeker projects. They don't know what to do with themselves, roam around at night, break into cars and steal shit: radios, CDs, you name it."

Raylan said, "What's with the vodka?"

"The meth sends them into the stratosphere," Big Country said. "And the vodka mellows them."

•••

AFTER STOPPING FOR A quick meal, they met in the marshals' offices to plan their strategy for the next morning: where and when they'd meet, and everyone's roles and responsibilities. Big Country introduced Raylan and Nora to the three deputy marshals who'd be with them on the take down—J. R. Harris, Cody Styles, and Jimmy Pond—and passed out wanted posters of Pelon.

When the deputies left the room, Nora said, "Who's the deputy looks like he's in high school?"

"That's Juice Box. It's what we call the new recruit right out of the academy," Big Country said. "Like he's a kid."

"I get it," Nora said.

"Juice has come a long way," Big Country said. "You'll see him in action when we hit Pelon."

Raylan said, "We can't call him Juice Box, what's his name again?"

"Jimmy."

TWENTY-EIGHT

They arrived wearing their UAVs, carrying shotguns and AR-15s—as the sun was rising over the flat parched desert. They'd met in a McDonald's parking lot fifteen minutes earlier to go over the plan one more time.

And now Raylan and Nora were at Pelon's front door with a breaching ram. Big Country, Juice Box, and two other deputies had formed a perimeter around the house.

The only wild card was the pit bull. Raylan had picked up a ham bone at an all-night market. "Hold this, will you?" He handed Nora the bone, gripped the breaching ram, hit the door sounding like a gunshot, and it burst open. Raylan could hear the dog barking somewhere in the house as he yelled, "US Marshals." He dropped the ram, drew his sidearm, and tossed two pounds of marrow-filled bone out in the dirt yard. The charging pit bull ran past them and went for the bone. They went into the house, closed the door, and made their way down a hallway that led to the bedrooms.

Pelon, a fat hairy man in his underwear, was sitting on the side of the bed, smoking a cigarette when Raylan entered, aiming his Glock.

A young girl asleep next to him opened her eyes and sat up, pulling the sheet to her bare shoulders.

Nora said, "Honey, what's your name?"

"Maria Elena."

"How old are you?"

"Fifteen."

She was a pretty girl with straight black hair to her shoulders and heavy blue eye shadow, trying to look older.

Nora stared at Pelon with rage in her eyes, and then softened her expression, talking to the girl. "What are you doing here? Where is your family?"

The girl didn't answer, she was shy, embarrassed.

"Where are your clothes?"

The girl nodded at the floor.

Nora crouched and picked up a tiny blouse and a pair of shorts. "You don't have to worry about him anymore." Nora pulled the blanket off the bed, wrapped it around the girl, and escorted her out of the room.

"Man, you're in a lot of trouble. Taking advantage of a minor, a fifteen-year-old kid," Raylan said.

"That why you here?" Pelon shook his head. "I don't think so."

"Where's your wife?"

Pelon stubbed the cigarette out in an ashtray on the bedside table, and lit another one. "In Mexicali visiting her mother."

"What's gonna happen she finds out you've been shaking up with this young girl?"

"I never touch her."

"You know where my partner's gonna take the girl when we leave here? The hospital. Why do you think we do that? You think it's to see, has the girl been molested or raped? Think there's a test they can do?"

Pelon made a face, took a heavy pull from the cigarette, blew out a stream of smoke. "You break in my house as the sun is coming up. What do you want?"

"We arrested your three friends at La Siesta. We're waiting for them to detox and tell us about your meth operation in exchange for leniency."

"I don't know what you're talking about."

"So far we've got you on sexual battery of a minor under sixteen, and trafficking a Schedule II drug. It's not even seven o'clock and you're looking at two life sentences. You miss prison, huh? Miss the CEN."

Pelon narrowed his eyes at Raylan. "You think I don't know what you doing? I ask again, what do you want? Break it down."

"Where's Jose Rindo?"

"Now we getting to it." Pelon's face lit up. "Rindo, sure. That's what this is about." Pelon finished the cigarette and stubbed it out in the ashtray. "The only problem, I don't know where he is. I was you, I would go to Mexico."

"Maybe Rindo's with your wife and her mother."

"You never know." Pelon lit another cigarette.

"I thought you'd want to help yourself, make a deal. Give us Rindo, I'll talk to the prosecutor on your behalf. You do a few years, or maybe with luck, you walk."

"One minute ago I was looking at two life sentences. Now maybe I walk? What you say makes no sense."

"We get the big fish, pull the hook out, let you go."

"Is not that easy. I do all day, or it's all over."

"We move you somewhere safe, set you up."

"Cross Rindo and there is nowhere safe."

"Okay, it's your choice. Get dressed, man."

Pelon picked up his Levi's and tank top off the floor, put them on, and stepped into a pair of sandals. "What you gonna do with Pepper, my pit?"

"Animal Services will take care of him till your wife comes home," Raylan said. "This is your last chance. You want to help yourself?"

•••

RAYLAN DROVE TO THE El Centro Medical Center, Nora and Maria Elena riding in back. He dropped them off at Emergency and sat in the waiting room. Two Latinas, mid-forties, were watching *Judge Judy* on a flat-screen. Raylan thought Nora was a bitch till he watched a few minutes of the judge's rant. When *Judge Judy* ended, *Maury* came on.

Raylan had never seen either show and was amazed how many dumb people there were on daytime TV.

After an hour, Nora appeared shaken, upset, telling him she'd held Maria Elena's hand while a doctor did a sexual assault medical exam, a rape kit. Took hair samples, fingernail scrapings, did serologic tests for hepatitis, syphilis, gonorrhea, chlamydial infection, HIV, and gave her a high dose of estrogen to prevent pregnancy.

"Pelon paid her father. Do you believe that?" Nora shook her head. "The poor kid's a nervous wreck. After going through what Pelon did to her, she had a doctor invading her privacy. I asked Maria Elena if Pelon had hurt her. She wouldn't tell me, wouldn't look at me. In private the doctor said she had been sodomized, there was rectal bleeding, and she had lacerations on her vagina. Maria Elena feels embarrassed, ashamed, thinks it's all her fault."

Raylan was angry too but knew the charges against Pelon were so serious—drug trafficking and now rape—that no judge would grant him bail. *Judge Judy* would've hung him.

"The situation is complicated. Maria Elena told me her mother had died during the crossing from Mexico, and she lives with her father. Arrest dear old dad, prosecute or deport him, what happens to her?" Nora took a breath. "She's close to her cousin, aunt, and uncle in Brawley, and might be able to stay there."

"Where's Brawley?"

"About fifteen miles north of here. If that doesn't work maybe I'll take Maria Elena myself, bring her back to Tucson."

"You don't know anything about her."

"She needs help, isn't that enough?"

This Mother Theresa side of Nora was something new and unexpected, not that Raylan really understood her.

•••

RAYLAN COULD FEEL THE tension as soon as Javier Ybarra opened the front door and they entered the small sparsely furnished house on the outskirts of El Centro. He could hear the window air conditioner laboring to cool the hot room. Maria Elena stood next to Nora, staring at the floor. She started to cry and had smudges of blue eye shadow on her cheeks.

Nora introduced them to Javier and told Maria Elena to get her things and stay in her room, they had to talk to her father. The girl shrugged, not sure what was going on, but did as she was told.

Javier Ybarra said, "What is this about?" He had the stooped shoulders and the suntanned arms of a field worker.

Raylan said. "How much does Pelon pay to have sex with your daughter?"

Javier Ybarra gave a heavy sigh and shook his head.

"How could you do that?" Nora said, her voice hard and angry. "*Mi dios.* A fifteen-year-old girl, a child. What value do you put on your daughter's virtue? What is it worth?"

"We need money to eat." Javier Ybarra licked his dry cracked, lips and wiped sweat from his face with an open hand.

"I think you need money for your habit," Nora said, not giving the man an inch. "And when you run out, you sell your daughter. What kind of a father does that?"

Javier was a mess, strung out and craving.

Nora said, "You're going to feel the *bicho* in your arms soon trying to get out. You're going to start scratching."

He already had. There were long white fingernail marks on top of his brown arms. Javier hadn't broken the skin yet but it was just a matter of time. Raylan said to the man, "You have a green card?"

Javier Ybarra stared at the floor.

Raylan said, "Where do you work?"

"La Brucherie, in the fields, picking peppers and potatoes, lettuce or whatever they got to pick."

Nora said, "You're making money, why do you sell your daughter?"

"Is not enough."

Nora said, "How long you been buying from Pelon?"

No response.

Raylan unfolded the mug shot of Rindo, held the page up to Javier Ybarra's face. "When was the last time you saw him?"

Javier studied the photograph and shook his head. "*No lo se.*"

"Says he doesn't know," Nora said.

"Sure he does. You see his eyes, the look on his face? He knows." Raylan stepped toward Javier. "What do you say, partner? Tell us where we can find Jose Rindo. We'll get you cleaned up, send you back to wherever you're from."

"Can I talk to you?" Nora had never looked more serious.

They went into the kitchen, Nora standing in the doorway, so she could keep an eye on Javier. "What're you talking about, send him home? I want to send him to prison. Selling your daughter is about as bad as it gets."

"You want Rindo? I'm trying to get some information. Telling him he's going to prison isn't going to get us anywhere. Maybe he has an idea where Rindo is and maybe not. Pelon isn't going to talk, and so far Javier, if he knows anything, doesn't have the motivation to help us. Let's give him a day in county, see if his memory comes back."

TWENTY-NINE

Nora said, "I talked to your aunt. She's excited to have you come live with them. She's a nurse, I understand. What is your uncle's occupation?"

"He is a manager at the Walmart store," Maria Elena said, sitting in the front seat on the way to Brawley.

Nora, hands on the steering wheel, smiled at her. "How about your cousin, how old is she?"

"Same as me, fifteen."

"Your aunt said she wasn't going to say anything about you coming." Nora, playing it up, smiled again. "It's going to be a surprise. Are you okay with this?

The girl nodded and said, "Can I ask you something? How did you know I was at Pelon's?"

"We didn't. We weren't looking for you. We were there to talk to him."

From the rear seat, Raylan said, "We're looking for a man named Jose Rindo. You know him?"

Maria Elena turned, looking over the seat at him, shook her head, and said, "No, I don't think so."

Raylan unfolded the wanted poster and handed it to her. She stared at the paper for several seconds, looked at Nora, and then over her shoulder. "I saw him one time."

Nora sat up straighter, eyes wide now, giving the girl a quick glance.

"Pelon picked me up and stopped at a house. This man in the picture came out and talked to him."

Nora said, "You're sure it's the same man?"

Maria Elena nodded. "I'm positive."

"How far away from him were you?"

"About twenty feet. He kept checking me out. Later Pelon said the man wanted me to come back and be with him, and I said no."

Nora said, "Is the house in El Centro, do you remember the street?"

"It's on the corner, South Fifth and Smoketree Drive."

Nora said, "You can show us?"

The girl said, "Yes, of course." She took a pink cell phone out of a pink purse that had Disney characters on it, brought up a street map of El Centro, gave them the address, and showed them a street view of the house.

Raylan said, "Did Pelon say why he was going there?"

"No. He gave the man in the picture something in a paper bag." She indicated the size of the package with her hands.

Nora said, "And after that you spent the night with Pelon?"

The girl nodded.

•••

THE AUNT AND UNCLE in Brawley, in Raylan's opinion, seemed like decent god-fearing people. As it turned out the girl's uncle and her dad were brothers, even looked alike, but couldn't've been more different.

On the way back to El Centro, Nora seemed relaxed and happy. "Finding Maria Elena was a blessing in disguise. Bringing her to her relatives was the best possible outcome. I think they've got their hearts and heads in the right place. They'll get Maria Elena enrolled in high school, give her life some structure. Who knows what would have happened to her if we had not come along? Sooner or later smoking meth, and maybe turning to prostitution."

"Were you serious about taking her with you to Tucson?"

"Why, you don't believe it?"

"I'm just curious is all. That's quite an offer."

"Would I have done it? Yes. But I'm happy for her. I think she's in the right place, where she belongs."

Back in El Centro, Nora went with him to see Big Country.

"The girl from this morning, Maria Elena Ybarra, positively ID'd Jose Rindo at a house in El Centro day before yesterday," Raylan said, sitting at a round table in the deputy marshal's office. He handed Big Country the address he'd written on the back of Rindo's wanted poster.

"It's close, a few miles from here. How do you want to play it?"

"Get a couple of your men over there," Raylan said, "keep an eye on the house."

Big Country said, "You want to hit tonight?"

"I'd like to make sure he's still there before we do anything." Raylan turned to Nora who hadn't said a word. "What do you think?"

"I agree. Let's take our time, do it right. I want to get him this time."

Big Country said, "What if they see him leave?"

"Follow him, but don't try to take him down unless he's heading for the border. You've seen his sheet, this guy is high risk." Raylan paused. "Finding him was dumb luck. This is our chance to bring him in before he goes south and disappears."

"If you ID him, let's hit first thing in the morning," Nora said. "Before he knows what's happening."

•••

It was a quarter to seven when he got back to the hotel. Raylan took a shower, walked down the street to a restaurant in the hundred-degree heat, sat at the cool dark bar, and ordered a beer. He took off the Stetson and placed it on the empty seat next to him. He'd invited Nora to come along. She was tired and wanted to take it easy but asked him to bring her a sandwich. He drank beer, reading the menu, decided on a cheeseburger, and a chicken quesadilla for Nora, both to go, and placed his order.

A good-looking Latina, mid-twenties, was sitting a couple seats away from him. The bartender brought over a small glass and a bottle and poured her a couple ounces of tequila. He saw her look at him a couple times before she said, "Are you waiting for someone?"

Raylan turned, eyes on her and said, "No."

"I have been waiting for you to buy me a drink," she said with a Spanish accent.

"You've got one in front of you." She didn't look like a hooker, so why was she wasting her time on an old guy like him? "It's been a long day," Raylan said.

"What does that have to do with buying me a drink?"

"Trust me, it does." Any other time Raylan might've been interested but there was too much going on.

She stood, lifted his Stetson holding it by the brim with two fingers like a dirty diaper, and sat next to him.

"You don't pick up a hat like that."

"You do when it full of sweat."

Raylan took the Stetson and rested it on the empty chair to his left. She signaled the bartender and held up her glass. And when the bartender poured her another measure of tequila, she said, "You a cowboy, here for the Cattle Call?"

"I don't know what that is."

"It's the rodeo. You look like a bull rider."

"I'd hate to find out how long I could stay on the back of a two-thousand-pound Brahman. Maybe a couple seconds, I was lucky."

"You're not here for the rodeo, what brings you to this thriving metropolis?"

Raylan wasn't gonna go into it, tell a stranger, even a good-looking one, his business in this inbred town. He sipped his beer.

"You don't say much, do you?"

"Much as I have to."

The bartender placed a white bag on the bar top along with a bill. "Here you go." Raylan handed the man a twenty and picked up the bag.

"What is it? You playing hard to get, or you don't like women?"

•••

HE KNOCKED ON NORA'S door five minutes later. "It's Raylan, I've got your food." The door opened, Nora in a robe, hair messed up, said, "I'm starving."

He could see her delicate neck and soft line of cleavage where the robe wasn't closed all the way. Conscious of his stare, she pulled the lapels closer together and adjusted the sash. Raylan handed her the carryout bag. "Chicken quesadilla with guacamole and pico de gallo."

"That's my chicken sandwich?"

"Close as they had. I'll see you in the morning."

Back in his room, sitting on the couch, Raylan had taken two bites of his burger when he heard a knock on the door. Had to be Nora. He got up and opened it. Holding the neck of a tequila bottle, the Latina from the bar said, "You forgot something."

"Yeah, what's that?"

"Me." She moved past him into the room. "You have some glasses?"

Raylan wondered how she knew where he was staying unless she followed him, which he doubted, and she didn't know his name— or did she? Whatever was going on, it didn't feel right. "Listen, I'm kind of busy at the moment."

"What are you doing that's so important?"

"Having my supper."

The girl smiled. "Man, you need a drink, loosen up." She put the bottle on the desk and her shoulder bag on the chair, walked into the bathroom, and came back with two glasses. She opened the bottle and poured a couple inches of tequila in each and handed one to Raylan.

Now she sat at the desk, fished a pack of smokes out of her purse, and lit one with a plastic lighter.

"You can't do that in here."

"Why do you have a gun? You a cop or something?"

His holstered primary was on the desk in front of her, and this crazy girl sitting next to it made him nervous. "You're gonna have to leave." Raylan put the glass of tequila on the coffee table and moved toward her.

"Not till I finish my drink." She smoked and reached for the Glock, slid it out of the holster, racked a round, and pointed it at him, cigarette drooping from her mouth.

Raylan froze, feeling like an amateur for leaving the gun out. Not that he could've predicted this was gonna happen.

"What's the matter, I make you nervous?"

"I'd feel better you put it down."

She slid the gun in the holster. "You got to chill, man." She dug a hand in her purse and came out with a small silenced semiautomatic. "I don't need yours, I have my own."

A long ash hanging from the end of the cigarette dropped in her lap. She looked down, swatted it from her clothes, and Raylan moved toward her, went for the gun, trying to take it as she squeezed the trigger blowing a lamp off the desk, shooting out the TV, putting a round in the ceiling before he was able to twist it out of her hand. She went for his eyes and he hit her, dropping her to the floor, woozy as he cuffed her hands behind her back. He dragged her to the bed, cuffed her ankle to the frame and called Big Country.

•••

HALFWAY THROUGH HER QUESADILLA, Nora heard three quick knocks on the door. She assumed it was Raylan, but he didn't knock that way. She looked through the peephole at a clean-cut teenage boy maybe fifteen, little guy about her height, holding a box of candy bars. Nora pulled the sides of the robe together, retied the sash, and opened the door.

"*Buenas noches,*" he said in friendly voice tinged with Spanish. "I am sorry to interrupt your evening," the boy said. "I am selling candy bars to make money for our church."

Nora thought it was strange to be selling candy bars at eight o'clock at night in a hotel but went along with it, decided to help his cause. "Six chocolate bars for three dollars," the kid said.

"Wait here, I'll get my purse."

•••

NORA WAS SITTING ON the end of the bed, looking fragile and afraid when Raylan entered the room. There was a boy standing next to her, the barrel of his silenced semiautomatic pressed against the side of her head, his finger pressing on the trigger. With his dark hair and dyed highlights, he reminded Raylan of a singer in a boy band. What had the world come to, there were no more men to hire? Rindo was now using women and children to do his killing.

A siren wailed in the distance. "You hear that? The police are coming for you. Put the gun down."

The boy didn't say anything but he was nervous. Raylan hoped to God he was, a high-caliber pistol pointed at him. The boy moved behind Nora and now there wasn't enough of him showing to get a target. Raylan lowered his weapon. He didn't want to spook the kid, have him pull the trigger by mistake.

Now the *woop woop* of the siren sounded like it was right outside. The boy turned and looked at the blind-covered window behind him and Nora went down on the bed. With a split-second opening, Raylan shot him center chest, the impact sending the boy onto the floor. Raylan rolled him on his back, touched his wrist, and felt for a pulse.

He was still alive but barely.

Nora was standing next to the bed, hugging her arms, looked like she was about to start crying. Raylan put his arms around her and felt her body tremble.

She sat on the bed. "He's a torpedo, young assassin who kills without conscience, no sense of right or wrong."

"There's another one in my bathroom, a girl. Get dressed while I check on her."

•••

BIG COUNTRY SAID, "I can tell you, based on what you say happened, your life was in danger and so was Agent Sanchez's. You acted in self-defense. Under the circumstances, you had no other choice. Regardless, you're gonna have to surrender your weapon, suffer a little bit of bureaucratic indignity."

"Believe me I know the drill," Raylan said. "I don't get it back till I've been cleared by the Office of Internal Investigations." Raylan drew his holstered Glock and handed it to him.

"I'll get you a spare." Big Country paused. "How many times has this happened?"

"You don't want to know," Raylan said, thinking about the last time, giving his primary to a field supervisor after he shot Diaz. That gun had yet to be returned and now he needed another one. "What about the woman and the kid?"

"Her name is Karen Flores, but goes by *La Bonita.*"

"The hell's that mean?"

"The pretty. I wonder how she got that," Big Country said. "This knockout young babe starts hitting on you—you didn't think something was up?"

"What do you mean? I get hit on all the time."

"Sure you do. Anyway, the Mexican police know her, say she does heavy work for the Taco Mafia. Boy's name is Jesus Cornejo."

"An assassin named Jesus, now I think I've heard it all."

"He's sixteen, lives in Mexicali," Big Country said. "If he makes it, his new home's gonna be Juvenile Hall till he goes to trial."

"He makes it, he's gonna be the princess of county lockup. They're gonna be standing in line for him," Raylan said. "How well do you know the federal judge?"

"Pretty well. He's taken me surfing a couple times. We go up the coast to San Diego—Imperial Beach, Sunset Cliffs. The judge has a house there he goes to on weekends, runs the court here during the week."

"You any good?"

"I spent the first couple times duck-diving and being rag-dolled. Now I can goofy foot and cross step." Big Country grinned.

Raylan picked up the glass of tequila the girl had poured for him earlier and took a drink. "When you talk to His Honor, show him their matching guns with suppressors. Convince him not to set bail or we'll never see Jesus or *La Bonita* again."

"I don't think that's gonna be a problem. Now let me switch gears on you, okay?" Big Country said. "You got something going with the FBI agent?"

"Why do you say that?"

"Cause of the way you look at her and she looks at you."

"I think you're seeing things."

"I figured you'd say something like that. Well, no French kissing on the first date, and you have to raise the kids Methodist." Now he smiled. "How's she doing?"

"Shaken up. That'll happen someone puts a gun to your head."

"She gonna be all right by tomorrow morning? In all the confusion I forgot to tell you. Rindo's there in the house. Stepped out to have a smoke, they got a positive ID. What time you want to take him down?"

THIRTY

IT WAS ALMOST MIDNIGHT when the police left. Raylan went into the bedroom, Nora was stretched out on the bed, eyes wide open, but distant. "I have to go back to my room."

"You can't, it's a crime scene. And the hotel's booked. You're gonna have to stay here with me. Your suitcase is in the living room. I'll sleep on the couch."

"It's your room. I'll take the couch."

"We'll figure it out," Raylan said. "How're you doing? How do you feel?"

"Stressed, I can't seem to shake it. I keep seeing that gun pressed against my head, and the look on the boy's face after you shot him."

"You know I didn't have a choice—"

"I'm not blaming you. I'm grateful." Nora swung her legs over the side of the bed.

"There's something else. The El Centro deputy marshals ID'd Rindo. We're gonna take him tomorrow at sunrise. Think you're up to it?"

"I wouldn't miss that for anything. I don't care what happened." Nora got up. "I'm taking the couch and that's final."

"Whatever you want." There was an extra pillow and blanket on the shelf in the bedroom closet. Raylan made a bed for her while Nora brushed her teeth. She came out in her robe and said good night.

Raylan was fading almost asleep when he heard the bedroom door open. Nora walked in, pulled the covers back on the other side of the bed, and got in. Raylan rolled over, facing her.

"Is this okay? I couldn't sleep, the couch is so uncomfortable."

"It's fine. I'm just surprised."

Nora scooted over closer to him, reached out and touched his cheek with her open hand. "I don't know how to thank you. You saved my life. That's what I've been thinking about."

"You don't have to thank me."

"What if I want to?" She moved closer to him, and now her face was coming toward his and she kissed him, and kept kissing him, their mouths finding the right angles, getting used to each other, tongues moving, exploring. And when they broke for air, Nora said, "Is this okay?"

"You're full of surprises, aren't you?"

"Did you think this was going to happen?"

Raylan shook his head.

"Did you want it to?"

"It crossed my mind." The sheet had slipped down her side and Raylan could see Nora's small perfect breasts and tight stomach.

"Can we talk about it later?" She pulled the covers back and sat on him. Raylan sliding his hands down her body, feeling her rib cage, feeling the smooth skin on her hips and thighs, cupping her soft breasts. Nora smiling, a look of pleasure he'd never seen before, leaned down and kissed him.

Raylan slid out of his briefs and entered her slowly, pushing through the friction, and then they were moving, Nora's eyes closed, in the moment as they found their rhythm. Raylan kissing her, feeling her hips gliding under him. And then unexpectedly she leaned to her left, hands on his shoulders, and they flipped over in one easy motion as if they'd practiced it a hundred times. Raylan on top now, both of them smiling, her hands on his face. Raylan sighing as he let go and lay on top of her.

He rolled on his back. "My God," Nora said. She put her hand on his chest, rubbing lightly with her fingertips.

"How do you feel now, you better?"

Nora smiled and brought her hand to his cheek. "I was attracted the first time I saw you. Though it probably didn't seem like it."

"That wasn't the impression I got."

"Why do you think I called your chief and told him I wanted to go with you to pick up Rindo?"

"You should've asked for Bobby Torres, it was his case."

"I didn't want to go with Bobby." Nora, maybe feeling self-conscious, turned on her back and pulled the sheet up to her chin. "Now what happens? Is this going to affect us working together?"

Raylan was wondering the same thing. "If we let it. I'm not gonna worry. Big Country thought we had something going based on how we look at each other. He knew it and we didn't. Right now we better get some sleep. We've got to be at the office in five hours."

The last thing Raylan remembered was Nora's warm body against his.

•••

HE OPENED HIS EYES and there she was on her back, asleep. He lifted the bedsheet, looking at her naked body. Now Nora moved, opened her eyes, and said, "What're you doing?"

"Making sure what I thought happened really did."

"It did, and it was wonderful." She glanced at the dark blind-covered window. "What time is it?"

"Five. You want the first shower?"

"No, go ahead, but let me brush my teeth."

Nora pulled the covers back, got up and walked to the bathroom. The light was dim but Raylan could see well enough, staring at her trim waist and small round fanny and started getting excited again.

THIRTY-ONE

THEY MET IN THE courthouse parking lot as the sun was rising. Raylan briefed the team, laid out the op plan, knowing it would probably change when they breached the house. "There's a high fence around the backyard. We go in the front door, Rindo's going to go out the back, so be ready." Raylan passed out wanted posters and reminded everyone whom they were dealing with. "I know you've all seen him, but take another look, and do not underestimate this crazy bastard. There's a reason he's top fifteen. Jose Rindo's murdered six people we know about, and probably more. He's escaped from custody three times, and he's not gonna go easy."

Standing at the trunk of his G-ride, Big Country pulled a worn Glock out of his gun box and handed it to Raylan. "Here's your on-loan primary. Anything else interest you? Shotgun, long gun?

Nora, in a chipper mood, was in her heavy vest and FBI wind-breaker getting something out of her car. She'd been smiling at him since they woke up together. Raylan at one point saying, "You've got to stop doing that. Big Country and his boys are gonna wonder what the hell's going on. Put on your game face till we get back to the hotel."

"What's the matter, don't you feel anything?"

"Sure I do, but we've got a fugitive to take down."

They drove to the house in two cars. Big Country, Raylan, and Nora in one, and the three El Centro deputy marshals in the other.

There were mature trees on the east side of the property blocking the hot rising sun. The house was well kept and blended in the neighborhood. It wasn't the kind of place you'd associate with a high-level drug trafficker, and that, Raylan guessed, was the idea. Rindo could come and go without attracting attention.

It was quiet at 6:22 a.m. except for a couple dogs barking somewhere in the distance. Big Country parked on Fifth Street fifty yards from the house and got on the radio saying: "Operation Early Bird. We're code five at Five Oh Six Smoketree Drive, negative ET. Apprehending a high-risk fugitive."

And the dispatcher saying: "Ten four, copy, code five, negative ET."

"All right," Big Country said, turning in the seat, first looking at Raylan next to him and then Nora in back. "Let's take him in or take him out."

•••

RINDO'S EYES WERE OPEN looking at the ceiling, mouth dry, head pounding from the blow and tequila. The girl was on her stomach on the other side of the king-size bed like she was trying to get as far away as possible. He couldn't remember her name. He got up and walked naked into the bathroom, turned on the tap, filled the glass with water, and shook some Motrin out of the plastic container. He swallowed four, trying to stop the pain, get back in bed and sleep for a couple more hours.

He heard the fence rattle, looked out the back window, saw a cop in a tactical vest, shotgun in hand, coming toward the house.

Moving into the bedroom, Rindo slipped on a pair of Levi's and a T-shirt, grabbed his nine, saw two lines on the mirror next to the bed, picked up the still-rolled hundred-dollar bill, geezed the mojo, and felt the rush. The girl hadn't moved. She was either asleep or pretending to be.

He grabbed the backpack in the closet, strapped it on, ran to the front of the house, heard a loud crash and a voice saying,

"US Marshals." And then footsteps and a flurry of bodies moving through the front door.

•••

Big Country kicked the front door open with his size-fourteen Tony Lamas, and they went in with their guns. Big Country moving down the hall to the first bedroom, Raylan and Nora covering him. The big black dude, Melvin Gales, Jr., was flat on his back on the king-size bed, taking up most of it, eyes alert and holding on the shotgun Nora was pointing at him.

"Melvin," Raylan said, "let me see your hands."

The big man lifted his arms out from under the sheet, exposing a bandage on his bare upper chest and shoulder.

"Turn over on your stomach, put your hands behind your back." Melvin did, groaning, saying he'd been shot. Raylan slapping on cuffs that barely fit his thick wrists. "Do you have a weapon?"

"Not suppose to say?"

"It's okay, you can tell *me*."

"Under the pillow."

Raylan found the .45 that was racked with one in the throat. He ejected the round and the magazine. "Where's Rindo?"

The big dude shook his head. "I hurt, man. Come on, take these off. Y'all violating my human being rights."

Big Country and Nora were pointing their guns at a teenage Latina in the rear bedroom when Raylan walked in. The girl, terrified, had the bedsheet gripped in her fists, pulled up to her chin.

They lowered their weapons. Nora, trying to calm her, said, *"Esta bien. Estamos buscando a Jose Rindo. Esta en la casa?"*

"No lo se."

Nora said, *"Has visto lo deje?"*

"Hace pocos minutos."

"Rindo was here a few minutes ago," Nora said. "She doesn't know where he went."

Raylan walked in the kitchen, looking at the sink piled high with dirty dishes, empty vodka and tequila bottles, and drug paraphernalia on the counters and table. Through the window he could see J. R. Harris in the backyard, Cody Styles and Juice Box on the driveway, holding the perimeter.

Raylan stood at the locked door in the kitchen, trying to turn the handle.

Big Country said, "Let me try," and kicked it with a boot heel a couple times, and the molding splintered. He opened the door, looked down the stairs and back at Raylan. "You see this?" He took a flashlight out of a vest pocket, turned it on, and started down, Raylan right behind him. It was a small empty room with cinderblock walls, but its purpose was clear when Big Country shined his flashlight in the tunnel. "I'm going after him."

Raylan ran up the stairs, told Nora and the deputies that Rindo had escaped, and ordered them to check the outside perimeter of the property and call the PD. He and Nora went to the garage and looked in the Suburban. No sign of Rindo, but Raylan found a metal grate in the concrete floor. He pulled it off, looked in at stairs leading to the tunnel, walked down a couple steps, and called to Big Country. "Hey, you in there?"

"You get him?"

"He's gone."

Raylan and Nora went north behind the property, running along the alley to the next block. Sirens shrieked in the distance, filling the quiet morning with distress.

•••

WITH THE FLASHLIGHT WEDGED between his shoulder and the backpack, lighting the way, he crawled on his hands and knees through the cinderblock tunnel that was eighty feet long. At the end he climbed up a couple steps, lifted the metal grate, and stuck his head through the opening. There were two men in green vests, US MARSHAL in white letters on the backs, standing on the driveway, holding shotguns.

He waited until they moved closer to the house, climbed up into the garage, lowered the grate into position, and went through the side door. He could feel the morning sun on his face moving down the alley behind the houses, taking his time, fighting the urge to run till he heard shouting behind him and took off.

With no idea where he was going, Rindo went left on Driftwood and right on Sixth Street. He could hear sirens as he ran across a baseball field at the elementary school. Still running, he cut between two houses on Aurora Drive and saw a van pulling out of a garage.

THIRTY-TWO

WIGGY SAW THE DUDE sprinting across the street, coming toward Lori's driveway. A few seconds later the dude was standing in front of the van, aiming a pistol. Wiggy hit the brake, dude got in the front passenger seat, put his backpack on the floor, pointing the gun, saying, "Get the fuck out of here."

"Where you wanna go?"

"Anywhere, just drive."

He stepped on the gas, turned right out of the driveway, drove a few blocks, waited for a cop car, lights flashing, to pass on Eighth Street. What in hell's name was going on? He glanced at the dude with the gun and said, "They're looking for you, aren't they? What'd you do, you don't mind my asking?"

The dude didn't answer, kept the big revolver pointed at him.

They turned left on South Imperial Avenue, and it was a straight shot to the freeway. He didn't think the dude would give him any trouble. What the hell for? Then the dude surprised him, took out a vial and did a one-and-one.

Wiggy didn't like to be under the influence when he was transporting a load, but he was tired, and it sure looked good. He glanced at the dude. "Hey, how about giving the driver some?" Dude glanced at him, eyes rolling back, getting off. "Think of it this way, I'm kinda doing you a favor."

Dude stuck the gun between his legs, unscrewed the cap on the vial, dipped the spoon in. Wiggy leaned over as far as he could and the dude put the spoon under his nose and blasted him off.

Awhile later the dude said, "What's in back?"

"Load a cargo," Wiggy said, rushing, heart pin-balling in his chest.

"What kinda cargo?"

That was some good blow. He was almost too fucked up to talk. Took a couple breaths, got it under control. "The human kind. Got eleven illegals, wets back there, hoping to find a new life in the United States of America." Wiggy let out a breath. "Hell, you look Mex, might know some a them."

They drove in silence for a few minutes, and Wiggy, on top of the buzz now, said, "Since we're sharing blow, talking, and are sorta buds, what're the police after you for? I mean you don't want to tell me that's fine too."

"Taking out some motherfuckers try to steal from me." He said it like he was telling time, no expression, no emotion.

"Oh…well, hey, sure, I understand. Who could blame you?" Wiggy was wondering why he opened his big mouth. It was the blow talking, not him. He had to be careful with this dude, try not to get too friendly, get in his business, piss him off.

•••

"ALL I CAN TELL you," Big Country said, glancing at Raylan in the rearview mirror, "we got lucky. Woman driving to work saw Rindo aiming his gun at some teenager in a van pulling out of a driveway on Aurora Street, called the PD, who called us. Turns out the house is being leased by a forty-eight-year-old former ex-con named Loreen Rondello."

Raylan said, "What's her claim to fame?"

"Did federal time, three years for trafficking illegals," Big Country said. "My guess, she's still at it. Someone brings a load in from Mexicali, drops them off at the Rondello residence. Teenager in the van stops by, picks them up and takes them to San Diego, Riverside, Chino, LA, wherever the hell they're going."

Big Country turned left on Aurora Drive and left in the third driveway. They got out of the car and walked to the front door. Raylan could see a woman looking out the window at them and heard dogs barking in the house.

"I'm gonna go around back," Big Country said, "make sure she doesn't try to run on us."

Raylan knocked and the door opened a crack. He identified them. "I know who you are, what the hell do you want?"

Nora said, "Are you Loreen Rondello?"

"No, I'm Angelina Jolie, you don't recognize me?"

She might've been good-looking twenty years ago, but now she had a wrinkled face and a rotten disposition to go with it. Nora said, "Ms. Rondello."

"It's Lori."

"We understand you had a visitor this morning," Nora said. "Young man driving a blue Ford Econoline van was seen in your driveway six thirty-eight this morning and was carjacked at gunpoint by a fugitive with a stack of murder warrants against him."

"What do you want me to do about it?" Lori took a box of Marlboros out of a Levi's pocket, tapped a cigarette out and lit it, blowing smoke at Raylan. He fanned the stream and stepped back. Lori swung the door open now. "Where's the other one? There was three of you."

Nora said, "You're not concerned about your friend's welfare?"

"I don't know who you're talking about."

Raylan said, "What was in the van? You're not still transporting illegals, are you?" He paused. "Know what's gonna happen if you're convicted again?"

"Marshals, FBI, regular dumbass cops in uniform, you're all the same. Any bullshit scam you can pull, you do it. Who needs evidence? You just start making it up. You just start slinging it."

"Anything happens to that kid, it's on you," Nora said. "What's his name?"

"Jerome Dentinger, goes by Wiggy."

"Why Wiggy?" Raylan said. "He sell product himself, or is he just wigged out?"

"Your name was Jerome, I think you might want to change it."

"What's he to you?"

"I knew his mother. She passed when he was a baby. I've taken care of him on and off for fifteen years."

"Where can we find him?"

"The Slabs. Lives in a little trailer out there in that god-forsaken place. I can't tell you why."

As they approached the painted rock formation, Big Country said, "This is Salvation Mountain, the entrance to Slab City." He stopped the SUV and read the painted words under a simple cross.

GOD IS LOVE
SAY JESUS I'M A SINNER PLEASE COME
UPON MY BODY AND INTO MY HEART

Nora, in the front seat, looking out the window, said, "What is this place?"

"General Patton had the concrete slabs poured as barracks foundations," Big Country said. "It was Camp Dunlop. He chose this stretch of earth to play war, get his troops ready for combat, ready to face the Germans in Northern Africa. The climates are similar. When the army pulled out, they left the foundations. There's no running water, no electricity, no way to grow food." Big Country pointed. "Four miles or so that way is the Chocolate Mountains Aerial Gunnery Range. The Navy uses it to drop bombs, fine-tune the skills of their pilots. And I understand the SEALS train somewhere over there."

Raylan looked out the window at assorted RVs, trailers, campers, and vans strewn across the flat arid acreage. He could hear the sound of a motorbike with a busted muffler somewhere in the vicinity, and then it came airborne over a hill, a teenage slabber with sand-covered goggles landed and drove off toward the mountains.

Nora said, "Who would want to live out here?"

"In winter, retirees come, set up camp, and soak up the sun," Big Country said. "They aren't paying utilities and no one's charging rent. Some of them are squatters, collecting disability and social security, living life in the slow lane. And like Jerome Dentinger, there are the coyotes. Locals who know the trails and roads through the Chocolate Mountains and where the Border Patrol checkpoints are at. It's an industry."

•••

WIGGY, JUST BACK FROM San Diego, was sitting in an aluminum lawn chair, his boney ass hanging through the middle where three straps had ripped. In spite of the 120-degree heat, he was comfortable under the camo netting, playing *Axiom Verge*, when he saw the SUV park next to his trailer. No one living in the Slabs, none of the regulars drove anything that new. He watched the three of them get out and come over to where he was relaxing after a long day, surprised one of them was a foxy dark-haired girl could've been a sister to one of the wets from earlier.

"Jerome Dentinger," a slim guy in a cowboy hat said. "US Marshals. We'd like a word with you."

Wiggy turned off the game and put the Playstation on the floor of his trailer and walked out from under the netting. "What could the law possibly want with me?" Wiggy working a length of rubber band between his teeth, dislodged a nub of hamburger meat he'd eaten earlier, and spit it out.

"The hell're you doing?" the big marshal said.

"Cleaning my teeth."

The woman made a face. "Do it later, some other time, okay?"

Wiggy dropped the rubber band. The cowboy handed him a piece of paper. "I'll bet he looks familiar. Man puts a gun in your face you tend to remember him. I'm surprised he didn't shoot you."

"Yeah, I picked him up hitchhiking."

"In someone's driveway, I hear," the cowboy said. "That's got to be a first."

"Seemed like a decent guy."

"Describe decent, will you?" the cowboy said. "We're on the fugitive task force."

"You know—friendly, minded his own business."

"While he was pointing a loaded gun at you, huh?" the cowboy said. "But you think he was decent. I think you've got a twisted view of mankind."

The woman said, "Where'd you take him?"

"Seely."

The cowboy said, "What's that?"

"Little town, seven, eight miles west of El Centro," the big marshal said to the cowboy. Now he locked his gaze on Wiggy. "Son, are you fucking with us? Cause if you are, there's a cell in county with your name on it."

"No, sir. I dropped him off at the Seely Club."

Wiggy wore rubber bands like bracelets on his skinny wrist, had a habit of pulling on them and snapping them. He did it without even thinking.

The big marshal was shaking his head. "Will you knock that off?"

"Doesn't make sense," the woman said. "Unless he was being picked up there. Rindo gets out of a hotspot, goes somewhere we'd never expect."

"Where'd you take the load of wets?" the big marshal said, surprising him.

"What?" Wiggy squinted looking at the hot afternoon sun. "Why do you think I'd be mixed up in that?"

"You mean cause you've already been caught twice, spent three months in the El Centro youth lockup?" The big marshal grinned. "That's when you were underage. Now you're an *ad*-ult, can mix it up with the big boys. Open the back of your van for me."

"It's open."

The big marshal walked over, swung the doors open, and backed away. "Jesus Christ does it stink in there. You been carrying dead meat or what?"

"Fertilizer," Wiggy said, winging it.

"Fertilizer my ass," the big marshal said.

"Homeowner in EC's trying to grow tomatoes, you believe that?"

"Not for a second," the big marshal said. "It's a human stench. Border patrol finds these people wandering out in the desert, brings them to the detention center. We've got to pat them down, people haven't touched soap and water for weeks, a stench that gets in your nose—that's what the back of your van smells like."

"Since we all know the illegals are gonna keep trying—let me ask you something—should we leave them out there to die?" Wiggy said, looking out at the vast sunbaked landscape. "Or should we try to help them, give them a chance to have a better life?"

"They're breaking the law," the big marshal said, staring at him.

Wiggy, staring back, said, "So what?"

•••

BIG COUNTRY GLANCED AT Raylan. "Let's have a pow wow."

They stood next to his G-ride.

"Who is this kid," Raylan said, "the Slab City philosopher?"

Big Country said, "You want to take him in?"

"What for," Raylan said, "cause his van smells?"

"Jerome's sympathetic, wants to help these poor people," Nora said.

Big Country frowned. "Three hundred a head buys a lot of sympathy. Tell me what the hell we're doing out here, will you?" Big Country gave him a dirty look. "You believe what the kid said?"

Raylan said, "What difference does it make?"

Big Country went back to Wiggy standing next to the van. "Show me your hidden compartment."

"What hidden compartment?"

"Where you put the wets or drugs when you cross."

Wiggy's face was blank.

"I can have a tow truck here in twenty minutes, we'll find it," Big Country said. "We'll tow it in, take it apart. Or you can save us all a lot of trouble."

"I bought the van in the condition it's in. If there's a hidden compartment, I don't know about it."

"Let's cut the bullshit, what do you say?"

The kid pressed a button under the driver's seat and the cargo floor raised up on hydraulic hinges, exposing a space that eight people could hide in.

Big Country glanced at Raylan. "Want to bring him in?"

Raylan shook his head.

"Well I guess this's your lucky day."

THIRTY-THREE

R INDO'S GONNA LET US know where he is," Raylan said. "It's part of the game. He thinks he's smarter than us."

"Based on everything that's happened," Nora said, "I think he is, too."

Big Country had just dropped them off in the hotel parking lot.

"Let's have a drink," Raylan said, "what do you say?"

"I'm not going anywhere till I take a shower. I feel like I've been wandering in the desert for days."

Walking in the lobby, Nora said, "Listen, I appreciate you putting me up last night, but I have to get my own room."

"You breaking up with me?" Raylan said. "Might be a new record. In high school Jessica Witkowski gave me the axe after going steady for a day and a half."

"What did you do?"

"I wouldn't give her my ID bracelet."

"Don't worry, your ID bracelet's safe. Let me share something with you. I work for a federal agency. I have to reconcile all my expenses when I'm out of town on a case. Now they're going to challenge me if

I've spent too much, or not enough. I can hear my supervisor asking why there are missing hotel charges on my per diem."

"Tell him—"

"It's a her," Nora said, cutting him off.

"Tell her you slept in the car to save money." Raylan said it straight and grinned.

"I thought I would get my own room, come down, visit you." Nora seemed embarrassed now. "If that's okay."

•••

AT THE RESTAURANT DINNER table an hour later, Raylan said, "Why were you at your partner's house the night he was killed?"

"Why're you bringing this up again?"

"I get the feeling you're hiding something."

Nora held her wine glass by the stem, giving him her full attention. "It had been a long day, sitting code on a house where Rindo was supposed to be hiding. Turned out he wasn't there. It was sorta near Frank's, where I'd left my car. So we stopped by to use the bathroom, have something to drink."

"Didn't you tell me Frank was married?"

"His wife was out of town on business. She worked in sales for a software company." Nora sipped her wine. "Anyway, we had a couple cocktails, and I didn't think I should drive. I was going to call an Uber to take me back to my apartment, and one thing led to another."

"Was that the first time?"

"Yeah, but I saw it coming, I think we both did."

"I have to tell you this doesn't sound like you, sneaking around while the guy's wife's out of town."

"I wasn't sneaking around." Nora paused. "Why do you presume to know what I will and won't do?"

"I'm just saying I think there's more to it." Raylan combed his hair back with his fingers. "What were you doing in your partner's house?"

"Having an affair."

"I don't think so," he said, not taking his eyes off her. "You don't do that."

"What do you mean? I did it with you."

"That's different."

Nora forced a grin. "Why, cause it's you, and you think you're better than everyone?"

"No, cause I'm not married and I'm not with the Bureau, and that makes it okay."

Nora sipped her wine, staring at the table.

"What happened?"

Nora looked uncomfortable, fighting herself to tell it. She held her wine glass, waiting while the waitress put chips and salsa on the table, and asked if they were ready to order.

"Give us a few minutes," Raylan said.

Nora waited till the waitress walked away. "Why don't you let it go? It's over and done with."

"You've got to be able to trust your partner." Raylan drank his beer.

"And you're saying you don't?"

"No, I'm not saying that. Look at it from my point of view. We're after Jose Rindo who was involved in Frank Tyner's murder. I just want to know what happened."

"Frank was a GS twelve bringing home seventy-eight thousand dollars a year, plus bonus. He told me his wife was making forty. So together they earned about one hundred thirty thousand and their mortgage was almost two grand a month. With me so far?"

"Should I be taking notes?"

Nora gave him a dirty look. "One day we're doing surveillance, his sleeves were rolled up, I notice he was wearing a gold Rolex."

"What'd you say?"

"Is that a real one? He said it was a present to himself for ten years with the Bureau."

"Maybe he'd been saving for a while."

Nora finished her wine.

"Want another one?"

"I better."

Raylan raised his hand, signaling the waitress.

"A couple weeks later—it was a Saturday—I see him at the farmer's market, driving a BMW, and now I'm wondering, what's going on?"

"What was?"

"I don't know. But I trusted Frank and decided to let it go."

The waitress brought them fresh drinks, glanced at Raylan's open menu on the table and walked away.

"Frank had been telling me his marriage, after seven years, was falling apart. Claire was out of town every week, and when she was home they didn't do anything together, slept in separate bedrooms. You get the idea?"

"So he was setting you up, huh?"

"You know how it is, you spend a lot of time working together and talk about your lives. We had been partners six months. Frank started flirting with me, started saying we should go away together. At first I thought he was joking, but he kept it up. Working the hours we work, it's tough to meet people, and even if you do, it's tough to maintain a relationship." Nora sipped her wine. "I joined an online dating service and went on a few dates. At first they were like, 'Wow, you're an FBI agent. That's cool. What kind of gun do you carry? Do you have it on you? Can I see it?' More interested in the gun than me. We'd be out to dinner and the guy would want me to draw my Glock and hand it to him. Let him pretend he was a kid again, playing guns." Nora picked up a chip, dipped it in salsa. "We would go out a couple times, I am guessing the guy wanted to make it with an FBI agent, tell his friends. Why didn't he just go to a gun store, get his rocks off, and save the cost of buying dinner?"

"You probably intimidated them. Or maybe you're too critical."

"It really doesn't matter, they weren't going to cut it anyway." Nora put the chip in her mouth, swallowed it, and said, "When's the last time you went out with a woman? I'm not talking about meeting a girl in a bar and taking her home."

"That doesn't count, huh?"

Nora picked up her wine glass. "Are you going to answer me, Mr. Smart Ass?"

"I'm thinking." Raylan sipped his beer. "It's been a long time."

"While you're trying to remember, let me finish my story. What I didn't tell you, Frank was a nice-looking man, and I was attracted to him. He liked to have a good time. He was fun to be with."

Nora stroked the stem of her wine glass. "We had dinner and a lot to drink, skinny-dipped in his pool, dried off, went inside, had another glass of wine, and got in bed."

"Listen, that's a wonderful story, but you don't have to tell me the rest of it."

"I'm coming to the best part." Nora's eyes held on him while she sipped her wine. "As it turned out I wasn't attracted to him, and he was a terrible kisser. I couldn't go through with it. I was trying to think of what to say when I heard him snoring and thought: there is a God."

"Why didn't you leave?"

"I was blowing a two. I got dressed and slept on the other side of the king-size bed away from him. It was either that or get in his wife's bed and that seemed like a worse choice. I thought I'd sleep for a couple hours, sober up and drive home."

The waitress stopped by again.

Raylan said, "Want to order?"

"I've lost my appetite. But I'll have one more glass of wine."

"And a beer."

"When I opened my eyes, it was just starting to get light. I was hungover, had a helluva headache. I got up and looked at Frank. He was on his back, snoring. I went into the bathroom and took three Excedrin. I was going back into the bedroom and thought I heard the sliding door in the kitchen close. I stopped and listened and heard the faint sound of footsteps on the hardwood floor in the family room. Somebody was in the house. I looked around for my bag, my gun, but didn't see it and remembered I left it in the TV room." Nora paused. "I looked through the open bedroom door and saw someone, the silhouette of a man approaching. I went back in the bathroom and lay down in the tub, holding my breath. I heard voices, someone talking to Frank. I heard, '*Plata o plomo.*'"

"What's that mean?"

"Silver or lead." Nora's eyes held on him. "The translation: take the money or you're dead."

"So Frank wasn't involved?"

"Or maybe he was but wanted out."

"The shooter said, 'Jose Rindo says is too late for explanations. *Que Dios te ayude*,' which means 'may God help you,' and shot him twice."

"Too late for explanations, doesn't that implicate him?"

"Or it means he couldn't be bought. After he shot Frank, I heard him come in the bathroom, his shoes making a clicking noise on the tile floor, coming toward the tub…"

Nora stopped talking as the waitress put their drinks on the table and walked away.

"I thought he knew I was there. My heart was about to explode, and he stopped at the toilet, relieved himself, walked out of the bathroom and left. I ran into the TV room, grabbed my gun, ran outside and down the street, chasing a silver VW sedan that sped away."

Raylan pictured Diaz on the train.

"Now you understand the problem." Nora drank some wine. "Frank was dead and I wasn't supposed to be there. I went home, showered, changed, went back a couple hours later, and called it in."

"What was Frank's connection with Rindo?"

"Same as all of us. He was after a fugitive with a couple warrants against him."

"Did you tell anyone about Frank's sudden wealth?"

"I thought about it and decided not to. I didn't have any proof, evidence of wrongdoing. I liked Frank. Why ruin a dead man's reputation and give the Bureau a black mark?"

"Did you ask his wife? Maybe she inherited money or won the lottery."

"She didn't."

"The man who killed Frank was a contract assassin named Joaquin Diaz.

I don't know if this'll make you feel any better, but he's dead. Came to Detroit after we arrested Rindo."

"Why didn't you tell me?"

"I didn't know he was the one who shot Frank till you mentioned the silver VW. That's what Diaz was driving."

They finished their drinks and went back to the hotel. Walking down the hall, Raylan said, "Want to come in for a nightcap?"

"I better not. I'm exhausted."

He watched her all the way to her room. Nora unlocked the door, turned, looked at him, and waved.

•••

HALF AN HOUR LATER, he was in bed, watching a movie, and thought he heard someone knocking on the door. He turned down the volume, put his Levi's on, looked through the peephole, and opened the door.

"You want some company?" Nora moved past him, untying the sash and letting the robe slide off her shoulders onto the floor. He followed her into the bedroom. Nora sat on the side of the bed. "I hate to barge in on you, but I couldn't sleep. You mind?"

THIRTY-FOUR

"Here's the latest from Bobby Torres." Raylan was staring at a Facebook photo of Jose Rindo sitting at a table at an outside cafe, posing, a drink in front of him. The caption read, *"Hola, amigos."*

Nora said, "Do you know this place?"

"It's a restaurant in Mexicali," Big Country said. "Dude's flaunting his freedom."

"Let's go down and get him," Raylan said.

"Whoa, time out." Big Country rubbed his jaw. "Rindo's now an international fugitive. There's a shitload of rules we've got to follow, and the first one is you've got to work with a deputy marshal, a Mexico Investigative Liaison who knows the Mexican authorities."

Raylan said, "You have one in your office?"

"You're looking at him," Big Country said. "There are things you can and can't do when trying to apprehend a fugitive in the Republic of Mexico. Basically, you've got to have your shit together. Is Jose Rindo a US citizen born in the USA?"

Raylan couldn't remember.

Nora said, "I am almost positive."

Big Country said, "Or is he a naturalized US citizen born in Mexico? If that's the case we can't deport him, we'll have to extradite him, which is more difficult."

"He was born in Detroit," Nora said. "Father was a US citizen. But his mother was a Mexican citizen, and Rindo spent time in Mexicali, growing up. Does that complicate the situation?"

"I don't know. But what can make it really tough is if Rindo has a Mexican wife and Mexican kids, owns a residence south of the border. It'll be harder to deport him. I'm gonna have to run all of it by the Marshals Internal Investigations Branch, get their approval."

Raylan said, "We give the Mexican authorities a copy of Rindo's résumé, you think they're gonna give him immunity?"

"You're forgetting one thing," Big Country said. "Rindo's got money. He can buy influence and protection."

Nora said, "All this Marshals Service bureaucracy is going to slow us down. What can we do keep the case moving?"

"Get a warrant with a judge's signature on it."

"I've got them from Detroit, Columbus, and Tucson," Raylan said. "Take your pick."

"I'm gonna need a copy of the dude's birth certificate, his driver's license, photographs of him, mug shots, distinguishing marks, tats, Facebook page, criminal history, border crossing history for the past couple years, and anything else about him you think's important." Big Country took a breath. "Oh yeah, and we need his address in Mexico."

"We don't know his address," Raylan said. "We did, we'd go down and get him."

Big Country frowned. "You hear anything I just said?"

•••

RAYLAN AND NORA SAT in the conference room across from each other with their laptops, getting together the items on Big Country's checklist. He came in a little later and said, "I've notified the Marshals Service in Mexico City. We're opening an International Lead on Jose Cardenas Rindo. I've reached out to the Mexican LEOs, good guys, state cops who've helped us in the past." Big Country sipped his coffee. "What do you have so far?"

Nora leaned across the table and handed him a stack of printouts. "Everything except the address of his Mexican residence."

Big Country's cell phone rang, He took it out of his shirt pocket, listened for a couple minutes, said, *"Que hora?"* listened and said, *"Gracias, amigo."* He turned off the phone and glanced at Raylan. "Memo, my Mexican liaison talked to a CI who has it on good authority that Rindo is going to be at a club in Mexicali tonight. It's the *fiesta de disfraces."*

"A costume party," Nora said.

Raylan said, "How're we gonna recognize him?"

•••

CROSSING THE BORDER THAT night, Big Country said, "I just want to make sure we're all on the same page. Without written consent from the Mexican government, Rindo can't be arrested or deported. Our objective is to find the man and locate his residence. Nothing else." He took a beat. "And watch yourself. Anything can happen in Mexico."

Nora said, "What does that mean?"

"It's a crazy place and you've got to be aware, on your toes."

Big Country introduced Raylan and Nora to Guillermo Cepeda at the Mexican immigration offices. "This is my buddy, Memo. He's with the Baja State Police." Big Country put his arm around the little guy who was about five six, weighed maybe one thirty and smiled a lot.

Memo wore Levi's, Ray Bans, and a Heckler & Koch .45 in a holster on his right hip. They followed him out to the parking lot, watched him open the trunk and unzip a duffle bag that was filled with guns: matte black semiautomatics and tactical shotguns. "My friends, whatever you like is for you."

"Why don't we each take one but be cool," Big Country said. "Last thing we want to do is injure an innocent civilian, start an international incident."

Raylan reviewed the situation. The Marshals Service had yet to give them permission to pursue Jose Rindo in Mexico, and here they were on a tip from a confidential informant. What they should've done was gone back to El Centro and waited till everything got sorted out. But Jose Rindo was in a club not far away and if they missed this opportunity, they might not get another one. So they took the guns and rolled the dice.

Next to the duffle was a bag of masks. Memo had thought it through, planned ahead, which made sense. If you were going to a costume party looking for an armed fugitive, you better disguise yourself. "Pick your favorite," Memo said.

You could be a zombie, a nun, an alien, a skeleton, Hannibal Lecter, Darth Vader, or the Phantom of the Opera. So they each took a mask.

Now they were in Memo's sedan parked across the street from the club. It was 10:20 p.m. The scene reminded Raylan of Mardi Gras in New Orleans, the crowd of costumed partiers spilling out onto the sidewalk, people drinking and dancing. The smell of cigarettes and marijuana hanging in the hot night air. There were lights strung high in the trees across the veranda where the mariachis were kicking it out, their bright festive notes floating up into the dark sky.

"Listen, I'll go first," Nora said. "If Rindo's in there I'll find him. He may be in costume, but I know him, how he moves, his voice, his tats."

"He knows you too," Raylan said. "That's the problem."

"But he's not expecting me and he's not going to recognize me." Nora took lipstick out of her bag and outlined her mouth dark red. Now she put her hair up in a bun.

"Who are you?"

"Wait," Nora said, turning her back to him, fitting the purple eye mask over her face and turning to show him. "What do you think?"

"I don't recognize you, so how will Rindo? All you have to do is spot him and walk out."

•••

NORA MOVED THROUGH THE tables across the crowded veranda. It was loud, the mariachis' horns piercing the night. She could see men checking her out as she pushed her way to the crowded bar and tried to get the bartender's attention. A voice behind her said, *"Algo de beber?"* Nora turned to see a man wearing a black eye mask, black hat, cape, and a sword at his side. These people took their costumes seriously. *"Zorro, a tu servicio."*

She smiled, Zorro, of course. Nora shook her head, signaled the bartender and ordered a margarita.

Now, with a drink in her hand, another man dressed as a *federale* in a khaki uniform, a brown military holster on his hip, stepped in front of Zorro. *"Este es problema."* It was Rindo. *"Tengo una tabla ven sientate conmigo."*

"Me estoy reuniedo una novia."

He smiled but didn't seem to have a clue who she was. *"Acompanarme hasta que ilega."* He lightly gripped her bicep and escorted Nora inside the club to a table where two men, one black, the other Mexican, were dressed as bandits, drinking tequila out of short jelly glasses. There was a bottle on the table between them. The black guy wore a straw hat low over his eyes and now she recognized him as Demarco Hall, aka Thunderbird. Rindo didn't introduce himself or his friends.

Nora said, "You speak English?"

"Why do you want to know?"

"My Spanish is a little rusty. I've been living in Phoenix the past fifteen years, just took a job with Gulfstream here in Mexicali." Nora drank the margarita, trying to calm her nerves.

"That's why I have not seen you here." Rindo poured himself tequila. "But with the mask, how can I be sure? Why don't you take it off?"

"That would ruin the mystery, don't you think?"

Rindo nodded at the Mexican with the mustache. The man got up and moved away from the table.

Nora finished the margarita and glanced at her watch trying not to be obvious. It was 10:46 p.m. Just a few more minutes, she told herself. She had to find out where he was staying. "Is there a story behind the uniform?"

"How did you know? My grandfather was *federale*. This was his. Now I am the *federale*, my friends are *banditos*. What do you think, uh?"

"I think you're having fun."

"But you don't believe it?"

The bandit returned and placed a margarita in front of her.

"*Gracias Lalo,*" Rindo said.

Nora picked up the glass, licked salt from the rim, and took a big drink. "You live here in the city?"

"Yes, of course, how about you?"

"I'm in a hotel for the time being, looking to buy a house. Maybe you can help me."

"It will be my pleasure."

Halfway through the second margarita, Nora was having trouble focusing. She looked at Rindo through the eyeholes of the mask, seeing two of him.

"You said you are working at Gulfstream." His voice sounded far away now.

"What?"

"I want to buy a jet. How much does it cost?"

Nora knew she was in trouble, tried to get up, and Rindo reached over, pressing on her shoulder so she couldn't move. "Hey, where you going?"

The bandits were enjoying themselves, laughing and drinking tequila.

"I really have to go." The words came out slow and elongated. What did they put in her drink?

•••

RAYLAN HAD SEEN NORA at the bar talking to Zorro and then walking across the veranda with a man in a peaked cap, wearing a khaki military uniform. He looked in the club and saw her sitting at a table with three men. The plan: when Nora saw Rindo, she would walk outside and give a signal. He told himself to be patient. It would happen, or it wouldn't.

Now twenty minutes later Nora was still at the table with the men. Big Country, wearing a zombie mask, was standing at one side of the bar. Memo, as the *Phantom of the Opera*, was just outside the bar, smoking a cigarette. Raylan, in a skeleton mask, wandered to the bar to get a beer. When he went back and looked in the club a few minutes later, Nora and the three men were gone, the table empty, and now he was worried. Raylan took off his mask, waved at Big Country and Memo. They rushed over to him.

"Where is she?" Big Country said, removing his mask now.

Memo said, "She didn't come out this way."

"Maybe she's in the can," Big Country said.

"Nora was sitting at a table with three men, now she's gone. They all are."

Memo said, "Come this way."

They followed him into the club that was filled with tables. There was another stage, another band, a few couples on the dance floor. They followed him through the kitchen to an alley behind the restaurant, but no sign of Nora.

Big Country said, "Was it Rindo?"

"I don't know. I only saw him from behind and he was wearing a hat. But let's assume it was."

"She saw him," Big Country said. "she was supposed to signal us."

"Well she didn't or couldn't." Raylan fixed his gaze on Memo. "We don't have much time. He's gonna find out who Nora is and what she knows, and then he's gonna get rid of her."

"Or maybe he use her to bargain," Memo said.

Raylan said, "Can we talk to your CI?"

"I ask him. He doesn't know."

Raylan said, "One thing I know for sure, Rindo likes the ladies, young and pretty. You know an escort service specializes in that?"

"No but I know a *casa de citas*."

"What's that?"

"A whorehouse," Big Country said.

•••

RAYLAN SHOWED THE MUG shot of Jose Rindo to the madam at the bordello called Baja Club. "You know this man?"

The heavily made-up woman, early fifties, shook her head.

"He's a regular, isn't he?"

"*No lo entiendo.*"

"She doesn't understand," Memo said.

The madam's bodyguard, a tough-looking former middleweight—Raylan couldn't think of his name—stood off to the side, staring at him, Raylan wondering what he was thinking. The woman sat behind an ornate desk in her formal, old-world office.

"How often do you see Señor Rindo? Man's a sex fiend, can't seem to satisfy his desires." The woman stared at him without expression. "That's right, you don't speak English, do you? Let me try something else. Give us Señor Rindo's address, we're out of here. Let you get back to running your house of ill repute. How's that sound?" Raylan glanced at Memo. "Tell her I want to talk to the girls. I want her to bring them in one by one."

The ex-fighter kept his eyes on Raylan.

"Is not possible," the woman who didn't understand English said in her angry Spanish accent. "They are with clients."

"Clients, huh? That's what you call them. Get the ones that aren't working, bring them in here," Raylan said.

"I call the police," the woman said.

"What do you think we are?" Raylan said. "We can put you out of business, lock your door, give all your customers the boot, drag this out, or we can talk to the girls and be on our way."

"Do what the man say or I'll will arrest you," Memo said.

They talked to them one after another, cute, innocent young girls with dark hair tied in pigtails and ponytails, wearing plaid skirts and white knee socks. The girls were shy, nervous, eyes on the floor as Raylan showed them the wanted poster of Jose Rindo, and Memo spoke to them in Spanish. "This man is a murderer wanted by the police. Do you know him? Do you know where he is? This man has kidnapped a woman. If we do not find her, she will die. Look at me." And now the girl would meet Memo's gaze. "Will you please help us? Someone must help us or the woman will die. Do you want this on your conscience?" Memo putting a guilt trip on them. The girl would eye the wanted poster a second time, shake her head, and say no. Memo gave each girl a card and told her to call if she remembered something.

THIRTY-FIVE

RAYLAN WOKE UP TO someone calling his name and touching his shoulder, opened his eyes, and saw Memo standing next to the bed in his underwear like the little guy was trying to jump in the sack with him.

"Raylan. Sylvia, a girl from the Baja Club, call asking did we find the woman? I tell her no and ask can she help us?"

They were in a bedroom at Memo's house, ten to six in the morning.

"The girl say she don't know where Señor Rindo is. But had a customer that works for him. The man's name is Eduardo Meza, but is called Lalo."

"Where does he live?" Raylan said, rubbing grit from his eyes.

"The girl doesn't know. Lalo came to see her later, after we go."

"Did she tell him we were asking about Rindo?"

Memo shook his head. "I am going to check has Lalo been arrested."

He woke up Big Country, who was asleep on the couch in the main room, his big Tony Lamas on the floor next to him.

Raylan made coffee, eggs, and toast, and the three of them sat at a table in the dining room, eating breakfast.

Memo, drinking coffee and looking at his laptop screen, said, "Meza was six years in the state penitentiary at El Hongo. Armed robbery. Now he work for Rindo." Memo turned the laptop around so Raylan and Big Country could see him, a Mexican with dark eyes and a bandit mustache.

At 6:47 a.m., they were parked on Avenue Puenta de Calderon, Eduardo Meza's last known address. Nora had disappeared eight hours earlier and Raylan could feel the stress to find her building. They still hadn't told the Marshals Service they were in Mexico, or that Nora was missing. Big Country had called the office and said he didn't feel well and wasn't coming in, buying them more time.

The single-story stucco house and open garage were behind a five-foot-high wrought-iron fence. They went through the gate, and Big Country went around to the back with a shotgun. Raylan, gripping a .380 Beretta, stood next to Memo at the front door.

"You going to tell him we're the police?"

Memo gave him a puzzled look. "You want him to know we are here?"

"We do it a little different in the US."

Memo picked the lock, opened the door, heard the squeal of rusty hinges, and entered a tile hallway, Raylan behind him, the morning sunlight, a filtered haze coming through grime-covered windows. To his left was the living room that had a couch and flat-screen but was otherwise empty. Raylan followed Memo down the hall to the first door, turned the handle, and went in, two hands on the .45.

Eduardo Meza, in bed, was reaching for a gun on the side table. Memo said, "*Policia,*" and something else in Spanish, and Meza raised his hands. Memo rolled him over, cuffed him, picked up his gun, and set it on the top of the dresser.

Raylan said. "Where is Nora Sanchez?"

Eduardo Meza shook his head. "Don't know any Nora Sanchez."

Memo stepped toward the bed and punched Meza in the face. "Answer the man."

"*No lo se,*" Meza said, trying to duck as Memo swung the .45 into the side of his head and now blood was streaming down his cheek.

Raylan said, "Where's Nora Sanchez? Give me an address, we can end this."

"She is with Jose. He say something about giving her as a present to a friend."

Memo, standing next to the bed, grabbed a pillow, covered Meza's face with it, pressed the barrel of the .45 against his head, and pulled back the hammer. "Where is Jose Rindo?"

"*Ir a la mierda.*"

Memo fired into the stained naked pillow, blowing out a cloud of feathers that floated in the air, Raylan's ears ringing from the thunderous report.

Big Country walked in the room with a Glock in his hand, glanced at Raylan and then at the bed. "Whoa."

Memo continued to hold what was left of the pillow over Meza's face. "*Su última oportunidad.*"

"Avenue de la Paz," came the muffled sound of Meza's voice.

"The number," Memo said.

"*Dos mil seiscientos sesenta dos.*"

"He's not there, we come back."

Raylan was thinking: so that's how you question a suspect.

"Okay, let's go," Memo said.

"What about him?" Big Country said.

"My friend, you want to shoot him?" Memo swung his arm toward Meza.

"*Por favor...*"

"Why don't we take his phone, cuff him to the bed frame," Raylan said. "Let Lalo contemplate his future."

When they were outside, Big Country whispered, "Mex kills another Mex, know what it's called? Misdemeanor homicide."

•••

THEY SAT CODE ON Avenue de la Paz, a couple doors from where Rindo was staying in a wealthy part of Mexicali. There were trucks parked up and down the street, landscapers cutting grass, trimming trees at 8:12 a.m. "Let's wait, maybe we get lucky, Rindo leaves to run an errand."

"What do you think?" Big Country said to Memo.

"I do whatever you want. Get tired of waiting, break down the door."

They didn't have to wait long. One of the three garage doors opened, and a Lexus sedan with blacked-out windows turned on the street fifty feet in front of them. Memo followed it to a convenience store a couple miles away.

Raylan was leaning against the driver's side door when Thunderbird, in a pork pie straw, came out carrying a grocery bag ten minutes later. "Thunderbird, I thought that was you? What're you doing in Mexicali? You're not running from those warrants we've got, are you?"

Thunderbird approached the car, grinning. "Motherfucker, you got no authority down here. The fuck you doing?"

"I don't, but he does." Raylan pointed to Memo coming up behind him. Thunderbird glanced over his shoulder and back at Raylan.

"What you want?" T-Bird was high, eyes barely open. Must've been an effort to get his brain in gear.

"Who's in the house with Rindo?"

"He gonna wonder where I'm at, suppose to be getting milk for the dude's cereal."

"Three murder warrants against you, that's what you're worried about?"

Big Country took the bag out of Thunderbird's hands and Memo cuffed him.

Raylan said, "Where's Agent Sanchez?"

Thunderbird seemed lost in his buzz now, eyes closed, then blinking open.

Big Country said, "What're we gonna do with him?"

"Got to have him picked up," Raylan said, "taken into custody." Memo, on his cell phone speaking rapid-fire Spanish, was making arrangements.

•••

RINDO WAS AT THE kitchen table, bowl, spoon, box of Cheerios, and a Colt Python in front of him, watching *Deep Throat*, the original, on a flat-screen with the sound off. The star Linda Lovelace wasn't much to look at but she had one major talent. Cost thirty grand to make, he read somewhere, and grossed $600 million. Maybe that's what he should do—switch to porn. Less risk, more fun. He heard the garage door open, watching Linda go down on the doctor, and then she saw fireworks. He heard Thunderbird come in the house. Still watching the movie, he said, "Man, where you been, can't find milk?"

"Sorry to keep you waiting."

He knew the voice, eyes on his gun next to the cereal bowl, and turned, looking at the crazy marshal, Stetson low over his eyes, a pistol tucked in his waistband, right side. The man, cool as always, in control.

"Show me your hands."

Rindo hesitated, waiting to see what the marshal would do.

"You think I'm playing?"

He raised his arms over his head. The marshal cuffed him, turned off the movie and turned the chair around, Rindo facing him. Now the marshal was looking at something on the counter, walked over, and opened the woman's ID. "Where is she?"

"Not here."

"You better start talking."

"What do you give me for her?" His gaze held on the lawman. "Problem is, you got nothing I want."

"I'm gonna deport you," the crazy marshal said, "take you back to Detroit."

"I am a Mexican citizen. I have a Mexican wife and a Mexican son. The mayor of Mexicali is a friend of mine. I call, ask for his assistance. Tell him US law enforcement is forcing me out of the country against my will. You don't see it, but the one in trouble is you. Go while you can, leave Mexico and don't come back."

"Nobody else in the house," the big man said, coming in the kitchen with the Mexican cop. "But I found this." It was his backpack filled with money.

The big man said, "Numb nuts here tell you anything?"

"He's saying how important he is, claims to know the mayor."

"No shit," the big man said. "I'm impressed. What about Agent Sanchez?"

The crazy marshal said, "Memo, what should we do with this fugitive, won't cooperate?"

The Mexican cop walked out of the room and returned a few minutes later with a piece of black cloth. It was a hood. The cop, trying to scare him, fit the hood over his head. *"Donde esta el agente Americano?"*

Rindo knew he wouldn't do anything in front of the marshals.

"La última vez que pido."

The cop was giving him an ultimatum.

"Put him on the counter," the Mex cop said.

They lifted him, one holding his legs, the other holding him down. What was this? He heard someone move to the sink and turn on the faucet, and now the water was soaking the hood. He was having trouble breathing, water filling his nose and mouth. He was losing consciousness, drowning, and then it stopped. He coughed out water and sucked in air through the drenched cloth.

"Donde esta el agente Americano?"

Still trying to draw a breath, he didn't have time to answer before it started again and happened the same way, and just as he was starting to fade, the water stopped and he heard the voice.

"Donde esta el agente Americano?"

And knowing they would keep doing it, he said, "Okay."

The hood came off. He spit water out of his mouth and snorted it out of his nose, trying to breathe, thinking of what he was going to say. "The FBI woman is with El Yiyo," he said, eyes holding on the crazy marshal. "Better hurry. You might be too late."

THIRTY-SIX

WHEN THEY WERE IN Memo's car, speeding through the neighborhood, Raylan said, "Who was Rindo talking about?"

"El Yiyo, the stew-maker's apprentice."

"You'll have to explain that."

"The stew-maker, El Pozalero, was an assassin for the cartels, responsible for the death of three hundred people—maybe more. They call him the stew-maker. He dissolve his victims in drums filled with acid—his stew—leaving only bones."

"He did this to them when they were alive?"

"Alive or dead, it did not matter to El Pozalero. The stew-maker was arrested years ago and is in prison. El Yiyo, a young apprentice who worked for him, now carries on the business."

They were in an industrial area, streets lined with warehouses and repair shops. Memo turned left on Avenida 29 de Junio, pulled over, and pointed to a nondescript building. "Is that one." There was a pickup truck parked in front.

Raylan got out of the car and followed Memo to an alley behind the warehouse. There was a loading platform. They climbed up on it and heard music coming from inside.

"They listen to Los Lobos," Memo said, "while they kill people."

There were half a dozen blue plastic chemical drums spaced apart on the warehouse floor. Raylan didn't see anyone. There was a pulley attached to a metal bar in the rafters and a length of rope attached to a pulley that extended to the concrete floor. It wasn't hard to imagine how the system worked. One drum had bubbling liquid in it, El Yiyo was getting ready to dispose of a body.

There was a young guy, maybe twenty, eating beans and rice in a makeshift kitchen. They surprised him, entering the room with guns drawn.

Memo said, "What is your name?"

"Refugio."

"Are you armed?"

"No."

Memo patted him down and shook his head. Then cuffed Refugio's hands behind his back.

Raylan said, "Who else is in the building?"

"A woman."

Raylan said, "American?"

Refugio nodded.

Memo said, "Where is El Yiyo?"

"*En su camino.*"

"He on his way here?" Memo said.

Refugio nodded.

Rayan said, "When?"

Refugio shook his head. "*No lo se.*"

Memo said, "How many men with him?"

"*Tres hombres.*"

•••

Nora felt sick, nauseous, opened her eyes. She was on a stained mattress in a small dingy room. She heard music and smelled vomit, saw traces of it on her blouse and on the bed. She tried to piece together the events of the night: remembered arriving at the club with Raylan, Memo, and Big Country, remembered sitting at a table with Rindo, Thunderbird, and a Mexican bandit, and remembered being carried out of the club and through the kitchen. Her memory was hazy after that, no recollection of coming to this place, wherever it was, no recollection of anything except the two men who came in the room earlier as the sun was rising. They stood next to the bed talking in Spanish.

"She's still out, man. How much they give her?"

"I don't know. But he wants her to be awake when we do it."

They walked out and Nora, still feeling the effects of the drug, closed her eyes and fell asleep.

•••

NOW SOMETIME LATER, AWAKE and more alert, she had a dry cough and a pain in her chest and wondered if these symptoms were related to what they had put in her margarita. She tried to sit up and felt dizzy, swung her legs over the side of the bed, and pushed herself up, searched the room for a weapon, something to defend herself. There was a toolbox in the corner. She opened it, picked up a screwdriver, sat on the floor, leaning against the wall, and waited.

Nora was dozing off when she heard voices, heard a key in the lock. The door opened. A man came in the room and stood next to the bed. It was Raylan. "Oh my God, I don't believe it." He turned and moved to her, picked her up and put his arms around her.

"I prayed you'd come and here you are."

"How do you feel?"

"I don't know."

"You don't have to worry. It's over."

Raylan carried Nora to Memo's car, sat her in the rear seat, and held her.

•••

AT RINDO'S HOUSE, RAYLAN took Big Country aside. "Listen, I need you to take Nora to El Centro, get her to a doctor."

"You're not coming with us?" Big Country gave him a questioning look. "You can't stay here. Let Memo take Rindo into custody, hold him till we work this out."

"I trust the little guy, he's been great, but as you said, the country's corrupt and Rindo's got money." Raylan paused. "Will you call your contact in Mexico City, find out what's going on?"

"They're trying to get clearance from the Mexican Government."

"You don't have something positive by tomorrow, I'm gonna do it my way."

"The hell's that mean?" Big Country said. "Let me refresh your memory, you take Rindo out of Mexico against his will, we're gonna have to give him back. That happens, we're never gonna see him again. Take it easy, will you? I think it's all gonna work out."

Raylan walked out to the car and got in next to Nora. "You need a doctor. Big Country's gonna get you to the hospital in El Centro."

"What about you?"

"I'm gonna finish up here, come see you."

"You better. Just do it fast, will you?"

•••

BIG COUNTRY PHONED RAYLAN an hour and a half later. "Nora's at the El Centro Medical Center. They've got her on IVs, trying to flush out her system. She's hanging in there. Doc thinks they gave her ketamine, some kind of anesthetic, says she'll be fine. No word on the Jose Rindo case yet. You're gonna have to be patient."

"What do you suggest I do with him, sit around, watch TV: *Judge Judy* and *Maury* in Spanish? Wait for *Jeopardy* and *Family Feud* to come on?"

"Find out what his interests are," Big Country said. "Start there."

"That's what I'll do. Thanks for the tip."

"I don't know what to tell you. I can come back, give you a hand if you want."

"I'll take care of it."

"Where's Rindo?"

"Cuffed to his bed frame."

"That's your signature move, huh?"

"You got something that works, why fool around?"

•••

ON THE WAY BACK from the border, Memo stopped at Eduordo Meza's house. There were Mexicali police cars, and an ambulance parked in front. Memo got out of his car, approaching the front door as a gurney carrying a body bag was rolled outside.

"What happened here?" Memo said to one of the cops.

"A man was murdered."

"Do you know his name?"

"Eduordo Meza."

"Do you know who did it? Do you have a suspect?"

"A neighbor heard gunshots, saw the killer come out of the house."

"Do you have a description of him?"

"We have a photograph—taken with a phone." The cop took his own phone out, pressed a couple keys, and angled the screen toward Memo. It was a grainy, out-of-focus shot of a man.

"Who is he?"

"An American."

•••

"LISTEN, THERE IS A problem," Memo said, walking in Rindo's kitchen. "Police found Eduordo Meza dead in his home, executed in the bedroom where we find him this morning. Is all over the radio. They have a photo of the killer and he look like you. They have a witness, saw you at the house. I think is time to go, leave Mexico. I can no longer protect you."

Early evening, Raylan was watching Memo chop tomatoes and onions and sear chicken in a skillet, making tacos, when he heard a knock on the front door. He glanced at Memo and they went into the bedroom. Rindo was on the bed, hands cuffed behind his back, ankle cuffed to the metal bed frame, duct tape over his mouth. Memo stayed with him while Raylan went to the front of the house, looked out a window, and saw a Mexicali police car, a marked unit parked on the street. There was another knock. Raylan looked through the peephole at two policemen.

Now the cops were moving across the front of the house, trying to see in the windows, moving around the side to the veranda, faces up against the glass panes, one of them shaking the handles of the French doors. Raylan watched them all the way around the house and back to their car. He saw Memo come up behind him. "Why would the Mexicali police come here?"

"No one has heard from Rindo for many hours. They look for him, or maybe you. Or maybe they are not the police. They have the car, they have the uniform," he said, "but this is Mexico."

"We should move him, get him out of here. I'm taking Rindo back to El Centro tomorrow."

"How you going to do that?"

Raylan told him his plan. "What do you think?"

Memo nodded and smiled.

•••

THREE IN THE MORNING, Raylan followed Memo to his house and pulled in the garage. No sign of the police. They brought Rindo inside and cuffed him to the bed frame in the room where Raylan had slept the night before. He went into the other room and stretched out on the couch but was too revved up to sleep. He stared at the ceiling, thinking about trying to bring Rindo across the border. It was a long shot, but it was the only one he had.

In the morning, Memo woke Rindo and gave him a piece of bread and a glass of orange juice with two sleeping pills crushed in it. Twenty minutes later, they carried him, barely conscious, to the garage and lifted him in the trunk.

"I don't know how to thank you," Raylan said. "You've risked a lot to help us."

"Is my job. Good luck, my friend. I hope we meet again."

Memo opened the garage door with a remote and drove out heading south to the outskirts of the city.

Raylan, in the Lexus, went next, heading north to the border. He'd gone a couple blocks when he saw a police car in the rearview mirror. He, made a couple turns, and now he was in the barrio. He looked again and there were two police cars behind him. Raylan punched the accelerator, speeding down a narrow street lined with parked cars on one side, hearing the sharp chirp of sirens.

From the neighborhood street, he turned right onto a city boulevard. Out of nowhere, a police car hit him broadside. The impact stunned Raylan and sent the Lexus bouncing over the curb onto a sidewalk, taking out several cafe tables, people scrambling to get out of the way. Raylan cut the wheel hard left and was back on the boulevard. He could see the border ahead, a sign that read:

LINEA INTERNACIONAL
CALEXICO/USA

Now a round blew out the rear window and punched a hole in the windshield. He could see a Mexicali cop leaning out the front passenger window with a pistol in his hand. Raylan turned left, driving along the seventeen-foot-high fence that separated Mexico and the US, and saw three Mexicali police cars, lights flashing, behind him maybe forty yards, and then he was braking hard, caught in the slow snarl of traffic waiting to cross the border.

Beggars washing car windows for spare change, and vendors selling tacos and Cokes, moved through the gridlock. In the side mirrors he saw four Mexicali police, guns drawn, coming up fast behind him. Raylan opened the door, got out, crouching, looking back at the cops, and now ran for the border. He heard shouts behind him and pistols discharge but kept going, seeing a US border agent watching what was happening, the man reaching down, raising an AR-15, aiming first at him until he said, "DUSM Raylan Givens," and showed his star.

"Better get over here quick."

Raylan ran, crossed the line. The border agent, a man about his age, aimed his long rifle at the Mexicali police, standing four abreast, pistols drawn, twenty feet from the United States border.

One of the Mexicali cops said, "This man is our prisoner, he is wanted for murder."

"This man is a United States citizen inside the US. You have no authorization, no jurisdiction."

The Mexicali police continued to hold their ground until three more armed US border agents appeared.

"This is the last time I'm gonna tell you," the old pro said, "lower your weapons and back away."

Now the Mexican police holstered their guns and dispersed.

"You couldn't have cut it any closer," the border agent said. "Welcome home, Deputy Marshal Givens."

Raylan would have some explaining to do. And the Mexican government might try to extradite him, but there was no way he was going back to Mexico anytime soon.

THIRTY-SEVEN

Wiggy had just taken a load of wets up to Anaheim when he got the call from Lori, saying Pedro, a coyote she knew, was offering them three grand to come down, pick up a wet in Mexicali, and take him to a house in El Centro. It was a two-and-a-half-hour job max, and he'd make as much as he usually did in a month or more.

Wiggy didn't exactly like bringing wets across the border. Too many things could go haywire, and he'd be the one holding the bag of shit. But if there was ever a time to take a risk, this was it.

His gaze held on the green sign ahead:

INTERNATIONAL BORDER
MEXICALI

Minutes later he was in line waiting to cross into Mexico. When it was his turn, a sleepy-eyed dude smoking a cigarette, tie at half-mast, glanced at Wiggy and waved him through. Getting in was a piece of cake. It was getting out that was tough.

Every time he came here, Wiggy was surprised how big it was compared to Calexico, which was a nothing border town on the US side. Mexicali had like a million people and went on forever.

Wiggy met Pedro and a skinny Mex with a big gun holstered on his hip in a dusty lot outside the city. The dude he was transporting, face under a baseball cap, was unconscious. Pedro said, "The man is okay, be awake when you get to El Centro." Pedro gave him an address. "Someone meet you."

•••

NOW APPROACHING THE BORDER on the return trip, Wiggy tapped on the sheet metal behind his seat. "Dude, can you hear me?" he said to the wet in the hidden compartment. "Be all chill, don't say anything till I tell you, okay?"

Wiggy handed the border guard his driver's license.

The man stared at it and stared at him. "Mr. Dentinger, what was the purpose of your visit in Mexico today?"

"I came down to have something to eat."

"Something to eat? We don't have food you like here in the US?"

"Yes, sir."

"Yes, sir, we do, or yes, sir, we don't?"

"We do."

"What are you transporting in the van?"

"Nothing, sir."

"Are you transporting illegal drugs?"

"No, sir."

"Are you transporting illegal Mexican aliens?"

"No, sir."

"You expect me to believe you came all the way to Mexicali for the food?"

"Yes, sir."

"Do I look gullible to you, son?"

"No, sir." Wiggy snapped one of the rubber bands on his wrist.

"What do you have on your arm?"

"Rubber bands."

"I can see that, why?"

"I don't know, sir."

"You don't know." The guard stared at him for a couple seconds and shook his head. "Are the rear doors unlocked?"

"Yes, sir."

The guard walked to the back, opened it, looked in at the empty cargo area, and closed it up. Now he walked around the van with some kind of a pole with a mirror on the end of it so he could see the undercarriage.

Wiggy thought he'd be on his way when the man came back to the side window.

"Pull over there," he said, pointing to a parking area.

"Is there a problem, sir?"

"Pull over and step out of the van, Mr. Dentinger."

Wiggy's heart started pin-balling again. He tried to kick-start his brain, trying to remember if there was something in the van they could bust him for: a few meth crystals, a roach, a pipe with a little weed still in the bowl. Was he forgetting something? Wiggy checked the ashtray. It was clean. Checked the aftermarket console between the seats. Nothing there either. What about the glove box? No idea. Why hadn't he thought about this earlier? Cause he was a dumbass. Wiggy could feel sweat on his face and sweat running from his armpits down his bare sides under the tank top.

He got out and the guard said, "Turn, face the vehicle, place your hands on the top of the door." Now the guard patted him down. "Son, when you leave here, I'd suggest you find a shower. Smells like something crawled in you and died."

•••

WIGGY FOUND 506 SMOKETREE Drive and pulled in the driveway. "Hey, you okay?" he yelled to the wet in the compartment. Jesus, he hoped the guy wasn't dead. He hadn't been there five minutes when the SUV pulled in. He knew why it looked familiar when the cowboy and the big marshal got out. Talk about bad luck.

"We're here to take him off your hands."

The cowboy said it like he knew Wiggy had the dude. He was trying to think of what to say. His first impulse was to bullshit the two lawmen and decided that didn't have a chance in hell of working. So he didn't say anything, opened the back of the van, lifted the floor, and there was the wet.

The big marshal pulled the dude—who looked dazed—out of the hidden compartment and cuffed him. Without the cap, Wiggy recognized him. This wet he'd just brought over was the dude they'd asked him about when they'd come to the Slabs, the dude with the gun he'd given a ride to. That's what this was about.

Wiggy said, "What about me?"

The cowboy said, "What about you?"

"What're you gonna do?"

"What do you want us to do?"

"Nothing. Let me go."

"Okay."

Wiggy couldn't believe it. What was going on? "You serious?"

The marshals left him standing on the driveway in total disbelief.

THIRTY-EIGHT

Rindo, sitting next to Raylan in the rear seat of Big Country's G-ride, tried to bribe them on the way to jail, and when that didn't work, he threatened them.

"Man, the fuck you think you're doing? Kidnap a Mexican citizen, take me across the border against my will."

"I don't know what you're talking about," Raylan said. "We didn't bring you across the border, and US Border Patrol has nothing that proves you entered the country at all. So that leads us to believe you've been here all along. Let me remind you, Jose, you're an escaped convict, a fugitive with several warrants against you. We had you under surveillance in El Centro—that's in the United States of America, last time I looked—and arrested you at Five Oh Six Smoketree Drive."

"Motherfuckers think you can hold me this time?"

"We're sure gonna try," Raylan said.

•••

HE WALKED THROUGH THE doors of the El Centro Medical Center, saw Nora in the waiting area, and couldn't get to her quick enough. She saw him too, got up, and ran across the lobby, fell into his arms, and held on, the two of them embracing in the middle of the hall as people walked around them.

"How do you feel?"

"Better now."

Nora was still pale but starting to get some color back. Raylan took her out to the car he'd borrowed from the El Centro motor pool. They got in and he leaned over and kissed her, and she kissed him back.

They held onto each other until Nora said, "I know Rindo's in custody. Tell me what happened."

"It got a little hairy there at the end. Local police accusing me of murdering one of Rindo's men." He told her about the showdown at the border.

"They thought you had him in the trunk?"

"That was the idea."

"And you used the kid from the Slabs? I don't believe it."

"It could've been a mess, but somehow it worked out."

"So as far as the authorities are concerned, Rindo was in El Centro the whole time. I have to tell you, it was brilliant." Nora paused. "What happens now?"

"You're not gonna like this. Investigative Services wants us to take him back to Detroit for arraignment and trial."

"I'm just happy we can put him away," the new mellow Nora said.

"Big Country and I are gonna do it once we get clearance. Probably be a couple days."

"In the meantime," Nora said, giving him a seductive smile. "I'd like to go back to the hotel and rip your clothes off."

"That can be arranged," Raylan said. He started the car and put it in gear.

ACKNOWLEDGMENTS

W HEN MY FATHER, ELMORE Leonard, passed away in 2013, he was writing a novel called *Blue Dreams*. For weeks after his death, friends asked if I had considered finishing Elmore's book. And the answer was always, no way. For me, *Blue Dreams* was sacred.

But my brother, Chris, had another idea. He said, why don't you write a Raylan novel. I thought, wait a minute, that's not a bad idea. It would be a tribute to our father, and a way to bring Raylan back for Elmore's fans and fans of the hit TV series *Justified*.

To research the book, I spent weeks riding and hanging out with the US Marshals Fugitive Task Forces in Detroit, San Diego, and El Centro, California. First getting a behind the scenes look at how the marshals discover the whereabouts of criminals with fugitive warrants, and then going on actual fugitive takedowns. It was an incredibly interesting and exhilarating experience. And the first time I've ever worn a bulletproof vest to work.

I also want to thank my agent, Jeff Posternak at Wylie NY, new publisher and Raylan aficionado, Tyson Cornell, and artful editorial director, Guy Intoci.